LAST SIGN

EMMA LAST SERIES: BOOK THIRTEEN

MARY STONE

MARY STONE
PUBLISHING

Copyright © 2025 by Mary Stone Publishing

All rights reserved.

No part of this book may be reproduced in any form or by any electronic or mechanical means, including information storage and retrieval systems, without written permission from the author, except for the use of brief quotations in a book review.

❀ Created with Vellum

For the entomologists and bug lovers—though creepy crawlies give me the shivers, I admire your love for all living things. And I swear —no bugs were harmed in the making of this book... just a few unfortunate humans.

DESCRIPTION

It's time to pay the exterminator.

After barely surviving the ghosts of her past, Special Agent Emma Last is desperate to move forward. But just as she starts to believe she can leave it all behind, her colleague makes a shocking claim.

She saw Emma in the afterlife. And she wants answers.

Now, Emma's sanity is in question, and she fears her career may be on the line.

But any questions about what really happened during her last case are put on hold when a mutilated body is found—a tattoo cut from his skin. Emma and her team suspect gang activity. Until they find a dead cockroach stuffed in his pocket, and a sinister email is directed to the police.

"Cockroaches overrun our city…and someone needs to do the cleaning."

When a second victim appears, it's clear this isn't a turf war—it's a vigilante's hunt. A predator collecting trophies. And now, Emma is the ultimate prize.

Last Sign is the gripping thirteenth book in the Emma Last series by bestselling author Mary Stone, where the most dangerous infestations don't crawl in the shadows—they walk among us.

1

Johnny "Juice" Duncan scratched an itch on his bare scalp as he walked, thinking about whether he should report directly in or stop at home first. This was his first major score and the biggest for his gang. The Skulls would be making bank now, running coke around the block.

He'd never seen so much money in one place before. Definitely not in his own damn pocket.

The boss, Seven-Oh, told him to make the score and get gone.

"Get there early, scout it out. See if you notice any cops or suspicious people showing up and hanging around. The buyer might try to roll on you and take his money back, so be ready."

Juice had been ready all right, carrying the ounces in his pocket and his gun tucked down the back of his pants. He had to wait three hours for the buyer to show, and Juice was twitchy and scared the whole time. But it all went down fine, money for blow, easy as pie.

Only, now that fat roll of cash weighed him down like a gold bar.

His fingers itched as he touched the bills in his pocket.

Maybe he should stop at home first, skim off the top so he and his sister could eat better this month. He'd promised Trisha doing these deals wouldn't be bad for them in the long run. Her response was to give him shit about being in the gang, saying he was putting them both in danger.

But she'd never earned real money in her life. Since they moved to D.C., all she'd done was take night classes and talk about being a nurse someday. Maybe she'd make it. She'd have it easier if he could bring home more money, though. If they could eat real food and not dollar-store crap.

Taking a bit off the roll, before Seven-Oh saw it…shit, he could probably take half, and that dude and his partner wouldn't know the difference.

Seven-Oh spent more time being drunk than doing anything else. His second-in-command, some dude everyone called "the Hippie," smoked so much weed, his eyes were permanently glazed and red. Juice figured the Skulls had a few months left before another gang straight-up steamrolled Seven-Oh and his stoner friend.

Idiots with more money than brains didn't stay on top for long in this world.

Especially now we're running coke. The Serpents, maybe what's left of the Drivers or Powders, gonna sit up and take notice.

Heck, maybe Seven-Oh would drink himself to death and somebody else in the Skulls would end up in charge. If that happened, Juice knew he'd be answering to a higher authority, and not the kind that got high before giving orders.

The Hippie's only around because him and Seven-Oh grew up together.

Juice paused to light a cigarette, taking a few puffs before he got going again.

Probably gonna be someone hard who takes over after Seven-Oh. Somebody who's done time. No chance of skimming with a dude like that calling the shots. It's now or never, Juice. Now or never.

He picked up his pace and took a left onto Chestnut Street, aiming homeward. He patted his pants pocket just to reassure himself the money was still there. Was he being stupid for thinking about stealing from the gang?

Seven-Oh would kill him if he found out, but that'd mean Seven-Oh was awake and alert enough to notice. The Hippie'd just nod and laugh.

Juice broke into a jog, just wanting to get home. Stuff some cash into the couch until he got back. Then he'd show his sister, and she'd stop riding him about getting into "dangerous shit" with the gang.

He turned a corner, relieved to find no one lurking in front of his apartment building.

Almost there. I'll just take a few hundred, maybe five. Seven-Oh won't miss that much.

Puffing on his smoke, Juice slowed to a trot before returning to a steady walking pace as he followed a path through the empty lot behind his building.

A strange sound—like a soda can opening—came from beyond the chain-link fence. An instant later, a sudden burning in his gut shoved him back a step. He dropped his smoke and stumbled against the fence before dropping to his knees. Juice stared at his stomach.

Something hurt real bad, like an explosion inside him.

The moon didn't give much light, but enough to watch a dark stain bloom across his white shirt beneath his jacket. Pain like nothing he'd ever felt radiated from his guts, and his brain went numb with the sight.

I just got shot. Somebody shot me.

Unable to control his body, he fell sideways, landing in the dirt. Wrapping a hand over the bullet hole, he tried to hold in his life, but blood, thick and sticky, poured from between his fingers, and every breath was agony.

His other hand found the bundle of cash in his pants pocket. *Still there.*

"Help." His voice was breathy. Too weak to make it far into the night. Nobody answered his plea. A whimper bled out of his throat, and he tried to sit up. Feebly, he reached around his hip, trying to get under his jacket to pull out his gun in case whoever shot him was coming to finish the job.

If he was going down, he'd take them down with him.

Juice got up on his side, grunting against the pain as his fingertips found the cold metal of the gun. But before he could grasp the grip, a kick landed in the middle of his back and sent him sprawling on his stomach. He caught himself, barely, but the gunshot wound scraped against the ground, and he cried out.

Fire raced through his midsection, worse than anything he'd ever felt. He tried to slide his hand down to put pressure on the wound, but his attacker's foot held him down. Above him, the guy yanked his gun from the back of his pants.

"What do you—"

"Shut up!" Another kick slammed him to the ground.

Juice's brain rattled. The dude he did the coke deal with must've followed him to get the money back, so he'd have the drugs and the cash. Juice rolled over to kick back, or to at least look his killer in the face when the final moment came.

The figure above him was a black shadow looming against the night—and not the guy who'd passed him the cash for the coke. This man was taller, stockier, and had both guns aimed at him.

The one with the silencer on it and Juice's little pocket Ruger Max-9 tracked up and down his body. "Show me your gang tattoo." Dressed all in black, the man was barely visible, though a shock of hair fuzzed the outline of his head against the night. "Where is it? Show me your damn tat."

"My what? I'll show you my foot in your ass."

The man's foot shot out, catching Juice in the face and smashing his nose. Blood gushed from his mouth as he fell backward.

Juice blinked tears from his eyes and scooted backward, knowing any minute the man might shoot him. But he had to at least try to get away.

His attacker stomped a boot down on Juice's ankle. "Filthy cockroach, trying to crawl back out of the light."

The man put the gun with the silencer in a shoulder holster under his jacket. Juice's Ruger went into his front pants pocket.

But instead of leaving as Juice had hoped, the man drew a knife from his belt. The blade glinted in the moonlight. "Show me your tattoo, or I make that bullet hole a lot bigger."

"Shit, man. Just finish what you started? I'm bleeding out. You gut shot me, asshole." Juice panted, each breath a stab of agony. "Skulls'll get you for this."

He groaned against the pain flaring in his stomach. Every breath was torture as more warm blood seeped from the wound.

Losing too much blood. Guy's gonna let me die like this, slow and painful.

"Why the hell you doing this?"

"You earned it." The man leaned forward and grabbed Juice's right arm, pulling it up. He slid the knife blade inside the jacket sleeve, drawing it up to slice the fabric open. The blade came down flat against the Skulls tattoo Juice had done two months ago, when he officially joined the gang—the same day Seven-Oh gave him the Ruger. "See, you're stained just like all the roaches scurrying around, making a mess of this city."

Juice swallowed hard, forcing his mouth to work against the pain as he spoke through gritted teeth. "Just take the money, man. Take it and let me go, all right?"

The man paused, his knife held above Juice's arm. "Money? What money?"

"In my pocket. Three grand. Go on and take it."

The man knelt and aimed his knife at Juice's right eye. "Don't fucking move." He felt around for the wad of money in Juice's pocket, pulled it out, and held it up in the sliver of moonlight. "Nice. Three thousand dollars'll go a long way, but it's barely enough to pay for what you've done."

"I ain't done shit, man. This is my first run. I ain't been in the Skulls that long and ain't done—"

Juice screamed as the knife sliced into his skin. With his other hand, the man shoved the wad of money into Juice's mouth. He tried to spit it out, work his tongue around it, but the guy forced the cash in deep.

Taking Juice's arm by the wrist, the man returned to his work, carving away the skin that held the Skulls tattoo.

Juice bit down hard on the roll of money, choking on a grunt of pain as his attacker continued slicing. He thrashed beneath the knife, trying to twist away. But the pain in his gut held him pinned to the ground.

There was no hope for escape.

His vision wavered as the blade finally left his flesh, only to be replaced by an agonizing, fiery pain as the last bit of flesh keeping his tattoo connected to his arm was peeled away like skin off an orange.

The inked portion of Juice's skin hung in the air above his face. Puke rose in his throat, and he heaved against the wad of cash pressing against his soft palate. Some vomit sputtered out around the money, but he swallowed most of the bile back down.

Juice choked and sobbed, unable to even gasp his last breath as the man drove the tip of the knife into his chest.

2

The last time Special Agent Emma Last saw her colleague and friend Denae Monroe, she'd appeared to Emma as a ghost in the Other, hovering between life and death. Emma and Leo had been in Boston, helping a shorthanded field office with a case, when Denae's family called him, urging him to come back as soon as possible. Denae had revived from the coma she'd slipped into after being shot in the side under her arm.

And she's coming back to work now, Emma girl. The world may not be perfect, but good things can still happen.

As she entered the familiar confines of the D.C. conference room, coffee in hand, she couldn't stop the smile that crossed her face when she found Denae sitting with their supervisory special agent, Jacinda Hollingsworth. She was beyond thrilled. "Denae—"

"Please sit down, Agent Last." Jacinda's voice was sharper than usual. "We need to sort something out."

Emma glanced from Jacinda to Denae. Jacinda sat at the head of the conference table, with Denae to her right. As Emma took a seat to Jacinda's left, opposite Denae, her smile died away. Their faces were both very serious. Across from them, Emma felt like she was in the principal's office. Her stomach swooped.

Denae lifted her chin. "It's about the ghosts."

"Agent Last, Agent Monroe requested this meeting." Jacinda had always been incredibly professional, even in the worst of times. And while Emma had been on the receiving end of her reprimands before, this was different. "She's given me permission to share that she's undergone a mental health evaluation to determine her fitness to return to duty."

"That's good, right? That means you can—"

"Agent Monroe failed that evaluation."

Emma bit her lips shut. Across the table, Denae's cheeks darkened in clear embarrassment.

Jacinda focused her gaze on Emma. "The evaluation will be conducted again in three months, to allow Agent Monroe the opportunity to rest and recover." She cut a sharp look over to Denae, then directed her attention back to Emma, who sat straighter. "In the meantime, Agent Monroe has stated that you can corroborate her claims."

Oh, shit.

Emma squirmed in her chair. Had her secret come out? If so, Denae would never be taken seriously again.

And neither would she.

Denae turned to Emma. "I need you to tell Jacinda the truth." Her voice was so scratchy, like she hadn't had a drink of water in days.

Emma held her breath, glancing from Jacinda to Denae and back, before the SSA jumped in.

"Denae believes she saw you in some kind of afterlife when she was in a coma."

Denae clenched her hands in her lap. "Please, don't talk about me like I'm a child who had a bad dream, Jacinda."

For a moment, the two women talked to each other like

Emma wasn't even in the room. Emma ping-ponged her gaze back and forth between the two of them.

"I'm explaining the situation to your colleague, who has no idea what she's walked into. And I need you, as a prized member of my team, to give yourself the time and space to recover from this traumatic event. People often experience vivid dreams or hallucinations or—"

"That's not what this was." Denae sounded like she'd tried to explain the situation a million times before and no one would listen and simply branded her unfit for law enforcement.

Her whole career was on the line, and Denae, truthful and honest, couldn't bring herself to lie about such a profound experience as dying.

"I didn't dream it up."

Once again, she turned to Emma, who could read the silent plea in her expression. Denae wanted her to confess. Her colleague wanted to know, for herself, that she wasn't crazy.

Emma bit her lip again, debating what to do. If she agreed with her colleague, her mental health would need evaluating as well. She could lose her job.

But so could Denae.

And Denae could lose even more. Her sense of self. Her confidence. She'd been through so much, and what she claimed was true. Emma Last could see ghosts.

So it was either lie and call Denae crazy—or tell the truth and be called crazy herself.

"I don't think it's a good idea to continue this conversation." Jacinda shifted in her chair, ready to stand up.

"Wait." The word was out of Emma's mouth before she could stop herself. As Jacinda settled back down, Emma exhaled a long, deep breath before taking another one in and looking the SSA right in the eyes. "I can see ghosts, Jacinda.

And sometimes talk with them. That's the 'other world' Denae mentioned."

The SSA stared at her. "Excuse me?"

"I can see ghosts."

A moment of silence descended as Supervisory Special Agent Jacinda Hollingsworth looked from Denae to Emma and back again.

Jacinda's going to have to fire us both, I guess.

Apparently sensing Jacinda was willing to listen closer now, Denae tried again. "I coded twice on the way to the hospital, and at least one more time during the open-heart surgery. Each time, I was technically dead, and I saw Emma. I was in this place that was all mist and fog, and we were surrounded by a bunch of other people with white eyes who were definitely dead."

Jacinda laced her fingers in front of her. It was the same position she took when interrogating suspects. "How did you know they were dead?"

Emma pressed her hands against her coffee cup, trying desperately to warm her suddenly frozen fingers.

"Some of them had bullet holes in their heads. Others were missing arms or legs. I could see blood coming out of them, and they didn't say anything. I've never seen a ghost before, but if I had to guess—"

"That's exactly what you were seeing." Emma couldn't let her friend continue to flounder or doubt herself a second longer. "Those were ghosts, and you were one too. I've been able to see them and talk with them for a while now." She met Jacinda's gaze full on. "When Denae was shot, I saw her. And each time she coded. That was when Leo and I were in Boston."

"Stop." Jacinda held her hand up. "I don't know if you're both punking me for some reason, but with your confirmation, Emma, I'm getting another set of eyes and ears in here." The SSA stood and went to the door.

Emma wondered if Leo and Mia would back her up if their jobs were on the line.

They definitely would, Emma girl.

Emma looked through the glass enclosing the conference area. Leo and Mia hadn't arrived yet.

Vance was just setting his bag down at his desk. The cast on his arm had been removed the day before, and he'd been cleared for full duty.

Great, the one person on the team who doesn't *know.*

"Jacinda, can we just keep this between the three of us? Leo and Mia already know too. I'm not sure Vance will—"

"Vance will act as a witness to this conversation, because I foresee a lot of long phone calls and meetings with HR. I need to protect myself as well as both of you, especially after Salem." Jacinda's mouth set in a hard line. "I'm sure you understand."

Jacinda had been handling the fallout from their last case, fielding phone calls from multiple internal affairs inquiries with aplomb.

Opening the conference room door, Jacinda called Vance into the meeting.

"Hey, Denae! Great to see you." He entered and walked around the table to his usual seat, facing the door. "We having a briefing without the rest of the team? What's up?"

Denae offered him a weak smile. It was clear she didn't want the others involved either. But at least she didn't look so unsure of herself anymore. That was important to Emma. At least Denae didn't have to doubt her own mental capabilities.

Emma reached over to lightly touch Denae's arm as she remembered the moment her friend nearly died. "Each time I saw you in that other world...you said to 'tell Scruffy.'"

"I did." Denae's dark eyes grew glassy with unshed tears. But her relief was palpable. "You heard me."

Vance sat up straighter and cleared his throat. "Somebody want to clue me in? What…'other world' are we talking about? Jacinda?" He turned to her.

Jacinda lifted a hand toward Emma. "I believe you had an answer for us."

"Hi, Vance." Emma twisted to face him. "I…have this ability. It's going to sound pretty out there, but I need you to hear me out." She searched his face for a moment before continuing. "I can see ghosts. When Denae died a few times after being shot, I saw her ghost. We talked in a place called the Other."

Vance's eyes widened so far, Emma thought they would pop out of his head. He didn't speak, so Emma pressed on, her words tumbling over each other.

She described how the ghost at the Ruby Red Spectacle Circus gave her the clues to talk down their perpetrator. She told them how the ghosts appeared at random, about the riddles they spoke in, and about the temperature changes. There were too many incidents to list in one meeting.

"A woman who used to live in my building…her ghost comes into my kitchen every morning and tells me to find a boyfriend. Oren…he comes to me. He helped us in Salem. When Denae was shot last month, her ghost came to me too."

Vance let out a jittery laugh, looking between her and Denae. "Emma, maybe the coffee hasn't kicked in yet. It's still early, but Denae's right there, at the other end of the table. She's alive, unless you're telling me I can see ghosts too."

"She's not lying." Denae leaned forward in her chair, her hands pressed tight on her knees.

"Leo will back me up."

I hope.

"Of course. He'd do anything for Denae. Come on…you

really expect me to buy this crap?" Vance's mocking look turned to pity.

Emma wanted to smack the expression off his face. "Mia knows too."

Vance slammed his mouth shut, his eyes darkening.

Standing up, Jacinda got everyone's attention with a clap of her hands. "Enough. Let's make this a team meeting. Confidential. Off the record. Leo and Mia just got in, and according to Emma, they can corroborate her story. Let's hear it."

The fact that Jacinda wasn't immediately dismissing them gave Emma a ray of hope. But Jacinda was an investigator, an agent trained to detect bullshit. She'd hear all sides and weigh all evidence before taking any action. Even when Emma had been reprimanded in the past, Jacinda had been fair.

Emma watched as her colleagues entered the conference room and settled around the table. Leo and Mia both sat straighter than normal. They were probably reading the seriousness on everyone's faces. She prepared herself to recount her story once more.

But Vance beat her to the punch. "You guys are just in time for story hour. Emma's starting, but I want to go next. I have a few good ghost stories saved up from campfire nights when I was a kid."

Leo steepled his fingers in front of him. "If this meeting is about what I think it's about, maybe try for a bit less derision and a bit more compassion."

Vance reared back as if he'd been slapped by the words. "Excuse me?"

"Free your mind, man."

Shaking his head, Vance laughed. "Fine, but I get to be Scully. Mia, you can be Mulder. I don't know about the rest of the team, but I'm sure we can figure something out." His gaze darted around to each of them. "Good one, guys. You got me."

"Vance!" Mia smacked her palm on the table.

Jacinda inclined her head toward Emma. "I'd appreciate it if everyone in this room could show everyone else some respect."

Disgust flashed across Vance's face, and Emma's stomach flipped over the omelet she'd forced down that morning. If even one of her colleagues thought her insane or reported her for being unstable, that could be the end of her career.

Emma looked at Mia and Leo, her throat drying as she searched for words. Mia's face had gone white with annoyance, but Leo was eyeing Vance like the other man had suddenly become a suspect.

"Hey, man, you might not have been in those woods outside Salem, but if not for Emma's dead friends, I'd have been one of them."

"Oh, really? Ghosty McGhostface popped out of the trees waving a sign that said 'Danger' or some shit?" Vance crossed his arms, his face pinched. "C'mon. It was funny for a second. Now I'm irked."

Mia reached across the table and grabbed his wrist, holding it until he met her eyes. "Give us a little credit? We were *running through those woods*. Even a trained survivalist couldn't have seen those traps in time to keep us out of them. Not with how fast we were running and how well camouflaged they were."

"And you're the expert?" Vance yanked his hand from Mia and faced Emma.

Jacinda held her hand up to stop him. "You weren't there, Vance. Neither of us was. And that wasn't the only case where things have…come up." The SSA frowned, then closed her eyes and rubbed her temple. "I knew something was off months ago. I didn't guess it was this."

Emma gnawed at her lip. It sounded like Jacinda… believed her?

"If not for Emma," Mia spoke quietly, offering her a nod, "Ned's killers would still be out there. He came to Emma in the Other, and that's how we knew he'd been murdered to begin with."

Vance jerked in his seat. "Does Sloan know too? Who the hell else is in on this carnival attraction?"

Emma flinched, his words stabbing through her. But the sharp glare that Jacinda sent Vance's way softened the blow.

"No." Emma tried to keep the tremor out of her voice. "Sloan doesn't know. Just the people in this room, and…a consultant on the Other I found. And the fortune teller from our first case."

As Vance drew in air to retort or spit another joke her way, Emma barreled forward. She spilled everything, starting with the time the fortune teller pulled her aside after her first case and warned her about a wolf and innocent blood.

She wanted to rest a hand on Vance's arm, to soften the blow of this new truth. She didn't. He was still staring at her as if she'd sprouted two heads. "I've had a wolf's howl haunting me these past few months. And Leo. We've both heard it."

Nobody, not even Vance, said a word, so Emma kept going. She filled in all the details about Salem that she, Leo, and Mia had left out of their reports.

"What happened in Salem had nothing to do with contaminated water. It was the work of Celeste Foss, who could also move through the Other and interact with ghosts. We stopped her, but she told me someone else would finish what she started."

Vance snorted, the sound full of derision. "Right. Can't have a wicked witch without a few flying monkeys to do her dirty work."

Emma pounded both her fists on the table. "I get that you think I'm joking. That we're all joking. But I'm telling the truth."

Denae clapped her hands together, drawing everyone's attention. She stared at Vance. "It might mean people think I'm crazy, but I know what I saw and what I told Emma when I died."

"What did you tell her?" Vance challenged, leaning forward onto his elbows.

"I told her to—"

"Tell Scruffy you'd keep the wolf quiet for a while." Emma finished the statement, repeating the words Denae had spoken each time her ghost appeared.

Leo looked from Emma to Vance. "That's why I believed Emma. There's no way she could've known Denae called me Scruffy. Or that I was having nightmares about howling wolves."

Vance waved a hand in the air, dismissing Leo's words and sinking back into his seat.

With a sigh, Leo turned to the SSA. "Jacinda, we've known each other a long time. I'm telling you, without Emma's...special type of help, we wouldn't have closed all those cases. We might not even be alive."

"I hear you, Leo." The SSA brushed her hair back, then turned to Vance as if daring him to speak, but he remained quiet. Jacinda's eyes met Emma's. "As I said, I've seen strange things. For right now, you and Denae have given us a lot to think about. And what you've both said will stay in this room, among our team, until I say otherwise...which I don't plan to do anytime soon."

Vance huffed a loud breath. The man was red-faced and all but vibrating in his chair with annoyance.

"Do you understand me? What was said here stays

between us. I want your word." Jacinda looked at Vance, waiting for a response.

"Right. Between us and the ghosts. I get it." He sneered. "Are they here now, or are they on a doughnut run?"

"Did you hear me, Vance?" Jacinda's voice went harder than it did with suspects.

Vance pressed his lips into a thin line. "Fine."

"Good." Jacinda sighed and stood up, stretching her arms above her head in a way that suggested she'd been just as tense as Emma. "Because while I admit I've never believed in ghosts, I don't have any better explanations. And if Emma's concerned there's still some danger looming from the parties responsible for the disaster that unfolded in Salem, we all need to be on the same page." She gave Vance a stony look. "Understand?"

It took several seconds, but Vance finally nodded. "Yes, ma'am."

The SSA checked the time. "I need to bring this meeting to a close. We've used up all the free time Denae has to offer."

Rising gently and favoring her left arm, Denae pushed her chair in and stepped to the door. She turned to face the room, meeting Emma's eyes. "Thank you. I'll see you all again soon, I'm sure."

As she left, the rest of the team all glanced around at each other, speechless and curious. Leo, in particular, seemed unable to grasp her quick departure. "Jacinda, is she…?"

"I'm not able to comment yet. I'm sorry."

The admin assistant for the floor stepped into the doorway, filling the space Denae had vacated. "SSA Hollingsworth?"

"What is it, Ray?"

He pointed to the conference phone on the table. "Sorry to interrupt. I know you'd asked me to take messages, but there's an urgent call. Line three."

She waved him off, and he left, closing the door behind him. Already reaching for the conference phone in the middle of the table, Jacinda gave Emma a quick glance. "We'll leave the conversation as it is for now. If this is important enough to interrupt us, I'm guessing it involves the whole team. Everyone stay here." She picked up the line. "SSA Hollingsworth. My team is with me. Who am I speaking to?"

"Agent Conrad Wurth, with Safe Streets Task Force. I have a body out here I think you should see."

Jacinda frowned. "Out here? As in, you're outside the Bureau right now?"

"Right across the street, in the alley next to the coffee shop. I didn't even bother to drive. Body's been mutilated and has apparent gang ties."

"Please tell me this has nothing to do with either the Powders or the Drivers."

"No, thankfully. The deceased seems to have angered a smaller gang that's been getting into the coke trade lately. Thought you'd want to see it, considering proximity and the violence involved." The line crackled. "Certainly fits the 'violent' part of your team's purview, and MPD has never seen a body dropped like this before."

Jacinda had her tablet out and used a stylus to take notes as the conversation continued.

Emma took notes along with her. She closed her eyes briefly, recentering herself. Another case was a good thing. Though given the subject matter, she wasn't sorry Denae had left the room. Her brother's involvement in their gang case two months ago had brought the dangers of the job far too close to home.

The phone conversation came to a close, and Jacinda signed off. Looking around the table, she pointed to each of them in turn. "What I said before still stands. Nothing that was discussed prior to this phone call is to leave this room."

Each of them had nodded their agreement.

After a long pause in which she seemed to weigh their commitment to her command, Jacinda then gave them their assignments. "Give Agent Wurth your undivided attention and see if you can help him process the scene."

Mia stood up as if she'd been spring-loaded into her seat. "You want us to take over?"

"Sounds like Wurth is either asking or offering." Jacinda's gaze lingered on the phone. "Use your discretion, but feel free to say we'll take lead if Safe Streets and MPD want the help."

Emma nodded along with her colleagues but lingered behind as the others filed out. She turned back to Jacinda, searching for words, but the other woman waved her off.

"Your story about a contaminant fouling the water in Salem still sounds easier to believe than anything to do with ghosts, but I'm going to keep an open mind." She gave Emma the shadow of a smile.

The SSA sounded so genuine, relief flooded Emma's system. She couldn't have dared to hope the meeting would end this way. "Thanks, Jacinda."

On that note, Jacinda followed the rest of the team out the door, leaving Emma alone for the moment.

As Emma stood there, in the silence of the empty room, her thoughts spiraled back to the events in Salem, where she'd come face-to-face with the reality of her family history.

She turned to consider the conference table, the center of almost every meeting she'd had with the team since Jacinda, Leo, and Mia had come on board in January. The people who'd just been sitting there were the closest to family she'd ever had.

And you might lose them, because you're not like them. You're the black sheep.

3

Mere minutes and a brisk walk later, Emma crouched beside the body, forcing the chaos of the scene to fall into the background behind her. The man was a white male in his twenties who'd been struck in the face, breaking his nose. Streaks of blood extended from his nostrils to stain his cheeks, mouth, and chin. He'd also been shot in the abdomen.

But the killing blow appeared to be a stab wound to his heart.

The victim was sprawled on his back, left arm outstretched, right arm alongside his body. Shifting into a squat, she inspected the victim more closely.

Leo remained standing. "His head's at an awkward angle."

"He might've been gagged." Even with the blood from his nose having dried over his mouth, Emma could identify a split in his upper and lower lips. "These injuries to his lips might've happened when he got hit in the nose, but I'm seeing flecks of dried vomit. I'd say he had something forced into his mouth before he died."

"Yeah, I see it."

Emma bent to examine the man's pallid face. "Contusions and lacerations on his right cheek and forehead but no blood around those marks."

"There's no blood around the body, so he must've been killed somewhere else, then brought here in a car, carried out, and dropped."

"Or thrown out. See the way his legs are spread and the left arm is stuck out?" Emma gestured to the victim's lower half. "It looks like he was maybe hauled here and flung forward, so he fell, but with some momentum behind him."

The position of the body could mean he'd been dropped quickly, and that would make sense, given how public the alley was. Even late at night, anyone dumping a corpse in the middle of a D.C. business district risked being seen on camera.

Emma repositioned herself so she could inspect his right arm, which lay half concealed by his body. Her gaze was drawn to a sliced sleeve partially covering his forearm. Pinching the fabric in her gloved fingers, Emma drew the sleeve away. Her lip curled. Someone had cut into the victim's flesh and removed around four square inches of skin.

"What do we think happened here?" She indicated the wound.

Stooping beside her, Leo peered at the wound. "Torture? Maybe removing a tattoo, brand, or birthmark? The guy has a few tats on his other arm, so maybe the killer was taking one away."

Emma spotted the telltale sign of tattoo ink above his wrist. She reached over and pulled that sleeve away, revealing a series of tattoos. Most were images she would associate with gang lifestyle, like bullets, knives, and dollar signs. "The killer was a trophy hunter, maybe. Or took a specific tattoo to send a message."

Agent Wurth stepped up beside her, his long nose and angular face pointing down at the victim like a pale arrow. Light-brown hair swept back from a broad forehead and clean square jaw only emphasized the effect, but the muscles bulging through his upper sleeves would make anyone think twice about pointing it out. "That was my first thought. The victim pissed off the gang, maybe betrayed them, so he got cut out of the membership."

"Which gang are we talking about?"

The task force liaison squatted beside her. "The missing patch of skin makes me think he was with the D.C. Skulls. That's where they wear their symbol. Best guess is our dead boy here got on their bad side, but we've never seen them mark a kill this way."

He stood, and Emma rose with him. "You've seen them mark kills in other ways?"

"No, which is why I called you in. The Skulls just started moving serious coke, graduating from dime bags to kilos. We're tracking their supplier and have a few leads." He lifted one shoulder. "If they're moving into the big leagues as dealers and escalating to this level of violence, we need help."

Leo pulled off his gloves. "Any other gangs wear a tat in the same place? Can we say for certain he was in the Skulls?"

Wurth shook his head. "No, we can't. I'll have to dig into our database of known associates."

"Could be he was in and pissed them off. Or whoever killed him wants us to pay attention to the Skulls, either as distraction or maybe as part of a vendetta against the gang." Emma jerked her chin to her office building looming above them. "They clearly didn't care about Bureau involvement, dropping the body across from our front door."

Nodding, Wurth clapped a hand on Leo's shoulder. "We'll know more once I've had a chance to look through recent arrest records."

While they discussed possible motives, Emma used a ruler from their crime scene kit to measure the wound for scale. "I can see why you called us in so fast. This isn't a normal gang killing."

Wurth sighed and turned away for a moment with his phone to his ear. "Sorry." He mouthed *the boss* and spoke quietly for a moment.

When he finished the call, she indicated the body's placement, pointing out the positioning of the corpse's limbs.

"Body gets dropped haphazardly, killer or killers depart. Whoever did this, they were clearly sending a message with the mutilation. He was alive for the…procedure." Emma pointed a gloved finger at the missing patch of skin. "See all this blood around the injury site? He'd been gut shot and was bleeding out, then the killer went to work on him."

"That could explain the vomit you mentioned before. The killer stuffed something in his mouth, then started cutting. Victim pukes from the pain."

Emma shuddered. She examined the victim's mouth again, noting the lacerations to both lips. "Whoever did this is friggin' sick, and if we're looking at gang activity…"

Wurth glanced at members of the task force lingering outside the alley, talking to Mia and Vance. "Yeah. Then it's organized, and that means more victims could be dropping like this."

Pulling on a fresh pair of gloves, Leo squatted beside the body, gently turning the dead man's head to reveal a tattoo behind his ear. "He wasn't a confidential informant for anyone in MPD, was he?"

"No." Wurth shook his head. "The chief confirmed that first thing, since he had the same idea. Asked around the force, and nobody had this guy as a CI. If the VCU wants to take lead right off the bat, we'll provide backup. I can send you everything we have on the Skulls."

With Jacinda's approval to take the lead, Emma experienced a rush of relief knowing the team would be focused on something other than her being a freak who talked to ghosts. "SSA Hollingsworth cleared us to take this case if you asked."

"Well, that's settled." Wurth removed his gloves and pocketed them.

"I'll get to digging into our database, but the Skulls just haven't racked up many charges as a gang yet."

Leo aimed his finger at the corpse. "That's going to change if this is what their future plans look like."

Emma squatted to examine the wound again. "The cutting here looks clean, no tearing of the skin except for right at this edge, like he sliced carefully all the way around. Our killer planned ahead. He knew to look for whatever was on the victim's arm, and he came prepared with a knife. He shoots the guy in the gut and takes his time collecting a trophy before he stabs him in the heart."

Wurth nodded and excused himself to talk to the MPD detectives. "They'll be happy to hear you landed on the same idea they did."

Vance and Mia came up from the alley mouth and took Wurth's spot. Scowling at Emma, Vance nevertheless dipped his head in greeting.

She stood and pulled off her gloves. "Nothing concrete to conclude, but we have some leads to follow."

Vance snorted. "Why don't you just ask his ghost who killed him?"

Emma clenched her jaw before she barked out something she couldn't take back. Beside him, Mia's face went white, with either annoyance or embarrassment.

"It doesn't work like that." She kept her tone carefully neutral. "And would you mind keeping your voice down?"

"Whoopsie." Vance threw his hands up, waggling his

fingers in a half-hearted sarcastic jazz hands. His voice shot up a few octaves. "Didn't mean to disturb the dead."

Emma darted a look over her shoulder, but the nearby cops and Wurth weren't close enough to hear Vance talking about ghosts. Even if they had been, at worst, she imagined they'd assume Vance was playing with gallows humor.

Unless he makes a habit of jabbing at you every time there's a corpse around. Then somebody's going to notice eventually.

Vance stepped closer to Emma, all mock serious now. "Sure would make our lives easier if you could, you know, get some inside information for us."

"Give it a rest already." Leo's hissed warning hung in the air as he stepped in front of Vance, face-to-face. "You want to forget what Emma and Denae told you, what Mia and I told you? Fine. Just don't forget we're a team, and we work together."

Mia poked him in the chest. "Which you agreed to do."

Vance stared at them all for a moment before shaking his head and moving back toward the detectives.

Emma couldn't find her voice. Her colleagues defending her was comforting, but Leo and Mia shouldn't be on the hook to mediate between her and anyone else, let alone one of their own. This was her own battle to fight.

Mia stepped closer and forced a smile. "He'll come around."

"Right." Emma glanced back to where he'd stalked off to, fighting to believe her friend. "Until then, maybe it's best we split up? The techs and M.E. need time to work, but Leo and I can start digging into the gang's background with Wurth. You and Vance want to hunt down surveillance footage?"

"You got it. I'll text Jacinda with an update." Without another word, Mia headed up the alley to connect with Vance.

Emma turned to Leo, who seemed to be waiting for

something more. She shrugged in reply to the unasked question. "I'm fine. He needs time to accept I'm telling the truth."

"We're all telling the truth. He'll come around. Same with Jacinda."

She only hoped that whatever helped her to convince both Vance and Jacinda wouldn't be as fatal as what had brought Mia and Leo around.

4

Leo flagged down Wurth, who'd leaned against a car and lit up a cigarette while talking on his phone. The man lowered the device as Leo and Emma approached.

"Do you have a photo of the Skulls tattoo handy?" Leo held up his tablet. "Be good to know what we're looking for, since our John Doe's was missing."

Cigarette hanging from his mouth, Wurth nodded and swiped through images on his phone. He held one up for their viewing—a skull and crossbones tattoo. "It's in our database. I'll send you the link."

As soon as Leo's tablet dinged with the notification, Leo clicked on it, zooming in so he and Emma could study the image.

Mostly drawn in black ink, the tattoo's one nod to color was in the skull's eyes, both of which were creepy green cat eyes. But the tattoo was artful and more detailed than what Leo usually associated with gangs.

He lingered on the photo. "That's detailed work."

Wurth took a drag and exhaled to the side before nodding. "Yeah, we haven't tracked them to a specific shop yet, but we figure they've got one experienced artist as their go-to. It's not prison-yard work, that's for damn sure."

Beside him, Emma bounced her weight between her feet. "Do you have any members in custody we could speak with?"

"We arrested a man on their payroll last week. A Darius Baker who goes by the name 'Diggs' on the street. We got him on cocaine charges, possession with intent to sell, and his arrest is the only one that's stuck so far."

Emma flipped through her notebook. "I thought you said they were moving into bigger scores. 'Dime bags to kilos.'"

Wurth ground out his smoke. "These guys are really good about not holding anything in their hands or pockets or even being near the drugs. Diggs wasn't so lucky. It was a first offense, and he only had a few little bags on his person, so the judge was merciful with bail. I can't see him trying to skip out."

Leo opened his mouth to reply, but Emma once again beat him to the punch. "We'll take that contact information."

Wurth nodded, taking her business card. He offered his own without another word.

As she verified the details of the gang member and his arrest, Leo took a step back, letting her take the lead. She seemed to need to be in control of the situation at the moment, and he couldn't blame her.

Vance's doubt had clearly gotten under her skin, and Leo knew she hadn't been prepared for it. After Salem, she'd been eager to have everything return to normal. Having to come clean about her secret that morning must have taken her by surprise.

Without Denae's unexpected encouragement, she might not have managed at all. Leo's heart squeezed when he thought about what it must've cost Denae to open up about her experiences.

Jacinda and Vance would need time and proof of their

own. Neither of them had a pet name, like Scruffy, or a Ned wandering around, like Mia, to help them along. At least, not that he knew of.

Yaya would know how to help her. Too bad I can't just take Emma home for dinner and a lecture.

The idea of presenting his ghost-talking friend to his religious grandmother was almost enough to make Leo smile. He shook himself to refocus as he watched Emma talking to Wurth. Maybe she would visit his family's home one of these days, but it wouldn't be today.

Emma and Wurth completed their conversation and shook hands. She spun on her heel and began stalking out of the alley. Leo waved to Wurth and followed his partner, jogging to catch up and walk alongside her. Once they crossed the street, he caught her elbow. "Slow down. No point in running to the motor pool."

She hesitated before slowing beside him, gently removing her elbow from his hand. "Something on your mind, I take it?"

He glanced behind them, making sure nobody had followed as they trudged down the Bureau's drive. "Well, yeah. Starts with you and ends with Vance. You might just have to give him space."

Her lips pursed, and her steps sped up again. "He can have all the space he needs."

"That's not what I meant, and you know it." He hurried to keep up as she began marching again. "You don't think I was still struggling when we were in Salem? This isn't a small thing you're asking him and Jacinda to believe in." He waved his arm over his head. "We're talking about worldview-changing stuff here."

Emma's nostrils flared. "I'm not asking them to do anything except treat me with respect, like a colleague. I'm not worried about Jacinda, but Vance is…he's being a dick."

Shit.

She wasn't wrong, but why did he feel like he had to defend Vance? "I'm just saying—"

"He's being a dick, Leo. Don't try to change my mind or pretend I'm wrong." Emma took a deep breath after cutting him off. She turned to face him, stopping in her tracks. "I'm sorry, but it's true. You saw him back there. If I could just ask the victim's ghost, I would."

"But the ghost wasn't there, was he?" They'd reached the Bureau garage entrance. He glanced at the building rising above them, wondering if Emma would face an uphill battle convincing both Vance and Jacinda. "All you can do is take the high road. Don't forget Vance almost died recently. He's been through a lot, just like the rest of us."

That was the understatement of the year. Thankfully, some of the bluster seemed to bleed out of Emma's expression at the reminder. Her lips softened, and finally, she nodded.

"He'll get there." Leo waved her ahead of him, and she entered the garage. "Just be patient."

Emma straightened her jacket, speeding up once more. "I can do that. I just hate that you and Mia are caught in the middle."

Leo couldn't come up with the right words for an answer. As Emma charged toward a Bureau SUV, he worried that his silence might have said more than he wished.

5

Vance and Mia took their time leaving the alley, mostly because he wanted to let Emma and Leo get on the road first. The idea of sharing airspace with their resident "ghost talker" got under his skin in a way he couldn't explain.

Not like I should have to explain. Ridiculous doesn't even go halfway to describing this nonsense.

He sat with Mia in the coffee shop beside the crime scene, fast-forwarding through footage Jacinda had sent to his tablet, showing the Bureau's perimeter cameras. But try as he might, he couldn't focus on the job, not after the way his morning had begun.

He paused the footage playback and leaned closer to Mia so he could speak lower. "You do realize that everyone will be calling us idiots, and worse, if Emma's so-called secret gets out." He sat back in his chair. "I don't like being lied to, and that's what this all feels like."

Mia's fingers clutched her coffee cup tighter. If she couldn't understand that, maybe they'd reached a crucial test in their relationship. "I know you're pissed, but nobody's lying to you." She inched her hand sideways and brushed his enough to catch his attention, offering the smallest of smiles. "It took me time, and it took Leo even more time."

"Denae had it easy, I guess."

Every bit of warmth drained from her expression, and her eyes turned hard. "That's cold, Vance. Really cold."

He looked away, unable to meet her gaze for a moment. "You're right. I'm sorry. You're sure this isn't some great big practical joke?"

"You know me. Would I do something like that?"

She wouldn't, and he knew that for a fact. With everything they'd endured over the past few months, they'd never make him the team's punching bag for a laugh. "I know you're not doing this just to mess with me."

"Nobody's messing with you or asking you to believe something that isn't true. We're asking you to trust Emma, like you already do." Her gaze softened. "This is just another, harder, level of trust."

"Another level?" Vance closed his eyes and shut down the tablet, giving up on the footage from the Bureau. "If Emma's lying, it's messed up that you're all enabling her. And if she's not lying, why'd she take this long to come clean?"

"Because she was worried about people treating her exactly how you're treating her." Mia's voice had a sharp edge to it that he rarely heard from her. "I don't understand why you're being so resistant. I really don't. Something this big...we wouldn't make this up. None of us would." She went quiet for a moment, staring at him with her arms crossed. "I'm not sure she would've come clean to me if it hadn't been for Ned reaching out to her in the Other."

"Let's assume I believe you." He put up a hand as if acknowledging her point. "Tell me this...Leo says Emma *saved* him. Well, she didn't save me, did she? I walked right into a trap, got blown up, and almost died. How's that supposed to make me feel?"

Mia's mouth opened in an O of understanding, but he went on before she could say anything.

"If Emma's..." He searched for a word that wouldn't alarm nearby customers. "If her *friends* warned her in time to save Leo, why weren't they around when it was my turn?"

Mia's brow crinkled. Her nose did, too, in the way Vance loved. But he didn't allow himself to smile. It had taken him most of the morning to understand what was really eating at him since the meeting, and now he'd finally voiced it. Mia's reply would tell him where they stood as colleagues...and as a couple.

"Vance." She scooted her chair around the table, closer to his. "She yelled your name and told you to stop, and I know you heard her because you turned back, and that helped save your life. If you'd continued running like you had been, you would've been inside the room when the bomb went off. You would've died."

He clenched his teeth, fighting back the urge to snarl at his girlfriend. "I had all of zero seconds to get to safety. Like the doctors said, I'm alive because of luck, not some message from beyond."

"Maybe so." She lowered her head to sip her coffee. When she looked back up at him, her expression was harder than he expected. "But we're a team, remember? And we have a job to do." She pushed herself up from her seat and moved to meet a man in a coffee-stained button-up and worn jeans who'd just walked in the door.

Vance rose and caught up just as she finished introducing herself.

The man shook her hand, then Vance's. "Mark Gimble. I'm the manager." He glanced at their IDs, barely bothering to read them. "I understand you want to see our security footage."

Vance was glad to do anything other than talk about Emma's "friends" and his feelings. "That'd be great."

Mark led them into the back, where a tiny desk in the kitchen supported an old computer monitor attached to a security system. Leaning over the desk, he didn't bother sitting down while pulling up video from the previous night.

The camera angle covered the alley entrance and picked up the far corner of the Bureau building across the street. However, they were treated to nothing but a blur of speeding cars, followed by some pedestrians who appeared to be arguing drunkenly over what bar to hit next.

"On a Tuesday night." Vance barely refrained from stomping his foot like a toddler. "This is all you got?"

Mark shrugged, either not noticing or choosing to ignore Vance's agitation. "Our cameras are set to catch anyone coming in or out in case we're robbed. We're happy to help if we do get footage of crimes taking place on the street, but that's not our primary concern. This is just the front camera, though. We have another one set at a different angle."

He moused to another window and brought that view forward, showing the front patio with several tables and chairs, then excused himself to help customers.

Vance sat at the desk and sped up the playback, but as the footage advanced, they saw little more than the edges of cars zooming by and the occasional group of pedestrians.

A stray dog peed on the patio around midnight.

Shortly after the dog departed, a young couple leaned against a table and began making out and pawing at each other.

"So much for curfew." Dammit. He'd switched from toddler mode to angry old man. "These kids—"

Headlights illuminated the lovers. They separated and fled from the camera's view. A second later, a dark van skidded to a halt near where they'd been standing.

Mia's breath hitched sharp and sudden in Vance's ear as she leaned in to see the screen. She put a hand on his shoulder and squeezed as they watched the van jostle slightly.

The vehicle sat inches from where the young people had stood. Only the driver's side was visible, but the headlights lit up the alley where their John Doe had been dropped.

"I couldn't catch a plate," Vance muttered, reaching up to cover Mia's hand with his own.

"Me either. You think he knew he'd be on film and aimed the vehicle that way on purpose, to conceal the plate from view?"

"Could be." He paused the playback, rewound it, and played it again from the moment the couple ran off camera.

"There." Mia pointed, and he paused. The van's front end came into view as the vehicle approached, but the headlight glare prevented them from seeing a plate. "Dammit. Maybe we can get this enhanced back at the Bureau."

"Maybe. Or maybe those kids spotted it."

"Good luck trying to find them." Mia grimaced. "But we can put out the word and see if anyone responds with an anonymous tip. Let's see what he does with the body."

Vance started the playback again. The weight in his chest lightened. This felt good, felt right—being a team again with Mia. Being partners.

They watched again as the van pulled up. The figure in the driver's seat pulled on dark gloves. Though the image was too dark to determine skin color, the unsub appeared male.

The man got up and moved deeper into the van. Moments passed, and the vehicle rocked gently. Then the man came around the front end, dragging a body by the armpits. He wore a hooded jacket or sweatshirt and kept his face turned down, away from the camera.

"Can't tell if I'm looking at a gang member or not, but his build looks kinda bulky. Like this guy is heavyset." Vance paused the playback and pointed at the man's back. "I'm almost ready to say he's wearing a vest. That line right there, see? Could have a plate carrier on, or at least a Level Three vest."

He hit the playback again. As they watched, the man hauled his burden into the alley and out of the camera view. The only other details they could see were his running shoes.

Vance flicked at the screen with his fingertip. If only he could angle the camera differently. Their man had either gotten lucky or knew where this camera was stationed and planned for it. "Can't see his face at all."

Mia squeezed his shoulder again. "At least we have this much." The presumed killer returned to the van, leaving the camera view before reappearing within the vehicle. He sat at the wheel, backed up, and sped away.

Vance stopped the playback. "So he opens the side or back doors, takes the corpse out, and hauls it into the alley, then retraces his steps, and gets back on the road."

"Seems to be what happened. The whole process took him maybe fifteen seconds based on the time stamps. I wasn't watching exactly."

He hadn't been watching the clock, either, but made note of the time at the end. "Twelve sixteen and thirty-two seconds. Let's see when he got started." He scrolled back to when the young couple darted away and the van came to a stop in the camera frame. "Twelve sixteen and eight seconds. Twenty-four seconds total, in and out."

Mia stepped aside, giving Vance room to stand up. "I'll ask Mr. Gimble for a copy of the footage."

Vance loomed over the screen, staring at the frozen image of the van. "Mia? You see that?" He pointed to a shadow at the edge of the screen.

"Looks like it could be...a person? Maybe two? Play it again."

When he did, the shadows were still there, but only for about twenty seconds before vanishing. Someone had darted out of frame—just moments before their suspect returned to his vehicle. He looked at her. "You think that was the kids we saw? Why would they stick around?"

Mia chewed her lip. "Maybe filming it to post online? We'll need to comb social media just in case. Or we have a different witness or witnesses."

"My money's on it being the kids. I bet we find this all over MeFace."

Sure would have been easier if Emma just pulled the truth for us out of thin air.

Vance's annoyance from earlier flooded back into him.

Whatever Emma said about ghosts, their killer was a living man who'd dropped a body in an alley as if it were nothing more than a sack of trash. She could talk to spirits all she wanted, but their next step was clear.

They'd get this footage to the rest of the team, and then they'd find a way to solve this case. With or without Spooky Last's input.

6

Emma pulled the SUV into the Berry Hill Apartment Complex parking lot. She'd been prepared to follow a series of signs, but the so-called complex was nothing more than an old streetside motel jerry-rigged into a small set of studio apartments.

She parked in the middle of the strip of fifteen apartments, choosing one of the few spots that wasn't taken or cluttered with trash. "Our guy's supposedly in number twelve."

Every car in the parking lot seemed to need repair, and none matched the description that Mia and Vance had texted. They'd seen a "dark-colored van" on security footage, but couldn't identify the make or model, much less confirm the number of occupants.

At unit twelve, she raised her hand to knock, and the door opened before she could bring her knuckles down. A lanky man with a shaved head answered. He wore a ribbed tank top, and the D.C. Skulls tattoo was in plain view on his right forearm. Even in the dim light of the covered walkway, the green cat eyes seemed to glow from his dark skin.

She was almost certain this was Darius Baker, aka Diggs Baker, aka Diggy B. She recognized him from a mug shot.

"Darius Baker? Also known as Diggs?" Emma opened up her credentials and offered him a clear view of them. Leo did the same beside her.

The man in the doorway stared at them for a moment and shook his head. "Don't know anybody by that name. Y'all have a good day now."

He started to close the door, but Emma held up a hand. "You aren't in trouble for anything, I promise. We're just trying to identify a victim and thought you might be able to help."

For a second, she thought he would close the door anyway. "What do you need?"

Emma put her ID away. "You are Darius Baker, also known as Diggs Baker and Diggy B.?"

He shifted his stance, considering her for a long second. "Yeah, okay. That's me." His voice trembled with nerves, though he did a decent job of keeping a straight face. "I'm just watching television and trying to get myself a job right now. Go ahead and ask your questions."

Emma's gaze wandered past him when he stepped to his right, revealing a card table with a laptop. She couldn't see exactly what was on the screen but recognized the logo of a popular job search website. "Like I said, you're not in trouble, Diggs. This isn't about you."

He coughed, discomfort contorting his face. "Call me Darius. Please. Diggs was my street name. I'm trying to put that shit behind me."

"Darius. Okay, we can do that. I'm Special Agent Emma Last. My partner is Special Agent Leo Ambrose."

Leo leveraged some of his charm into a smile. "We're here to find out what we can about one of your fellow members of the D.C. Skulls."

"Whoever it is ain't no fellow of mine." Darius crossed his arms. "Like I said, I've put all that behind me. I don't hang with those guys anymore. They hung me out to dry, and I'm past it. Separate ways and all that."

"You're not affiliated with the Skulls anymore?" Emma eyed him, waiting for some tell that he was lying. "Sounds like there are hard feelings between you and the gang. How did they 'hang you out to dry?'"

He narrowed his eyes on her. "Uh-uh. You want details, you can look them up in your database, I'm sure."

Leo offered an easy grin. "What can you tell us about the Skulls? Have you had any contact with anyone from the gang recently?"

Darius shifted his gaze between them before shaking his head.

Sensing the discussion taking a downward turn, Emma tried another approach. "We'd like to take as little of your time as we can, Darius, so how about this? Can you account for your whereabouts last night, between the hours of nine o'clock and one in the morning?"

He startled and backed up a step, putting his hands out as if to ward off her implied accusation. "I was here, by myself. I know that don't mean a thing to y'all, but I can prove it." He motioned to the laptop. "If you let me bring up my search history, I can show you what I was doing last night."

Emma nodded and kept a hand ready to grab for her weapon if need be. Leo stood relaxed beside her. "Go ahead."

He grabbed the laptop and brought it over to the doorway, tabbing over to his email from the job search website. "See, right here? I was sending these applications out all night long. Finally gave up around midnight, I think."

Looking at the screen, Emma spotted time stamps on a number of emails, all titled "Employment Inquiry" and sent to various addresses.

Good for you.

She gave him an encouraging nod, genuinely pleased that he was working toward creating a new life for himself. "You're taking this seriously. That's a good sign, and I bet you'll have someone calling you for an interview soon."

His smile was beautiful. "Already did. They didn't hire me, but the next one might. Just gotta get through my probation hearing next week." The smile faltered, falling into a mask of worry at the reminder.

Emma's heart softened for the man. He had the attitude of someone looking for a new path forward, away from the life he said he'd left behind. Tattoos might be permanent, but a person's mind and heart could change.

She shot a quick questioning look at Leo.

He gave a tight nod in reply. "Darius, we're here because a man was murdered last night, and we believe he had some connection to the Skulls. If you help us identify him, that could go a long way toward proving to the judge that you're serious about turning over a new leaf."

He closed the laptop and held it against his hip, nodding. "I am. Promise made is a promise kept."

Emma pulled her tablet out and tapped the power button. "As Agent Ambrose said, we're investigating a murder. Can we show you the pictures? See if you recognize the victim?"

"I don't like blood." He grimaced. "You gotta show me all of it?"

Emma paused. She was so used to crime scenes that she often forgot most people weren't. "I'll just show you his face, how's that? But his nose was broken, just a heads-up."

He nodded, and she swiped past the bloodiest photos to get to a close-up of their victim's face.

Darius peered at the screen reluctantly, but by the way his eyes went wide as he flinched backward, Emma knew they had something even before he spoke.

"Yeah, I know him. Don't know his name, though. Joey or Jason, maybe. A *J* name?"

"How long were you in the gang?"

"About a year. Maybe two."

"Did you interact with this *J*-named individual while you were with the Skulls?"

He kept his gaze locked on hers, avoiding looking at the photo again. "No, I didn't."

Emma didn't roll her eyes, but she sure wanted to. "You were in the same gang for 'about a year' or 'maybe two.' Are you sure you don't know his name?"

Darius shifted his feet, nudging the tablet away from him with one finger until Emma lowered it to her side. "I mean, we weren't all besties, you know? This guy was new and just did low-level stuff. Pretty sure he only joined a few months ago. I think he knew one of the dudes who ran the crew and just kinda wandered in as I was trying to get out."

Scrolling on her tablet, Emma pulled up Darius's statement from his arrest records. "You said the Skulls were 'a small, tight-knit group' when you were arrested." Emma checked his face for recognition, but so far, Darius remained calm and unwavering. "You also said 'nobody was into anything serious because it was more of a club than a gang' and you all 'hung out together, telling jokes and getting high.' That sound familiar?"

Darius winced. "Maybe. But I didn't hang out with Juice except..." His face drooped as Emma smiled at him.

"Juice, huh? His name was Juice?"

Meeting her gaze, Darius frowned and lifted the laptop. "Let me put this down on the table?" He tipped his head toward the card table behind him, and Emma nodded.

He put the laptop down, then came back with his hands in his pockets. "First off, I didn't know Juice that well. I wasn't lying about that."

"Why were you lying about knowing his name?"

"Like I said before, I'm trying to get past all that. I didn't want to come off like I knew any of those guys, because I don't want to know them. Not anymore."

"We're not trying to jam you up, Darius." Emma lowered her voice, wishing she'd just worn a regular jacket instead of her FBI cover. "I promise."

He took a step back, holding his hands up. "I don't want to talk anymore."

"We know that." Leo sighed. "But this kid got murdered. We just want his name so we can tell his family and hopefully find out who killed him. Is his name Juice? Not Jason or Joey or something else?"

Darius glanced back and forth between them again, then over Emma's shoulder toward their SUV. When he brought his gaze back to her, he swallowed hard, as if the sight of the official vehicle had brought him to some decision. "His street name's Juice. But that's all I've got. Most of us had street names that started with the same initial as our real names, so he probably is *J*-something."

Leo nodded, writing down the name. "What else? There's gotta be something else you can tell us to help us out here. You said Juice 'mostly did low-level stuff.' We understand the Skulls are moving into cocaine in a big way, bigger than the four dime bags you were caught with. You think Juice was killed over coke?"

He shook his head, lips tightening. "Look, man, I have no idea. Like I said, that shit's behind me, and it's gonna stay behind me. I wasn't even around when Seven-Oh made the call to move kilos instead of baggies. Just heard about it from some other guys who thought that might get me wanting back in."

"Who's Seven-Oh, and who are these 'other guys?'"

Darius hunched his shoulders. "Seven-Oh's the leader.

Dude spends his days getting high and his nights getting wasted. I don't know where he is, but I wouldn't be surprised if you find him OD'd somewhere, to be honest."

Emma had her notes app open and was taking all the information down. "What about the 'other guys' you mentioned?"

"Just dudes in the gang. They came around and said the Skulls were moving major product soon and did I want to get back in with them. I said no, and they left."

"That's it? They just left?"

He stared at Emma for a moment. "I don't know what y'all learn about gang life, but it ain't like *The Sopranos*. At least, the Skulls ain't like that. If you want out, ain't nobody gonna stop you from leaving, really, long as you keep your mouth shut." He shifted his gaze between her and Leo. "Which I am trying to do."

Leo motioned with his pen and notebook. "You said these other guys mentioned the Skulls were going to move 'major product soon.' How soon? When did they come around?"

"A few days after I made bail. But I didn't go to where they were. I came straight home and started looking for work."

"How did you get home? Take the bus or drive?"

Darius shook his head. "Ain't got a car. I rode the bus to the nearest stop two blocks away and walked from there."

Looking up from her tablet, Emma ran with Leo's question. "You said some Skulls members came around. Did they also take the bus and walk, or were they in a car?"

"Why're you asking about how people get around in this hood? Ain't it obvious nobody here can afford a chauffeur?"

"Just part of the process, Darius. The dudes who came around...they drove their own vehicle? Took the bus like you?"

He nodded at Leo. "Didn't see 'em in a car, and they

walked away when I told 'em I wasn't interested in their offer."

Emma jotted the information down, noting that so far, Darius had told them nothing that might connect the Skulls to a dark-colored van. She focused instead on the nature of the gang's visit. "What did they offer?"

He looked at his feet for a moment before answering. "Just came by and said Seven-Oh sent 'em. Like I was still in the gang. One dude said last night was gonna be a big score and did I want in."

Before Emma could form a question, Leo jumped in. "What kind of score was it? Did they say?"

Darius shook his head and kept his gaze on his shoes, prompting Emma to knock her knuckles against his doorframe.

"Hey, Darius. We're not accusing you, just trying to get answers that'll help us find Juice's killer. Do you know who the deal was supposed to be with? Was it coke? Anything you have could help us."

He stuffed his hands back into his pockets. "It was coke, yeah. Couple thousand worth or something like that. I'm being honest when I say I don't know who the dudes were, though. They were Skulls, but all new guys. Nobody I'd seen before, even when I was in the gang."

Leo lowered his tablet and leaned against the doorframe. "Darius, I feel like you're leaving something out. You could end up right back in that cell for withholding information."

Darius pinched the bridge of his nose, closing his eyes. "Johnny Duncan, okay? That's Juice's real name. I don't know anything else, I'm tellin' ya. I swear on *my* name. Now, I'm going to ask the two of you to leave, because this really isn't about me."

Emma stood still, wondering if she should push back on him. If she did, that would burn the thread of a bridge they'd obtained here. And she didn't want him to take off running if they had to come back to him for another identification.

We got a name and enough to help Wurth update his file on the Skulls. He can always come back here if he needs more.

"Okay." She pulled out a business card. "If you remember anything else, here's my card."

He backed up, shaking his head. "I ain't takin' that. Y'all can drop 'em on the doorstep if you need to. I'm sure my lawyer'll know how to get in touch." He started to close the door.

Emma and Leo stepped back into the hall, and Darius slammed the door behind them.

On the way to the SUV, Emma considered their visit a small win.

"At least we have our victim's name and some information about the gang's activities. Wurth will appreciate that." She settled into the driver's seat. One way or another, she wouldn't be surprised if Darius earned another visit from law enforcement before landing himself a job. "He might've been reluctant to help, but he seemed genuine in wanting to leave gang life far behind him. Fingers crossed that's the last time he needs to talk to one of us."

"No disagreement here." Leo buckled himself in. "I just hope he stays alive in case one of us needs to talk to him."

7

I woke up in my recliner with a sore back and a slight hangover. The TV was still on, with a pair of talking heads mumbling about nonsense as usual. The thin blanket I'd pulled over myself was half on the floor already. I tugged it back, and the events of last night rushed to my mind. I started laughing softly, then louder, until I thought I might fall out of my chair.

Flinging the blanket aside, I got up and steadied myself with a hand on top of the television. A charming brown-haired gentleman was now interviewing a celebrity about their latest charity effort. "Idiots. You don't know the first thing about helping the people who really suffer in this city."

But I did.

After exterminating my first cockroach, I was just about jumping out of my skin. I'd finally done it. But in the moment, the adrenaline was almost too much. I could barely keep still enough to drive at the speed limit. And my vest made me over-warm. Sweat prickled along my back and chest, but I forced myself to ignore it.

I'd headed to the closest drinking hole, hoping a shot or

two of cheap whiskey would calm me down enough to think straight and get myself home safely.

Plus, I needed an alibi. Squatting in a dive bar was the best way I could think of to build one.

Those two kids I scared off might have spotted me, but I was pretty sure they just ran without looking back. Another couple of gawkers showed up, though, and I thought one of them might have taken a picture.

My hangover wasn't helping as I rewound my memories, trying to focus on how many people I'd seen when I dumped the cockroach in that alley.

I'd worked fast, throwing his useless corpse onto the ground and rushing back to my van. That was when I saw the two guys standing outside the coffee shop. Maybe it had been one guy. I couldn't remember.

Think, dumbass. Think.

I got back in my van and peeled out of there, then slowed down at the next corner and drove as normally as I could until I found the bar I'd used to establish an alibi.

You went in, grabbed a stool, and ordered a double.

On my second whiskey, a single shot, I was calm enough to look around me. I'd needed to remember faces if I ever got called in front of a judge.

There were a few losers, guys just like me. Lonely drunks all but sobbing into their beers. A few friends had a game of pool going. Two ladies sat in a booth chatting.

A woman, beautiful in a plain kind of way, offered me a smile from the end of the bar. This, I remembered. She smiled, and when I gave her a nod, she came over.

"You look like hell, if you don't mind me saying so." She held her beer with both hands. I noticed she took tiny sips. It would take all night for her to finish at the rate she was going.

Considering what I'd done, I probably did look like hell.

I'd at least had the presence of mind to wipe the blood off my hands. Baby wipes to the rescue. "Rough night."

"Did you get mugged?"

"Something like that."

"This town, man. Surrounded by thugs and gangsters. And the cops don't do a damn thing."

And in that instant, I knew we were kindred spirits. She was someone who understood what the good people in this city were up against. I'd assumed she was waiting for someone, but no one walked in, and she bought us another round—even though her glass was still half full—and we just kept talking.

I told her everything I'd ever believed about crime and the cockroaches who committed it and how the cops were just failed exterminators. She agreed with every word.

When I was younger, I might've been bold enough to ask for her number. But I wasn't younger, and she was out of my league with her mysterious dark eyes and rosy cheeks so full of…life. She seemed electric. I couldn't believe I'd originally thought of her as plain. I didn't think I'd ever looked as alive as she did to me last night in the dim bar lights.

And I hadn't even asked her name.

Somehow, I'd made it home safely. I didn't remember driving myself. In fact, I wasn't even sure I got home in my own van.

I ran to the window and pulled the curtain aside, looking for my van in the parking lot. There she was, just where I always parked her near the exit. I relaxed and let the curtain fall into place again.

My head was still fuzzy, so I got the coffee maker started. The woman from the bar kept coming to my mind. I thought of her as the scent of coffee filled my kitchen.

Turning to the fridge, I spotted the bloody blanket on the

counter, with my shirt and vest strewn haphazardly beside it, and last night's adventure came flooding back again.

Ignoring the coffee, I set up the spindly wooden drying rack in my kitchen sink. The rack had been my mom and dad's idea of a going-away present when I graduated college. No car for me, or anything that might've been helpful to a young guy getting his feet wet in the real world.

They gave me a piece of kitchen junk.

One move after another, even after I met my wife, and we'd moved in together, I'd had the thing with me.

Maybe I couldn't bring myself to throw out the only physical object that tied me to my parents.

The house fire that killed them and destroyed my childhood home had been set by an idiot trying to cook his heroin in the driveway. He'd tucked himself between my dad's truck and the garage door, out of sight of anyone.

The neighbor's house had turned into a rental that was used as a shooting gallery, with junkies coming and going all the time. If that one dumbass hadn't tried to cook his dope next to my dad's old truck and dropped his lighter into a puddle of oil, I might have a place to live other than this shitty apartment.

My wife...my ex-wife...got to keep our place in the divorce.

The only things I took with me were my clothes, the baseball bat I got my son for his eighth birthday, my bulletproof vest, my pistol, and this dumbass drying rack.

If my folks were alive and could see the rack now and what I was about to do with it...they'd probably call the cops or stage an intervention.

Or they just might applaud. Finally, someone with the guts to do something about all the cockroaches making a mess of our neighborhoods and this city.

Gently as I could, I lifted the bloody blanket I'd used to

carry the trophy home. Holding it from the corners with my gloved fingers, I laid it across the drying rack. The skin would take time to cure, and I'd need to get the right kind of salt or maybe construct a drying cabinet. For now, this would have to do.

I was disappointed in myself that the hunk of decomposing flesh was a dozen hours old, but I'd never killed anyone before and couldn't have predicted how I'd react. The blanket had kept the maggots off, but I'd need to make sure nothing else came along and tried to nibble on my prize while it dried. I left it there and went to look up ways to preserve it for posterity.

In the room behind me, the television spouted news about inept politicians and the city's drug problem. I adjusted the tattoo on the rack and laughed. "Keep yapping, you morons. The city's drug problem hasn't changed one bit in the past thirty years."

That was God's honest truth, and I, more than anyone in Washington, D.C., knew it for a fact. My parents were dead because of a junkie who fumbled his lighter.

And my son was dead because he'd had the misfortune of walking around the wrong corner. He'd been on his way home from baseball practice and witnessed a drug deal going down. The dealer and buyer both pulled guns and shot him dead, right there on the street.

In broad fucking daylight.

My hands clenched into fists as I remembered that day. The phone call from the police. Having to call my wife and tell her, and the way she blamed me for choosing a bad neighborhood when we moved in.

That was the only thing that made me laugh in those dark days. Our neighborhood was fine, and she knew it. She had no problem keeping the house when I offered it during our divorce. Our son wasn't dead because I'd chosen the wrong location. He was dead because cockroaches spread like wildfire unless there was someone willing to stomp on the little bastards.

All because some gangbanger and his junkie friend had been afraid Ethan would rat them out to the cops. I knew he wouldn't have said a word. He was a good kid and a smart one too.

Ethan knew when to open his mouth and when to keep it shut. But those assholes never gave him a chance. They were in his neighborhood, on his street, not their own run-down turf.

He should've been the one to survive that day, not them. But they'd moved in, spread to our neighborhood, and acted like they owned the place.

That was what this city would never understand.

Cockroaches didn't discriminate. For them, a street was a street and a house was a house. Food was food, and they'd take everything and ruin it unless they were stopped.

My son didn't deserve to die like that, and I'd be damned if I wasn't going to get him justice now.

Standing, I collected the wadded-up blanket I'd used to transport my trophy. The blanket was stiff with blood and no doubt full of my DNA from all the times I'd handled it without gloves. I should wash it or find some way to dispose of it completely.

I had time to figure that out, though. For now, I'd wash the blanket in my bathtub. I knew cops could find trace evidence from the drains, but they'd need to know who I was first, and I wouldn't let that happen.

I was more careful than that. No way would the cops ever suspect me, even with my history and the horrors of my past.

With visions of what was yet to come, I set the blanket on the kitchen counter and paced back to the television. I wondered if the yapping dogs would bother to talk about the boy I'd killed. He'd probably killed dozens of people himself. But this city was so corrupt, I could see them talking about how sad it was that he'd been taken so young.

A cockroach like him doesn't deserve half the sympathy Ethan got.

Sure enough, a woman with long brown hair and a dark blazer showed up in a side-by-side image with the news anchors at their desk. The ticker along the bottom mentioned *mutilation* while the reporter babbled about a possible gang-related revenge killing.

I turned up the volume and smiled as she described the scene.

"Police have just now allowed pedestrian access to the other side of the street. I'm told the FBI...their offices are behind me...will be heading up the investigation."

The news anchors nodded, saying all the things they were supposed to say. I dropped into my chair and stared at the television, not liking that one bit.

The Feds are involved. This is going to get messy.

My concern faded as quickly as it'd come. As if the Feds would be any more competent than the MPD. They could barely contain a gang war that'd raged last month.

And I wasn't the only one who thought that way.

That woman at the bar did, and I knew there were more people like her. People who understood the cops would never solve the city's crime problem. Not with all their steps and rules and courts and trials.

"That's not how you fight cockroaches. First, you turn off the lights, so they think it's safe to come out. Then, when they've started feeding, getting fat on the crumbs, that's when you strike. That's when you squash them under your boot heel."

I slammed my foot into the floor, the rage burning inside

me again. None of the druggies and dealers out there had any idea what was coming for them.

I patted my pocket, where I'd stuffed that wad of money from the cockroach. I needed to clean it off, since while I was cutting him he'd spit up his guts around the roll of cash I'd used to keep him quiet.

"Guess I'd better get started on the laundry." With a laugh, I headed for the kitchen to grab the blanket. Once I had the money washed off, it'd be time to go shopping. I wanted that brand-new Level Three vest I'd seen, which had been just out of my budget before, to replace my current one. More ammo would be a good idea too.

I peered between the front curtains and examined the parking lot. The sun was steadily climbing in the sky. My operation couldn't get started until after dark. Laundry first, then a trip to my favorite sporting goods store and some food to fuel me for the evening's activities.

And then I just have to wait for the sun to go down and the roaches to come scurrying out from hiding.

"Look out, you disgusting vermin. The Bug Man's coming."

8

Emma had just pulled back onto the expressway, heading toward the Bureau, when her phone buzzed to life. Jacinda's name blinked at her, and she pressed the button on the steering wheel to take the call. "You have me and Leo here. Just heading back."

"Anything from Darius Baker?"

"Just the name we messaged you. We also passed along info to Wurth about the Skulls getting into the coke business in a big way." Emma put her blinker on and moved over a lane. "Darius mentioned last night's deal was supposed to be close to a couple thousand dollars. That explains why Johnny Duncan was killed."

"I wish I could agree with you."

Emma's hands tightened on the wheel. "What do you mean?"

The SSA sighed. "Thank you for keeping Wurth in the loop. I'm calling about a new development that seems to preclude Johnny's death being related to a drug deal gone wrong."

Emma turned up the volume. "We're all ears."

"The killer, or someone pretending to be the killer, sent us an encrypted email, directed to the VCU specifically. Mia and Vance are on the other line. You ready to hear this?"

Leo reached for his tablet. "When you are, Jacinda."

"'Dear failed exterminators.'" Jacinda paused, allowing the opening to sink in before she went on. "'I'm sure that you've found my contribution to ensuring the city's safety. It wouldn't have been needed, but that's what you get when police ineptitude is allowed to run rampant and fail the good people of the city.'"

Emma's foot stuttered on the gas pedal. "Please tell me we have a return address. I'd love to send a list of our most recent cases to this idiot."

"You know better than that, Emma. And there's more." Jacinda cleared her throat before continuing to read. "'You've seen what I do with our city's cockroaches. What I've trained and learned to do on my own. You've seen me squash one of the city's worst pests into a smear of useless paste on your doormat. And why? Because you couldn't be bothered to lift your own shoe to do it. Cockroaches overrun our city—'"

"I'm sorry, is this guy for real?" Anger oozed from Vance's tone. "Jacinda, tell me this is a fucking joke."

"It's not a joke, I assure you." Her voice was tight with annoyance.

"Sorry, SSA. Keep going."

Jacinda repeated the last bit she'd read. "'...overrun our city. These bugs crawl in the darkness. Can you hear them scurrying under your feet? I'll bet you do, and you just don't care, because you've given up. Well, I haven't.'"

Emma and Leo exchanged a glance. He mouthed *this is crazy* to her. She agreed.

Papers shuffled on the line, and Jacinda whispered to someone nearby before continuing to read the email. "'If anything about you is impressive, it's how utterly useless you are at stopping the tide of vermin crawling over our city streets. Our whole city is a cesspit, thanks to your ineffectiveness, and someone needs to do the cleaning.'"

Is this an email or a manifesto?

For a half second, Emma thought the SSA was done, but Jacinda had only paused to take a breath.

"'I'll even deliver their slimy remains to your doorstep. Just stay out of my way and let me do my work.'"

The words hung in the air, having painted the intended picture. The way the unsub had written his note, Emma couldn't help picturing cockroaches scuttling up walls and into cracks. Even the cars in the surrounding traffic suddenly seemed like bugs. Her skin itched, and she fought the urge to scratch the nonexistent vermin. "That's...creative, to say the least."

"Ha." Jacinda mumbled something to someone before coming back on the line. "You can say that again. Don't worry, I'm emailing it to all of you."

Leo stretched in his seat, absently scratching at his elbow, and Emma took some slight satisfaction from the fact that she wasn't the only one whose skin was crawling.

"This doesn't sound like a rival gang." Emma sped up again, shifting in front of a sedan that had been moving at a slug's pace. "So it feels like we can wipe that idea off the table. Agreed?"

"Agreed." Mia's voice came through immediately. "We're looking at a vigilante who sees himself as better than us. Just based on the language he uses, 'ineptitude" and 'ineffectiveness.' Calling us 'failed exterminators.' I mean—"

"We could be dealing with a smart rival gang." Vance jumped in, excitement in his tone. "Maybe someone's trying to throw us off the scent. We need to keep an open mind."

"It's possible." The last thing Emma wanted was to argue with Vance, but he didn't have all the information. She kept her tone casual. "We should also consider the Skulls' recent step into the arena, from small-time dealers to moving 'major product.' That's what Leo and I got from talking with Darius Baker."

She explained the bulk of their conversation, including that the Skulls were led by a man named Seven-Oh, and that the gang had a big coke deal planned for the night Johnny Duncan was murdered.

"That deal might've been a setup, is that what you're thinking? I don't see how that ties in with this vigilante message." Vance's frustration came through loud and clear, though whether it was with the case or with Emma, she didn't want to guess.

"I'm saying we shouldn't ignore the possibility that Johnny Duncan was killed as part of a deal gone bad." Emma navigated around a slow-moving delivery van. "Maybe the Skulls are working with a supplier whose competition didn't like the idea of another gang getting involved in the coke business, so they target the small-time gang member instead of the more dangerous and established supplier."

"Mia and I saw at least two potential witnesses to the body drop on the security footage we reviewed. If any tips come in, we could get a visual on our unsub. Or you could ask Emma to ask one of her—"

"Shut up, Vance!"

Before Vance could fire back at Mia, Jacinda put a stop to the debate. "You both make good points, and we will pursue every lead. Agent Jessup, you will also curtail any impulses to ridicule your colleagues. All of them. Is that clear?"

"Yes, ma'am. Clear as can be." Vance was quick to agree, but Emma was pretty sure the argument would come up again.

"Good. As for potential witnesses, we will continue monitoring social media, with help from Cyber, in case someone did get video of the body drop or if any anonymous tips come in." Pages ruffled in the background. "Meanwhile, let's change things up. Emma and Mia, the new medical examiner has finished up with Johnny Duncan. Introduce yourselves and follow up on the autopsy. I also want you to check with Agent Wurth about the tattoo. He was looking into artists who've done work for gangs in the city."

"He's thinking we might have a collector going for a particular artist's work?" Emma took the exit to get them back to the office. "Or...?"

"That's one possibility. The unsub could also be an artist who selects targets based on what they've overheard while working on gang members. Wurth might also be grabbing at any available straw before another body hits the pavement."

"Got it. We'll ask him about the coke angle, too, see if he knows anything about suppliers who might be pushing against each other."

The SSA gave her approval and continued detailing assignments. "Vance and Leo, check with Cyber for any updates, then start building a profile for our unsub. Get a suspect list going on the vigilante angle."

Without another word, Jacinda hung up. Mia and Vance signed off an instant later, effectively ending the conference call and leaving Emma and Leo in silence.

9

Emma knocked at the glass window of the medical examiner's office door, plastering a smile onto her face despite still having the creepy-crawlies from all the talk of cockroaches in the email Jacinda received.

The woman inside rose from her desk, waving at them as she opened the door. Her gray-blond hair hung down over her shoulders in two braids, and her glasses were bright blue, but her starched white coat and thin smile still made her look professional. "You must be from the VCU. SSA Hollingsworth called to let me know you were coming. Medical Examiner Miranda Hartford at your service, fresh from Tucson."

She stepped out of her office rather than inviting them inside, and Emma moved aside to give the woman space in the hall. "Special Agent Emma Last, and this is my partner, Special Agent Mia Logan."

Miranda shook their hands and waved them to follow her. "I like meeting the local agents face-to-face, so I appreciate you coming down. I was just finishing up my notes of the external visual inspection, but I think it's worth us looking at the decedent."

"That's what SSA Hollingsworth said you preferred." Emma hurried her step to keep up with the lithe woman. "Do you have time of death for us?"

The M.E. opened the door to Autopsy and held it open, gesturing to a small box of masks on the sideboard. She took one for herself and put on gloves as she spoke. "Time of death is estimated at between eleven thirty and midnight. We were able to corroborate the name, too, thanks to a fingerprinting drive thirteen years ago. Our victim is Johnny Duncan. No record in the system other than the fingerprints his mom had recorded at a mall when he was ten years old."

"We understand he went by Juice on the street." Emma followed the M.E. toward a covered body at the center of the space, doing what she could to ignore the chemical smell seeping into her senses and her clothing.

Better than bugs. She shivered.

Miranda drew the plastic cover down to his hip bones. "Gunshot wound to the gut. No exit wound, so the bullet's still in there. I'll dig it out during the post and send it to ballistics. Maybe we'll get lucky with a match."

Emma mentally crossed her fingers, wishing it were that easy.

"When the decedent was brought in this morning, it was already exhibiting symptoms of mid- to late-stage livor mortis, and you can see where the skin's discoloration had already become fixed by that point. Considering the temperature outside, I don't believe he was killed any earlier than eleven p.m., or we'd be dealing with later-stage decay."

Emma watched as the medical examiner pointed to the discoloration. Beside her, Mia took a step back, her discomfort visible even around the edges of the mask.

"If you look at where someone peeled away, or rather,

sliced away, the skin here," Miranda touched a gloved fingertip to the wound on Juice's forearm, "you'll see evidence that the victim was either still alive or very freshly dead, based on the degree of bruising. I'd say the killer used a straight-edged knife, very sharp, based on the cleanness of the cuts. Except for here, at the upper portion of the wound site, where you see slight tearing."

Emma took the magnifying glass the M.E. held out and took a closer look. Yep, the tearing was there, just as she'd determined at the scene.

Miranda indicated the stab wound over Johnny's heart. "Based on the depth and texture of this wound, which pierced his right atrium, tricuspid valve, and inferior vena cava, I'd say you're likely looking for a blade that's outside of legal limits and plain edged."

"That doesn't narrow it down much." Emma handed the magnifying glass to Mia and scratched her forearm. She wondered whether she was imagining cockroaches or a blade. "Legal limit is three inches, but the unsub could've used a kitchen knife or hunting knife."

Miranda pointed at a nearby monitor, showing close-up images of the wound in Johnny's chest. A ruler alongside the incision marked the dimension at close to one and a half inches in width. "Most chef's knives will reach that dimension along their length."

"Great." Emma was hoping for more useful news. "So we're looking for just about anyone with a knife block."

Miranda shrugged. "Possibly, but look at the wound edges. They are remarkably clean and precise, with minimal tissue trauma. This suggests the knife used was exceptionally sharp, possibly professionally honed or meticulously maintained. While not conclusive, such a level of sharpness is often maintained in professional kitchens, but serious home chefs or collectors could also keep their edges this sharp."

Emma took the magnifying glass back from Mia and leaned over Johnny's body to examine the wound again. At either end of the incision, the skin puckered slightly, the edges pulling outward. "But these spots...it looks like tearing. Would a really sharp knife do that?"

Miranda gave Emma an approving nod. "That's not tearing. It's wound distortion. The blade was twisted inside the wound before being withdrawn. A clean cut like this wouldn't naturally widen at the ends unless the knife was turned deliberately."

Peering closer, Emma understood. "I see."

The medical examiner traced a gloved finger near the edge of the wound but didn't touch. "This wasn't just an attack. Whoever did this wanted to cause pain. The twist would have torn deeper into the muscle, making it excruciating."

Emma pictured it—the smooth entry followed by the deliberate, agonizing twist before the blade slid free. Cold, calculated.

"Now look at the blood pooling." Miranda moved around Johnny's torso, pointing to the mottled patches spreading beneath the skin, staining his pale flesh in deep purples and reds.

Emma followed with Mia trailing behind. She loved how patient this doctor was with her explanations. She didn't appear rushed or annoyed to have them there.

"See how lividity has settled along his back, buttocks, and legs? That tells us he was on his back for a while after death. But notice how we also have some pooling on the front? That means the body was moved before livor fully set."

Mia crouched to get a better angle. "So he wasn't dragged around?"

"No." Miranda shook her head. "But I believe he was

repositioned. Not rolled, not tossed around, but briefly lifted and transported."

Mia rolled her neck, stretching the muscles. "He was moved in a van."

Emma exhaled, piecing it together. "So our unsub wasn't just killing…he had a plan. He knew what he wanted to do, took his time, then moved the body and dumped it where he knew we'd find it."

Mia studied the discoloration again. "Careful with the knife, but sloppy with the body."

Miranda nodded. "Exactly. Either he didn't care once the job was done…or he wanted him found." She frowned. "You're certain the dump was purposeful?"

"We weren't at first, but a message came in a little while ago, accusing MPD and our office of being inept and incapable of fighting crime."

"The murderer's rubbing your faces in it, then?"

"Seems that way." Mia straightened, sighing. "Whoever did this is convinced we can't do our jobs 'exterminating cockroaches.' His words, not mine."

Miranda reached down to a shelf beneath the body. "Well, that explains this." She lifted a glass jar for them to examine.

Emma's gut clenched. Her fingers itched to scratch at her lower back. "Is that what I think it is?"

"A dead cockroach. American species, *Periplaneta americana*. Quite common just about anywhere in the city, including well-maintained and clean homes. They're most common in restaurants and alleyways, or anywhere grimy."

Mia gagged, backing away. "I'm never eating in a restaurant again."

With a snort, Miranda turned the glass, inspecting the insect. "This lovely specimen was deliberately placed into the victim's left front pants pocket. Based on residue and…other substances in the fabric, I suspect it was alive when placed there, then crushed. Your killer came prepared. Left it as another message." She tapped the glass. "Great gift, huh?"

Yeah, message received. This case can't end soon enough. At least we're not dealing with a cannibal this time, though.

Miranda placed the glass jar back on the shelf and drew the sheet back over Johnny's corpse. "If you want more than fingerprints, we also have his dental records and a home address."

Relief loosened the tension in Emma's shoulders. "We'll take anything you have. When do you plan to begin the postmortem?"

Miranda glanced at the clock. "In about two hours. Like I said, I'll send the bullet to ballistics and also let you know if I find anything that might be immediately helpful for your investigation."

"Thank you."

Minutes later, Emma and Mia exited the building, and Emma inhaled a lungful of fresh air. She glanced at the address in her hand. Time for the part of the job she hated the most. Letting a family know their son wasn't coming home.

"According to the records, his only surviving family is a sister. Same address on file for her."

As they settled into their SUV, Mia wrapped her arms around herself. "I'll tell her, okay? I've been in her shoes before."

Putting a hand on her friend's arm, Emma nodded her agreement before pulling onto the road.

She drove quietly, considering just how well-suited she was for the task of informing survivors of their loved ones' fates.

You did okay with Mia, but Ned made it easy for you. So far, Johnny Duncan hasn't offered anything that will help.

In the passenger seat, Mia was talking about what she

planned to say when they got there. Emma only caught a few words and nodded along with sounds of agreement.

None of her colleagues, not even Denae, could really understand what life was like for Emma. Always anticipating someone's death as a source of information and the frustration that came from knowing that anything a ghost might say to her would be of limited value. At least until she could put all the pieces together.

She wouldn't say ghosts were entirely unhelpful. But they had a history of granting her much less help than she'd have liked, considering they'd always been the ones reaching out. And as the only member of her team who could regularly see or interact with them, she'd always been alone.

Maybe the only person alive who can do that now that Mom, Monique, and Celeste are dead.

Of course, the one person who might be able to relate to Emma's situation would be a sister. If she did, in fact, have a sister, as Celeste claimed. Celeste's warning rang over and over in her head. *"When your sister learns what you've done to me, she will find you, and she will end you."* Those had been the woman's dying words.

Emma couldn't tell which was worse—knowing she'd always be the odd one out among her colleagues or knowing the only person alive who might truly understand her could also be out to kill her.

10

Leo sat at his desk, jabbing his fingers at his keyboard. He and Vance had spent a few hours searching up recent vigilante cases, poring over messages sent to the police department and FBI offices, and looking for similarities in word choice and phrasing.

Since none of that had paid off yet, he decided to call up Keaton Holland at the Richmond BAU. Maybe their team had come across a similar case.

He answered on the first ring.

"Hey, Keaton. Leo Ambrose here, wondering if I can pick your brain for a minute." He explained what they were up against and read excerpts from the email they'd received that morning. He hoped the Richmond team's ace profiler would have some insight.

"Sorry, Leo. That sounds…disgusting. Cockroaches are the worst. The real ones, I mean."

"Nothing sounds familiar to you? You guys haven't had any threat letters or vigilante messages come in?"

"Not even by courier pigeon, nope. The last vigilante case we had was the Crucifier, and his version of communication was more...well, he let his victims do the talking for him. He's about to be transferred to max security."

Leo'd caught news of the case. The Crucifier had, as his nickname suggested, crucified his victims on wooden crosses he planted in the ground.

Leo thanked Keaton and hung up. Across the room, Vance continued pounding on his keyboard, angrily clicking and scrolling with his mouse, and generally making more noise than progress.

"Hey. Get anywhere yet?"

Vance hit a key on his keyboard hard enough to break it. "I'm finding plenty, but nothing I can tie to this case. You have any idea how many people out there think we're shit at our jobs? Dammit!" He shoved his chair back. "Ignore me. Just blowing off some steam."

Leo watched Vance stalk out of the room before he went back to his own searches. Whatever Vance was dealing with, he wasn't sure he wanted to stick his nose into it. He added another name to the list he had going on a notepad.

The problem was they had too many damn names to follow up on, and so far, none of them had panned out. The first dozen Leo had looked at were all currently serving time, which had him both relieved and frustrated.

Easy enough to cross those names off the list, but where does that leave us?

Vance returned, a soda in hand, and cozied up to his computer again. His typing was still forceful, but Leo didn't think he saw any smoke pouring from the man's ears.

"Any thoughts on whether this guy is a criminal or someone within law enforcement?" Leo marked down another suspect with a military background who'd also worked as a private security officer at a parking garage downtown. "Seems like half the people on my list are ex-military or retired cops just voicing frustration with how the city's gone downhill."

Vance shrugged. "I dunno, but the way that guy talked about squishing cockroaches in his email sounds like it could be cop-speak. Violent cop-speak but cop-speak nonetheless."

Leo scanned his list, nodding. It wouldn't be the first time he'd heard a cop refer to a gang member as a cockroach. But at the same time, the body had been parked directly on the Bureau's doorstep.

"He dropped Johnny Duncan where we'd find him, but in his email, he calls us out alongside MPD." Leo tapped his pen against the list. "Maybe he's using Hollywood logic, thinking the cops and Feds hate each other."

Vance spun in his chair to look at him. "Where are you going with this?"

"I mean, what if the guy's trying to rub both our noses in it and sow discord at the same time?" Leo fiddled with the pen. "He not only drops a body in a public place, but he chooses our doorstep. It's like he's saying the cops are too inept to catch him in the first place, and he's going to prove it by dropping the body in the place that's most likely to cause them embarrassment."

"Why not use their front door, then?"

Leo picked up his notepad and wheeled his chair over to Vance's desk. "That excludes us from the picture."

"Still not following you, Ambrose. Explain it like I'm five." Vance laughed, and for the first time that morning, Leo felt a genuine reason to enjoy working with the man.

He cracked a grin and turned his notepad for Vance to see. "Almost every insulting message I've read this morning has targeted MPD, with just a handful mentioning the Bureau." He tapped his forefinger against the notepad. "Of those, all but one implies the city would be better off if the cops stepped aside and let us handle everything."

"As if that'd fix anything. Fewer badges on the streets just means more crime."

"You're right, but that one message mentions our 'inability to cooperate.' The person who sent it thinks the reason crime is so high in D.C. is because the Feds and the cops don't work well together."

Vance sipped his soda. "I don't know, man. That's slim. It could mean something, and I'm not saying ignore it. But you're reaching here."

Leo couldn't argue, but after several hours of searching names and cross-referencing with prison records—and, in some cases, death records—he was up for any lead that had even a hint of possibility attached.

Spinning away from his computer, Vance slapped his hands on his thighs. "Hey, about what Emma said this morning. Tell me you're not really on board with all that."

Leo ground his teeth together. Not only had Vance diverged from their investigation, he'd also gone back to harping on Emma instead of being a team player like everyone else. Even Jacinda, though she had yet to confirm her acceptance of Emma's ability, was willing to treat the woman with the respect of a colleague.

And Emma needs all of us behind her, now more than ever. If what Celeste Foss said was true, she's still in danger.

Swiveling his chair, Leo held Vance's gaze and took a breath to calm himself. "The woman who caused the chaos in Salem made something of a dying declaration. She told Emma that her sister would come after her for revenge."

"Oooh, a wicked sister?" Vance's eyes rolled into the back of his head. "Do we have a name?"

"No. And Emma has no knowledge of any siblings. As far as she knows, her parents only had one child."

Vance rubbed his chin, his eyes glinting. "I'm calling her

Dorothy. If she turns out to be real, we'll already have an alias for her."

"Look, man. Even if you don't believe her about the ghosts, just keep quiet about all this." Leo narrowed his eyes at Vance. "If Emma believes there are people who still want her dead, then I'm liable to stay cautious after what happened in Salem. If nothing happens, we haven't lost anything. But if something happens, we'll be in a better position to deal with it. So chill out, please."

Vance waved in Leo's direction as if to dismiss the entire conversation, then returned to his keyboard and got back to work.

Leo watched Vance labor in silence for a long moment, shoving down the urge to shake the hardheaded bastard and make him believe. The man would just have to come around to the truth on his own time. With a sigh, Leo went back to his own suspect list, pulling up the ex-cop who'd sent that message about the cops and Feds working together.

Dalton Renfield. Okay, Mr. Renfield, let's see what you've been up to since you left the force.

11

Emma and Mia sat in the SUV outside the last known address for Johnny Duncan. Mia's phone was on speaker while she talked with Wurth, getting everything he had on the Skulls and their supplier before she and Emma went up to speak with Johnny's sister.

"And you're sure the Skulls have never moved large amounts of product before last night?"

"As sure as I am that the sky's blue. The gang has been peanuts for their entire existence, except for one member doing time for second-degree murder. The victim was another gang member who was in bed with the killer's girlfriend at the time."

Emma scratched her chin. "They eat their own. At least that matches with the idea that Johnny Duncan was killed for making a misstep."

"I'd say that's your best angle here. We've had no news of suppliers getting into turf battles, but that's something we'll watch out for."

"What about the tattoo? Jacinda said you've been looking into artists who did work for the gang."

Wurth grunted. "Nothing so far. A lot of these gangs have their work done in-house. Sometimes by artists who also maintain a storefront, but they'll ink the gang members on their own turf instead of at the business location."

"Smart and makes it that much harder to track down the artist who did the work. But could we be looking at an opportunistic killer who happens to be a tattooist as well?"

"I had that thought and put some folks on the hunt. They're going through every registered tattoo parlor in the greater D.C. area." He let out a resigned sigh. "Should only take them a week or two."

After promising to follow up with any new information he obtained, Wurth ended the call.

Emma and Mia exited the vehicle and headed up the walk to Johnny Duncan's apartment building. The asphalt path was cracked and sprouting weeds, not unlike the concrete block stairs leading up to the vestibule entrance. An old oak loomed beside the path.

With her hand at the call box, Mia glanced at her notes for the Duncans' apartment number, but Emma reached past her.

"The lock's busted." She pushed the door open, releasing a cloud of air that smelled of cooking grease, cigarette smoke, and wet dog. "Looks like we just head up and see if anyone's home to notify."

With Mia on her heels, Emma led the way inside and up a narrow staircase covered in patchy, worn carpet. The building smelled similar to a gazillion other run-down complexes she'd entered, if slightly worse. Rotting garbage, pot smoke, and the scent of something rancid trying to be covered up by something floral permeated the air. She barely flinched at the sight of a large rat scurrying around a corner as they rounded a landing and continued upward.

"Remember, I'd like to be the one to tell her. Okay?" Mia

stepped over a large puddle of what Emma hoped was spilled soda.

"Sure thing." Emma wasn't going to argue. She knew Mia would handle the notification professionally and would give Trisha Duncan more than mere sympathy for her loss.

Her brother was murdered too.

Grief worked in weird ways. It could come and go like the tides or be a sudden flash flood. While she hadn't lost a sibling, Emma had her own experiences with loss. The thought got her spiraling into internal questions about what Celeste had told her before she died.

"This isn't done, Emma Last. When your sister learns of what you've done to me, she will find you, and she will end you."

She knew her mother had only given birth to her. If her father had a child by another woman, she'd have to check with his colleagues. Maybe his classmates at law school.

Since Celeste's revelation, Emma had built up a battle plan for digging into her father's history, hating herself for suspecting him and at the same time feeling oddly closer to him than she ever had when he was alive.

Her mind was still drifting over the easiest way to reach out to her father's former classmates when Mia moved in front of her. They'd reached the fifth floor and were approaching the door to unit 505.

Johnny Duncan and his sister had lived at the very end of the hall. Like most of the apartments along the hall, no welcome mat graced the doorway.

The woman who opened the door after Mia's knock wore a sports bra that framed her protruding clavicle bones and oversize sweatpants that hung loose on her hips. Emma and Mia held up their IDs as Mia introduced them. The woman immediately started closing the door. "He ain't here. I don't know where he is."

Mia lifted a hand. "We know Johnny's not here, Trisha. He's...we just want to talk."

Trisha's face fell. Her brown eyes went liquid and sad as realization seemed to dawn on her. She fell back a couple of steps, letting the door swing open. "Yeah, I'm Trisha. You're here to tell me Johnny's in jail or dead, aren't you?" Before Emma or Mia could answer, she waved them inside. "You can come in."

Pulling her brown hair into a loose ponytail, Trisha moved over to a threadbare recliner and gestured Emma and Mia toward the couch catty-corner to it. Mia remained standing, but Emma perched on the couch, taking in the apartment.

Small but neat, the space held a mishmash of furniture and dated technology, most of it probably secondhand, based on the wear and tear. An old boombox that had probably been playing music before Emma was born sat on a sideboard with a stack of CDs beside it.

The cracked flat-screen television reminded Emma of one she'd had in college. The kitchen itself sported a chaotic mix of whitewashed cabinets and orange laminate, as if someone attempted refurbishing a seventies-style kitchen at some point in the nineties but gave up when it came to the more permanent fixtures.

Johnny and Trisha Duncan's apartment was a sad space, clean or not, and seemed to leave a curtain of heaviness on them even before the conversation began.

Emma knitted her hands loosely together and met Mia's eyes.

Mia nodded before crouching beside the recliner. "Trisha, I'm sorry to be the bearer of bad news, but your brother was found dead this morning."

She stiffened in her seat, parting her lips and closing them again. She looked more confused than surprised. "How did it happen?"

Emma's mouth had dried to a crisp. The empty-eyed expression coming over Trisha's face reminded her too much of the young man they'd found in the alley.

Mia put a hand on Trisha's shoulder. "He was murdered. We're hoping you might be able to help us get some leads on who would have wanted him dead."

Trisha hiccupped as a tear slid slowly down her face.

Emma leaned forward. "Trisha, we are sorry about your brother. If you need us to call someone for you…"

She shook her head, lips tightening before she sat back in the seat. "No, I'm okay. I'll…tell our family after you leave."

Mia flashed a look at Emma, who pulled out her tablet. "You have more family in the area?"

"No." Trisha shook her head. "They live down in North Carolina, in a small town. Here in the city, it was just me and Johnny. We moved up here once we were both eighteen. Neither of us wanted to live out in the country anymore."

Emma rested her tablet on her knees.

Mia spoke even more quietly. "Trisha, if you can tell us anything about who might've been upset with your brother, that could help."

The young woman tugged at the band of her sweatpants, fidgeting. "I mean, I knew he was running with a bad crowd, but I didn't know it was *this* bad. I thought he was smoking pot and pawning stolen goods and shit. Selling coke…" She closed her eyes.

Emma gave her a minute to process before speaking. "You knew he was in a gang?"

"The Skulls." Trisha grimaced, refocusing on Emma and Mia. "Us living together and all, he couldn't exactly hide the tattoo, and he told me the truth when I asked about it. Same with the coke…we had a big fight when he joined the gang, and then another one the night he brought home a couple ounces he was going to sell. He said his cut would 'set us up good' and if he made another score soon, we wouldn't have to live in this dump anymore."

Since Trisha seemed calm and willing to talk, Emma probed for a little more info. "When were these fights, the night he joined and the night he brought home the cocaine?"

Trisha thought for a moment, staring at her hands. "He joined the Skulls maybe two or three months back. I don't remember exactly, but it wasn't that long ago."

"And the cocaine?"

"Two days ago. He went out last night to make the deal. When he didn't come home, I figured he was out with the gang partying and getting high."

"And you said a couple ounces? Did you see it?"

"Yeah, it was in little baggies about this big." She held up her fingers to indicate the size.

Emma traded a look of confirmation with Mia. Neither of them did much work around vice issues, but they'd both encountered cocaine dealers on cases before, notably their rogue effort with Special Agent Sloan Grant to bring down the men who killed Mia's brother.

Based on Darius Baker's report of "a couple thousand," and Emma's knowledge of the drug trade, Trisha's estimation of a "couple ounces" checked out. She made a note in her tablet.

Mia got up from her crouch and took a seat beside Emma on the worn couch. "Did Johnny ever tell you about his gang? The people in it? Anyone he had beef with?"

She shook her head. "I wanted nothing to do with that part of his life, and he knew it. I told him I was gonna move out come the end of the year. I wasn't comfortable with him being in the gang, and then knowing he'd have drugs in here. I'm studying to be a nurse."

"That's what you fought about."

Trisha stiffened and nodded, holding in tears.

Emma sat up straighter and looked Trisha in the eye. "What time did you fall asleep last night?"

"A little before eleven. I don't know, really. I take a sleep aid around half past ten like I always do. It puts me out like a zombie, so I get in bed right after. I was reading a textbook and woke up with it lying next to me. I was probably asleep by eleven at the latest."

Trisha wiped at tears of sorrow or anger. Emma's heart tugged. *Probably both.*

Mia shifted to the edge of the couch. "What about before you took your meds? Can you walk us through your evening? Let's start with the time your brother left."

"Around five. He said he was going to make the deal and promised he'd be back in time to say good night."

Mia traded a quick look with Emma, then turned to the young woman across from them. "But he wasn't."

She shook her head. "No. He didn't come home." Tears steadily fell from Trisha's eyes, trailing down her cheeks.

Worried they might lose the interview before learning anything, Emma focused on concrete facts that Trisha might recall. "Did you hear anything last night? A gunshot, maybe, around or after eleven? We're still trying to determine where he was killed."

The young woman stared at the floor for a moment. "No. I didn't hear anything."

"I'm sorry to ask, but it's a matter of protocol." Emma kept her voice gentle. "Can anyone vouch for you being here all night last night?"

Trisha sighed, closing her eyes as if in defeat. "The short answer? No. Does that mean you need me to come to the station?"

"Not yet." Emma glanced to Mia, who nodded. Family

members might be the first suspects in a lot of cases, but this woman's sorrow was real, and she'd invited them in with barely a thought. Maybe they couldn't take her off the suspect list, but she wasn't near the top of it.

Emma rubbed her chin. "Did your brother have a vehicle we should be looking for? Or do you know the bus stops he frequented?"

"We don't have a car. He liked to walk and hated the bus." Trisha ran her hand through her hair, and Emma noticed how her fingers trembled. "Look…if you don't have any other questions, I need to call my family. I can barely think right now. I'll call you if I think of anything?"

As Emma stood, Mia handed the girl her card. Trisha showed them to the door. As she closed it behind them, Emma heard her mutter, "We should've stayed out in the country."

Emma swallowed down a sudden lump in her throat. As she led the way out of the building, she half expected Johnny Duncan's ghost to pop into existence.

Mia's voice broke into her thoughts halfway down the stairs. "I feel like we just got ten steps forward and the same number back. We still don't know where he was killed or why."

But another thought had percolated in Emma's mind. "It's more about the when for me."

"The what?"

"The when." Emma sped up as they descended the stairs, speaking over her shoulder. "Johnny Duncan left around five o'clock, saying he'd be home to say good night, which he'd know would be close to eleven because Trisha goes to bed at the same time every night."

"And?"

"Johnny didn't come home."

Mia nodded. "Maybe he was out with the gang, living it up after he sold the coke."

"Does that track with a guy who promises his sister they'll be 'set up good' and promises her he'll be home?"

Mia shot her a look. "You're thinking Johnny was going to make this score as a way to make up for putting Trisha in harm's way."

"Exactly. I think he was coming home when he was killed, which means we might be looking for a crime scene close by." She nudged Mia in the elbow. "How do you feel about looking around before we head out?"

"Makes sense."

Outside, she kept waiting for ghosts to show their faces. After the trip to Salem, she expected to see them everywhere, but she'd only seen Mrs. Kellerly since coming back to D.C.

Emma wasn't sure whether to be thankful or annoyed by that. She'd finally come clean to her whole team about her experience with the Other, but Vance was still acting like she'd made him the butt of a massive practical joke, and she hadn't been able to produce any kind of results to prove herself to him.

She led the way around the building, down a sidewalk that bordered a browning patch of lawn and the parking lot. A chain-link fence divided the lot from the lawn and wrapped around the back of the building. "I really hope I'm right about this. If Johnny was killed somewhere else, we could be wasting our time."

"We should canvass the area, see if anybody heard or saw something."

She was about to suggest they start with the residents in Johnny's building when a drift of Other cold enveloped her. Emma's first thought—with the memory of Salem still fresh in her body and mind—was to back away and avoid the deep chill.

Her heart leaped into her throat. Johnny's ghost wandered across the parking lot toward them. Seeing only a single ghost, and one she recognized, lightened her mood so much, she almost broke into a run to meet him halfway.

"He's here after all."

Mia spun around and walked alongside Emma, throwing her hands in the air with a laugh. "Just lead the way. It's not like I can see where he is or where he's going."

Sharing a brief laugh with her friend was almost enough to make Emma forget they were on the trail of a sadistic killer.

She followed the ghost across the lot, back in the direction they'd come from. Johnny turned around at one point and shivered before darting for the chain-link fence. He aimed for a gap in the fence that allowed access to the lawn on the other side. When he got to the fence, he staggered and dropped to the ground.

"I ain't a cockroach. Shouldn't have squashed me like that."

Emma paused and put a hand out for Mia to stop. "He's sitting down by the fence, at the gap there." They headed over.

"He's right here. Maybe this is where it went down." She stooped beside the ghost and examined the ground, pulling gloves from her pocket and putting them on.

Mia did the same but remained standing. "Is that a cigarette?"

"Where?" Emma turned, and her gaze caught on a dark patch of ground next to Johnny's ghost. "Better question. Is that blood?"

Johnny's ghost looked at her, shaking and holding his hands over his abdomen. "Ain't a cockroach. Shouldn't squash a guy like that." Then he vanished.

"He's gone."

Mia backed off. "I'll get the kit."

She raced to the SUV and was back just as fast. While Emma videoed the process, Mia carefully collected a soil sample and tested it for the presence of human hemoglobin. Within minutes, they had a positive result.

"Bingo. But there's no way to tell if the blood that was spilled here belonged to Johnny Duncan. Even a lab may not be able to extract DNA from what's here."

The dark patch of ground crawled with insects. Emma's skin itched again.

She photographed the test result, then took pictures of the soil area. "Even so, this is a large quantity of blood, so we might have better odds than you think. And I'd bet those dark patches leading toward the parking lot are a trail to where our unsub parked his van."

They followed the path, with Emma taking pictures along the way.

"We need forensics here. Let's put up the cordon in the meantime."

While Mia returned to the SUV and got the crime scene tape, Emma marked the cigarette Mia had spotted for the crime team to collect.

Her ghosts had come through after all.

❈

When the forensic techs arrived, Emma and Mia had already marked additional evidence. A 9mm shell casing and additional blood spatter all but confirmed they'd found the location of *someone's* murder.

And Emma would bet her Prius the *someone* was Johnny Duncan.

The lead tech waved them down as she was carrying evidence bags to the forensic van. "You did most of our work for us, but we found additional signs of recent gunfire." She brought out an evidence bag with what looked like slivers of metal. "Considering how long the blood was on the ground, I don't think we'll get a match to your victim. But we might get it off these. Found them in the grass, on the other side of the fence. First glance, I'd say this is what's left of the bullet."

"People around here would've heard a gunshot." Emma met the tech's eyes as she brushed hair from her face. "Most of these apartments are occupied."

The tech shrugged. "You know this type of neighborhood. Nobody hears anything. You ask long enough, everyone here will swear they put in earplugs each night before going to sleep."

"Or the gun was suppressed." Mia examined the evidence bag, frowning. "Our unsub must've planned things, to be ready to take that tattoo and move the body. Getting a suppressor on his weapon wouldn't have been the hardest thing in the world if he wanted to be careful."

Emma sighed, knowing that Mia was right. Acquiring a suppressor legally would be as simple as getting a gun. And if he had the funds, he could certainly get one on the street, assuming he didn't use a homemade one.

A Bureau SUV pulled up across the lot, with Leo at the wheel and Vance beside him. The men had been mired in research when she and Mia checked in earlier.

They thanked the tech, then made their way to the vehicle as Leo shut off the engine. He and Vance climbed out and met them by the hood.

"The techs are still collecting evidence, but it looks like we have our crime scene." Mia's voice was clipped when she addressed Leo and Vance outside the vehicle, and Emma wondered if she was still sore with Vance. "But there's no footage along this street, and we could probably door-knock all day without getting answers."

Emma forced a smile, directing it more at Leo's cocked head than Vance's thin-lipped expression. "What about you two? Anything useful?"

"We do have the makings of a suspect list, and it's a long one. But I think I have our first person of interest."

Leo brought up the list he'd generated and showed it to them.

Reading down the names, Emma wondered again why their unsub wanted the FBI's attention. "You marked this list as folks who think law enforcement isn't doing its job. These people all have complaints about the FBI or local PD?"

Vance barked out a sound that was halfway between a snort and a laugh. "You have no idea how many people feel that way, and you don't need any ghosts to tell you so. The shit Leo and I saw today would make you think twice about wanting to stay with the Bureau."

So Vance still wasn't ready to be civil. Ignoring him, Emma pivoted to face Leo. "Forensics identified the weapon as a nine-millimeter, based on a shell casing. They also got bullet fragments. And the medical examiner will be digging a bullet from our victim soon."

"Though plenty of civilians have them, a nine-millimeter weapon would fit with the unsub being former LEO or ex-military. A lot of the people on this list have those backgrounds, but this guy, Dalton Renfield, strikes me as worth looking at."

"What's his story?"

"Former cop who thinks the Feds and MPD would be more effective if we teamed up, but look at his social media." Leo held out his tablet. "One day, he thinks MPD has their heads in the ground. The next, he's singing their praises and claiming we're the ones who are 'overpaid and undertrained.'"

Emma read through a few of the posts Renfield had made

online. "He's all over the place. He loves us, or he hates us. Is there a pattern?"

"None that I could see, but out of all the names Vance and I dug up, this is the only guy who has an intense love-hate vibe for us and MPD and isn't wearing an orange jumpsuit." Leo's mouth twisted. "A couple of mob associates fit the bill, but they've been doing time on Rikers Island for the last two years."

Mia suggested they return to the Bureau and update Jacinda with what they'd discovered, but Emma was antsy to check on Dalton Renfield. She expected Leo to argue, but he was up for a visit to Renfield's address as well.

"We could split up again. Vance, Mia? Do you want to head back to the offices?"

"Actually," Vance stepped forward, "I was hoping to talk with Emma for a minute. I haven't been my best self today, and I'd like to clear the air."

Emma's stomach flip-flopped. She searched his face for a moment before nodding toward the side of the parking lot.

Whatever he has to say, Emma girl, just remember what he's being asked to accept. And if you're lucky, somebody he used to know might pop out of the Other and help you convince him.

12

Vance walked past the point where Emma stopped. He'd kept his cool while they all discussed Leo's list of suspects, but with things winding down and the looming prospect of going back to the Bureau, he just couldn't wait any longer.

He kept going until he stood at the edge of the parking lot, near the street. Emma looked at him with her arms crossed but finally joined him.

Maybe a dimming street near a crime scene wasn't the best place to barrage her with questions, but what place would be better? Certainly not the Bureau, and he wasn't about to follow her home or take her to some coffeehouse for the talk.

"Thanks, Emma, for giving me a chance to explain. I also wanted to ask a few questions. If that'd be okay." He forced himself to smile, though he doubted the expression was believable.

Emma just stood there like a statue. "Go ahead. What do you need to get off your chest?"

He swallowed, fighting to keep his voice low and allow her the privacy she obviously wanted for this conversation.

"First, I'm sorry I've been…tense about things. I know you're coming from a place of…" He searched for the words and couldn't find them. And then all his frustration came bubbling up. "I need the truth, Emma. This thing you call the Other? These stories you're telling about ghosts. What's really going on?"

A sigh escaped her, but she nodded and stepped closer. "I told you that I have this ability, or gift or curse or whatever you want to call it, that allows me to see ghosts. I haven't had time yet to share my family history or everything that happened in Salem, so I completely understand that you have so many questions. But, honestly, if all you plan to do is make fun of me, I'm not sure I want to bother."

He glared at her, already losing patience. "That's the big catch, isn't it? You have everyone else ready to eat this up, and they have easy outs. Mia's brother. Leo and Denae almost losing each other. Hell, I almost lost Mia on that same case and almost died myself. But for some reason, I don't get to know what you know or see what you see." He kicked at the ground. "Why? What's the secret?"

Emma bristled and dug her hands into her pockets. "I'm not keeping secrets. I thought I made that clear. I don't have an answer for your question, and I'm sorry I don't. This is all pretty new to me too."

His mouth twisted. "Which feels convenient."

"I—"

"You only gave me and Jacinda pieces of what happened in Salem, and this morning…I'm supposed to believe that was all because of ghosts?" He jabbed his finger at her. "I want to know how exactly you expect me to believe anything you've said today, especially that you're able to talk to ghosts."

Emma ran her hands through her hair. "I'm not sure I can tell you, but I'll try."

She kept going, but the story blurred in Vance's mind, despite how he tried to take her seriously. Mia would want him to, he knew. He tried to keep an open mind as she talked, but everything she said sounded like a fairy tale.

As Emma went on and on about her mother's childhood friendships and an amateurish girl's fantasy of a blood pact, admitting she really had no idea how all this worked or why she had such contact with the Other—beyond guesses—his blood only boiled hotter.

Finally, he broke in. "And you could always talk to ghosts?"

"No! I didn't really understand what I was even seeing until last year. Though, the first time it ever happened, I was young. This guy I was in school with died in a car accident, and I saw his ghost." She shook her head. "But I only recognized that in hindsight."

"Okay, so what happened last year that changed things? When was that?"

"Right after my twenty-eighth birthday. And then on our first case in January, at the circus." She drew in a shaky breath. "I saw the victims, and...I knew what I was seeing."

"Ha. When Leo and Mia showed up?" He sneered, ignoring the flush that rose to her cheeks. "How convenient. You get a new ability to share just in time to impress new team members and a new SSA."

"I didn't tell anyone at first." Emma stepped closer, her face within a foot of his as she attempted to stare him down. "You think I made this up? To impress people?" She pointed her finger at him. "That's bullshit, Vance, and you know it."

He waved off the attack, backing away. She wasn't exactly the most logical person he knew. Maybe she believed all this crap, but that didn't make it true. "But you went back to Salem, and you took Mia and Leo with you, so you not only told them earlier, before me and Jacinda, but you knew something bad was about to unfold. And, what, you put your secrets above innocent lives?"

Emma's face went white, and she faltered backward as if he'd punched her. He took a different approach, not wanting to force her into a defensive position. If anything, he needed her at her best.

I'll have an easier time believing her if she's standing up straight and looking me in the eye.

"Why did you go to Salem initially if you didn't know what was going on?"

"I had a vision involving my mom's other friend, Monique Varley. The woman who died on the hilltop right before you and Jacinda arrived."

"A *vision?*" Vance laughed louder than he meant to.

"Keep your voice down." She glanced back at the cops swarming the crime scene.

Emma's own voice had been raised, though he chose not to point it out. That said, the sneer on his face might've done it for him. All thoughts of having a collegial chat left him, and he went on the attack. "I thought you only saw ghosts?"

"It was a onetime thing. It happened in the Buckskin Wilderness, in Virginia. Monique was trying to contact me because *she felt* something was about to happen. I had no idea how bad it would be in Salem, but I'd already planned to go back there."

She went on, telling him about the time she and Leo were in Boston while Vance and Mia were in the hospital, recovering from their separate ordeals.

"Each time Leo and I drove past Salem, I got…it's hard to explain unless you've ever suffered hypothermia. But it was worse." Emma hugged herself. "I could barely move, let alone breathe."

"And that all happened in Salem, so you went back? Help me understand."

She threw her hands in the air. "I went back to find out *why* that happened and to see if I could stop it from happening again. It felt like something I needed to do. I don't know how else to say that, so don't ask." She narrowed her eyes at him. "And before you accuse me of 'taking' anyone with me, Leo and Mia volunteered to go along. Insisted. It's that simple."

"Simple." Vance turned and paced a few feet away, trying to keep his emotions contained. She'd saved herself and others, clearly, but nearly let him die, and she called all this simple.

"Vance…"

"Give me a damn minute, would you?" His demand silenced her, finally, and he kept his eyes closed. He counted to himself, trying to even out his heartbeat.

Every word out of Emma Last's mouth only added to what sounded like extremely elaborate fantasies she'd concocted.

But why? To make herself feel special? To stand out on the team?

The fact that she was playing it so straight, staying calm while talking about this, should've put him at ease. But no matter how hard he tried to believe her, his doubt remained.

"I don't know." He kept his back to her. "I thought we were friends. Colleagues and professional partners."

"We are! I've been piecing together the insanity of my life for a while now, and it's been all I can do to stay on top of it." Her voice cracked, but he didn't turn. "To try to figure things out while working cases and dealing with the Other intruding whenever I let my guard down. I'm doing my best here. I know it's a lot, but I need you to trust me."

"Trust." He faced her, breath evening out. "That goes both ways, right?"

She nodded, flinching. "Yes, but I don't think we're talking about trust in the same way."

For a moment, she looked weak. Hollowed out like she'd been after her boyfriend died. Vance's blood pressure had come down a few notches, but he still couldn't take her at her word. No matter what she said.

"I trust you to do your job while I do mine. I trust you not to stab me in the back, literally or figuratively. As for ghosts and visions," he shook his head, "I'm gonna trust you to just keep that stuff to yourself for now. All right? Just…leave me out of it."

"Vance, we're a team. We work together every day, and that won't change unless one of us decides to transfer or quit."

"Maybe you're right." He put his hands on his hips and looked down at the pavement. "I'm hungry." He jutted his chin back in the direction where Mia and Leo were likely still waiting for them. "Mia and I are going get some dinner and figure our shit out. Maybe a night off will have us all coming back together fresh tomorrow morning, like nothing happened."

She opened her mouth, but he walked away before she had a chance to speak.

13

Emma sat at her desk, reading over the unsub's note once more. She and Leo had picked up tacos on the way back to the offices and were almost ready to head over to Dalton Renfield's apartment.

As their primary person of interest, based on the messages he'd posted to social media, criticizing both the Bureau and MPD, Renfield stood out. That wasn't saying much, though, as making accusatory comments online was not, to Emma's knowledge, a criminal offense.

But right now, I'll take anybody who stands out more than me.

She'd spent the last twenty minutes fighting with the part of her brain that wanted her to find Vance and plead for him to believe her.

To keep herself distracted from those entirely useless thoughts, Emma picked apart the email Jacinda had received from the killer. She was looking for repeated phrases, anything they could use to help make their interview go smoother.

If Renfield was the author, she'd be ready to use his own

words and, she hoped, spark enough of a reaction that he gave himself away as their killer.

Leo was at his desk, having just returned from the bathroom, and had his nose in his laptop. He was doing the same as her, reading and rereading the email. "You know what I find most compelling about this message?"

"Tell me. As long as it doesn't involve cockroaches." She pushed the remnants of her tacos away.

He laughed. "Aren't we reading the same thing? Anyway, I was saying…this feels personal. Like the writer's been directly attacked or harmed in some way and sees law enforcement as the responsible party."

She kept staring at it, focusing on the language. "Renfield's an ex-cop, and we know he was dismissed for a bad shoot."

"Yeah." He scooted his chair over to her. "The investigation revealed the man he killed had gang affiliation and that he'd been carrying a can of spray paint, which Renfield claimed he thought was a gun."

"He lost his badge because of it. So there's our personal reason for being mad at MPD. But how does the Bureau figure into things? Better yet, are we looking at a guy who can't resist telling us he's the killer?"

Leo stared at her, mouth agape. "What makes you ask that?"

"The bug thing." Emma's lip curved up. "You ever see *Dracula*? Read it?"

It took a second, but then Leo smacked his forehead. "Renfield was the guy who ate bugs, right? Dracula's pet human. If Dalton Renfield is our killer, maybe he's asking to get caught. Wouldn't be the first time that's happened."

Emma had already started digging into Renfield's personal history. "Or thought he was being clever. Well, Mr. Renfield, maybe you got too clever for your own good." She pulled up public records about the man and whistled. "Look at that."

Leo grabbed a notepad and crossed the aisle between their desks. He crouched beside her chair. "I'll be damned. Personal and direct as can be."

Emma summed up her findings out loud, so Leo could jot down the details on his legal pad. "Dalton Renfield's son, Paul Renfield, was killed in an act of gang violence five years ago. The boy was only fifteen but an active member of the Hollow Bones gang, a small outfit operating out of Baltimore. There's not a lot of information, but the kid wasn't a random victim. He was found with a bloody knife and, apparently, had been in the process of cutting a rival gang member's arm, attempting to mutilate his gang tattoo." She let out a low whistle of satisfaction. "He was slicing an X over the ink job."

When Emma tried to make eye contact with Leo, he was busy writing.

"Dammit, Leo, we have him. This all but confirms it. Renfield's trying to exact vengeance for his son's death."

"Let's slow down a bit." Leo stopped writing and held up his hand. "I agree this makes him look good, or…bad, I guess. But it's not going to stand up in a courtroom. It's not proof of anything except that he has a reason to hate gangs."

Emma scanned the active-gangs list Agent Wurth had sent over, her enthusiasm waning just a touch. "Nothing connects the Hollow Bones and D.C. Skulls, and the Hollow Bones aren't active anymore. We'll have to check with Wurth and see if they moved on or got absorbed into some other gang." She jerked her chin at the computer screen. "You know D.C. still has over a hundred and forty, even after the Drivers and Powders busted up?"

"Yeah, I know." Leo sighed, already typing out a text to the Safe Streets liaison.

"Listen, we have a note from Renfield's personnel file." Emma saved it as a PDF but left it open on her computer. "If he's our guy, we'll want backup with us when we go interview him."

"I'll ask MPD for support. Anything else we should nail down, or are you ready to roll?"

Emma paused before answering, her gaze tracking over the email again, noting the author's repeated references to "cockroaches" and police "inefficiency" and "ineptitude."

The wording and phrasing reminded her of her father's way of speaking at times. Especially when he and his colleagues conversed over the phone. The back of her neck prickled.

Whoever wrote this probably went to college, maybe even law school, neither of which are a match for Renfield's background.

According to the records she'd accessed, he'd attended one semester at a community college, taking classes in the Criminal Justice program, before he applied to the academy and began his career in law enforcement.

"Do you know anyone in the BAU who's an expert on writing analysis or linguistics?"

Leo shook his head. "You'd know someone local before I would."

Emma pulled up the Behavioral Analysis Unit directory and searched through the different departments. "Got her. Renee Bailey, two floors up."

She checked her phone. The time was coming up on seven o'clock, but maybe she'd get lucky and find Renee at her desk.

She printed out the email as well as the note from Renfield's personnel file, grabbing an envelope just in case she had to leave the materials at the admin desk. "I'm gonna go up there. Want to join me?"

Leo had been shifting in his seat like he might stand but

waved her off. "I'll let Jacinda know what we've found. You can fill us both in when you get back."

Emma nodded and headed upstairs, stretching out her stride to get the blood pumping back in her legs after sitting for so long.

Outside of Renee Bailey's office, she was gratified to hear the sounds of soft jazz floating from an open door. She knocked on the frame and received a lilting, "Come on in."

Renee Bailey sprouted pretty brown curls in every direction, and her clear round glasses made her eyes shine, even in the dim light. She gave Emma a friendly, big-toothed smile. "Can I help you?"

"I hope so." Emma handed the two notes across the desk to the woman. "I'm Special Agent Emma Last with the VCU. We have a note from a killer, and this other note came from a potential suspect. Any chance you could tell us if the same person wrote them?"

Renee motioned toward a chair with an afghan blanket folded across the back. "Grab a seat." She pushed away the folder she'd been paging through. "I've spent so much time going over the evidence for this trial I have coming. My eyes can use a break from it. Let's see what you have."

Emma waited and watched, keeping quiet to avoid bothering the woman any more than she already was. The sole of her foot itched, bringing to mind the picture of a roach's antenna grazing it before she could cut it off. She squashed the image and forced a bland smile onto her face.

"Okay, well, maybe?" Renee turned the notes around so Emma could view them, too, running her fingers to different sentences as she spoke. "You have similar sentence lengths, paragraph lengths, and vocabulary. But that won't hold up in court. Two people with similar upbringings or education levels might use the same phrasing, sentence length, and so on. We also have 'there' misspelled in both, but that's a commonly misspelled homonym, so again, we could easily be looking at a coincidence."

Emma's gaze lingered on the two words. She hadn't paid attention to the mistakes, but still, she'd hoped for more. "Anything else?"

Renee's focus remained on the notes, scanning back and forth, but she finally shook her head. "You can leave these with me. I'll upload them tomorrow and run them through some software. The subjects are so different...one a threatening note and one that looks like a semiformal resignation or something that went along with one...I'll be surprised if we get anything definitive, but I can try."

Passing the woman her card, Emma stood up. "Anything you can do, we'd appreciate it. Thanks."

Renee waved goodbye with the card in her hand. "You got it. I'll be in touch if I find anything. And if another document comes up, just send it my way. Card's on the bookcase there."

Emma grabbed the woman's card and headed back out the door, tamping down a sense of annoyance. A real connection between the notes would've been too simple, but didn't they deserve a simple win every once in a while?

Back downstairs, she gave Leo the quick and dirty version of what Renee Bailey had told her. "Inconclusive at best, but she's going to keep looking at the notes and will let us know if anything jumps out. How'd it go with Jacinda?"

"Fine, but she wants us to hold off on questioning Renfield until tomorrow. She left before you came back."

"Everything okay?"

Leo picked up his bag and pulled it over one shoulder. "She's still underwater dealing with Salem, but so far, so good. Nobody's calling for your head, in case you're worried."

She was. But with Jacinda running interference, Emma

knew she stood a good chance of avoiding any public embarrassment around her ability.

Taking a moment to shut down her computer, Emma thought about how far the team had come since their first case together in January. Not even five full months, and they'd brought down over a dozen serial killers, stopped a gang war from overtaking the city's poorest neighborhoods, and even prevented a mass murderer from destroying Emma's hometown of Salem.

Maybe you've had more wins than you give yourself credit for, Emma girl.

With her bag on her shoulder, she followed Leo out of the office, her steps a little lighter. At least they had a lead.

Heading into the stairwell to the garage, she thought about the wisdom of waiting on an interview with Renfield. She knew better than to take off on her own and attempt to contact a potential suspect, and she couldn't very well ask Leo to go rogue with her.

At the garage, he waved goodbye and climbed into his truck. The engine roared to life as Emma headed for her car. Tomorrow morning, with the whole team refreshed, they'd look into this Renfield character.

For a moment, her skin itched, but for once, the sensation wasn't due to the creepy-crawlies from thoughts of roaches. Instead, she was remembering Vance's words from their little chat. She hoped his sincerity could be trusted.

Standing in the nearly empty garage, alone, she was struck by another thought.

I wanted for so long to just tell everyone. Now that I have, I'd give anything to go back to how things were before.

14

Marty "Murda" Kaine left the fun house on the corner and headed down the sidewalk. He took a moment to adjust himself in his pants, glancing both ways to make sure nobody noticed. The houses around him were mostly dark. A few places showed TV screens flickering behind curtains, but the street was quiet. Made sense, as it was half past midnight.

Empty, except for Marty, of course, as he made his way back to his crash spot. He could've stuck around the fun house, the brothel that his gang, the Serpents, was running, but he'd never get a wink of sleep in that place.

Ain't no sleeping going on there.

Marty kept walking, unable to stop picturing that girl with freckles who'd given him her time for a handful of cash. She'd just turned eighteen, or so she said, but he had his doubts.

And he was twenty-seven.

Bad enough his gang was running this business in competition with the Blue Devils from the next neighborhood over. Sooner or later, that was going to start a turf war, and Marty'd seen enough to know he didn't want any part of that.

Having a kid who "says she's eighteen" up in there was asking for even more trouble. And he knew if the gang got taken down for child prostitution, they wouldn't survive on the inside. Jailhouse justice for dudes who hurt kids was swift and full of pain.

Moving faster, he made sure his gun was fully hidden by his jacket, though he told himself nobody in this neighborhood cared. That was why the Serpents picked these streets to set up the fun house.

Somebody said the guy who owned the house lived down the way, and he was cool with whatever the gang wanted to do, as long as the cops stayed out of it.

That meant keeping the neighbors from getting suspicious or angry enough to call the cops in the first place. But anybody watching had to be ten kinds of stupid not to know what was going down in that house.

Dudes coming and going all through the night up and down suburban streets where people have play sets in their backyards and Ring cameras? No way the neighbors don't know what's up. Matter of time before they get shut down for good.

Tonight would be Marty's last time going around there.

Marty paused after crossing the last street before the neighborhood ended. The railroad tracks were up ahead. Just across there, and he'd have two more blocks to get back home. His apartment was waiting for him with a fridge full of beer and some leftover takeout.

A black van slowed to a crawl at the intersection up ahead. From where Marty stood, he couldn't make out the driver, but the way it just sat there, it was damn sure suspicious.

He casually changed course, turning down the street he'd just crossed instead of going forward. The van surged after him, and he started running. Marty was about to pull his Hi-Point Model C9, but the vehicle sped past him and turned at the next corner.

Marty pressed his hand to his chest, trying to calm his racing heart. Even without the van, the night seemed to be closing in on him. He turned back the way he'd come, heading for the street that would get him out of the neighborhood, over the tracks, and on his way home.

At the corner, he looked right, then left. Empty streets in both directions, cars sitting on the curbs or in driveways. Life in the suburbs was nice for people who could afford it.

Marty kept walking, out of the neighborhood and across the railroad tracks, finding himself on more familiar streets.

The streets his dad used to run on when he was in the gang back in the day. Serpents used to own a whole lot of D.C. territory back then, when Marty was a kid. He could find his way home now with both eyes closed if he had to.

All around him, apartment buildings and empty storefronts rose up like monuments. He laughed when he thought about a U.S. president one day having a statue sitting inside an old apartment block. Like that'd ever happen.

Turning down the next street, Marty froze in his tracks. That same black van from before sat just a few yards away, with its side door hanging open.

Marty spun around, running back the way he'd come. He slammed into the doorway of a closed-up barber shop, sheltering under its eave. Reaching for his gun, he fumbled, and the weapon dropped to the ground.

Footsteps on the street told him he had maybe a few seconds before whoever was coming would get him in their sights. He snapped up his gun with both hands and braced the weapon as he stood up.

A black-clad figure loomed in the street, its arm raised toward him. Marty fired, but not before something tore into his guts. He fell backward against the door and slid down to the ground, dropping his gun and grabbing at his stomach with both hands as he cried out in pain.

Agony like he'd never felt took over, blotting out all sound and blurring his vision. He knew he had to sit up, so he could find his gun and see the shooter, but every movement put a stabbing pain deep into his guts.

Blood poured from the wound, slicking his fingers, warm and wet.

Gotta be the Blue Devils. I bet they're pissed about the fun house.

He swallowed slow, struggling to control his breathing so he didn't move his stomach muscles too much. The pain was like fire tearing through him. He flailed around with one hand, trying to find his gun.

Whoever'd shot him hadn't come up to finish the job yet. Maybe his own shot had struck true and the dude was lying dead in the street.

Marty tried to lift his head and managed to get a glimpse of where the shooter had been standing.

He was gone. The street was empty. A shadow shifted to Marty's right, and he turned his head in time to find the barrel of a gun with a silencer on it aiming at his face. He tried once more to find his own weapon, but the man kicked it away from his searching hand.

Marty's stomach was a blaze of pain and torment. He lifted both hands in surrender.

"Please, man. I don't want to die. I don't even want us running that house …"

The man loomed over him, and Marty could just make out what looked like a bulletproof vest with a big mark in the middle. The man wore a mask that only revealed his mouth.

"You shot me." The man wheezed as he drew in a breath. "You're gonna pay for that."

"Wait, man, please. Don't!"

The shooter aimed at Marty's stomach and fired, putting another round right beside the first.

Marty jolted on the ground, gasping out words that didn't make sense. He screamed and scrabbled at his wounds. Blood flooded up and out of his body.

The man knelt beside him. There was a flash of silver, and Marty grunted as a knife plunged into his chest.

He shook once, staring at the blade as his killer pulled it free. Blood bubbled up from the wound. Marty slumped forward, his face landing in a puddle of his own blood. Fiery pain consumed him, and he welcomed darkness as he closed his eyes.

15

Dragging the gangbanger to my van was harder than it should've been. My chest hurt like hell where he'd shot me, and I could barely move my left arm, even without the pale-faced scumbag's heft weighing on me. He didn't look like much. Either I was in worse shape than I'd thought, or he was all muscle.

I couldn't believe he got a shot off before I could take him down, and he'd hit me center mass. Lucky I had my vest on, but dammit if I wasn't surprised by how much that shit hurt.

Getting the cockroach into the van took too long, but the street remained empty. A run-down row of shops like this wouldn't have anyone around it this time of night.

Adrenaline helped me shift his body all the way into the van, but one glance back at the sidewalk showed a long slick of blood.

And his gun. I ran back for it.

Racing back to my ride, I slammed the door shut and dropped the roach's gun into my duffel bag. I had to get out of here. This area was more public than the last spot I'd chosen, and our little gunfight had to have been heard by someone.

Starting the engine, I got moving, keeping to the speed limit. I lowered my window and hung an arm out, just like if I were a regular guy wanting to get where I was going.

Down the street, a set of headlights swung in my direction. I couldn't tell if it was a cop or not, but the height of the beams meant I was looking at a truck or SUV.

I kept to a steady speed, just in case a cop had turned this way. Pulling my hand in to grip the wheel, I tucked my other hand under my jacket. The grip of my gun felt solid and safe, like an anchor. I didn't want to kill a cop. As useless as they were, I wasn't a cop killer. That'd make me just as bad as the roaches I was stomping out.

But if this wasn't a cop and was a car full of roaches instead, I needed to be ready.

The vehicle slowed down as it got closer, and I readied myself to draw and fire out my window.

I caught the vehicle's profile in the dim light. An SUV, and a black one at that.

Shit, it's probably an undercover cop or even the Feds.

With my eyes on the road, I kept driving, resisting the urge to speed away and disappear into the maze of streets around me.

The SUV rumbled by at an easy speed. I only got a quick look at the driver. Long hair, so maybe a woman, but Feds and cops wore their hair up.

Whoever it was, they turned on the next block and sped off. Their engine faded out of earshot.

Letting out a slow breath, I relaxed my grip from my gun and put both hands on the wheel as I drove on.

Watching the odometer, I let the night guide me until I got a few miles from where I'd killed the cockroach.

I pulled into a parking lot behind an electrician's shop, out of sight of the street.

First things first. I dug into my duffel bag and pulled out the bag holding my change of clothes. I moved my gun and the one I'd taken from the cockroach into that bag. Then I stripped down fast, tossing my bloodstained stuff into my empty duffel.

When I got a look at the bruise on my chest, I almost choked. The dark blossom rippling around the impact point just above my heart was huge. No wonder my arm hurt so damn much.

I patted my vest's bulk inside the duffel bag. "Good girl. You saved my life tonight. Gotta replace you, though."

Moving fast, I pulled on clean socks and pants. I reached for the extra shirt but decided to wait. Even if the shirt was black, I might as well wait until I'd done the rest of my work.

No sense making more laundry for myself.

Kneeling beside the dead cockroach, I used my phone's screen to light up his face and neck.

An image of my son flashed to mind. He was younger than this guy when he died, and nothing like him. He might've worn similar jeans and sneakers, favoring neon shoes and wide, baggy denim, but my son had been a light in this city.

"He wasn't a criminal. He was a good kid, doing his best to survive in this shitty world, and some piece of shit like you took that away from him. Took him away from me."

I couldn't resist the urge to stab my knife into the cockroach's chest again. The blade went in deep, between his ribs. I tugged the knife free and began my work, removing the snake tattoo and the writing with his name.

I kept my blade tight to the snake's outline.

When I'd gotten the tattoo off, making sure not to tear

any of the skin this time, I used the cockroach's shirt to wipe my knife.

I sat back on my haunches to marvel at my work, breathing deep with satisfaction.

Damn, my chest hurt like a bitch. But now I had a battle scar. Further proof that I'd waded into the shit of this city, squashed a filthy bug, and survived. Not by luck, but by skill.

"It's time to send you on your way, little insect. But let's see if you brought anything useful with you first."

Digging through his pockets, I looked for any cash he might be carrying. All I got for my trouble was a cigarette lighter and pack of unfiltered smokes.

With a snort of disgust, I reached for the little pickle jar I'd brought with me. I used it to collect one of the actual insects that tried to make my apartment their home. First, I rattled the jar a bit to disorient the bug, then I opened the lid. The bug almost got away, but I poked it back in with my fingertip.

I took out the pack of smokes, wriggled the little beast into the half-empty box, shut it tight, and shoved it back inside his pocket. Then I slammed my hand onto the guy's hip, feeling and hearing the crunch of the bug and cigarettes squishing together.

"You can both go where you belong now."

I spent some time wiping my hands clean with a towel and some disinfectant I'd brought. Then I wrapped up the tattoo in the towel and laid the bundle carefully inside the duffel bag, atop my dirty clothing.

Another piece of art for my collection.

After pulling on my spare shirt, I climbed into the driver's seat and gazed around the area, checking as far as I could see in both directions. The street was still dead and dark. No people wandering around, since it was half past one now.

I started the engine and slowly rolled out of the gravel lot I'd parked in, coming around the electrician's storefront.

I'd dropped my first kill across from the FBI. This one had a different destination.

The cops and Feds could use geo-location to narrow down my base of operations, so I'd picked my drop spots with care.

A half mile from D.C.'s shittiest police station—at least, if you judged its quality by the crime stats from nearby streets—I pulled the van to the side of the road. I was parked between a shuttered bakery with a For Sale sign across the window and a storefront church that probably hadn't seen more than a handful of parishioners in months.

I got myself into the back, shifted the side door open, and rolled my latest kill onto the sidewalk. He flopped out and landed on his chest.

Holding onto the van for leverage, I hopped down beside him and kicked him over onto his back. I grunted with the effort because my chest hurt like hell. The cockroach's eyes were closed, and the blood on his chest blazed against his pallid skin.

With the door slammed shut a second later, I jumped back into the driver's seat and got moving, making a slow U-turn and taking a different route than the one that brought me there.

The streets flew by, despite my abiding by the speed limit. Once I got home, I'd planned to go out and set up another alibi, maybe see that same woman at the bar again. But my chest…the pain put a wrench in that plan. Damn, did it hurt.

At a stop sign, I looked behind me and groaned at the blood staining the floor. "That's too much to clean up tonight." Especially with my chest aching the way it did.

I turned down a street that took me back toward the warehouse district and found a shitty parking lot next to an even shittier building. Shingles hung from the roof, and the front window was cracked. Somebody would notice my ride eventually, but it'd take a while.

Before abandoning the van, I made sure to wipe down the wheel and every surface I'd touched using glass cleaner and a rag. Those went into my duffel bag with the tattoo and dirty clothes. The guns were in the smaller bag, stuffed down at the bottom of the duffel.

I shuffled my way home moments later. Now that the adrenaline of the kill was oozing away, exhaustion and pain were taking over.

Having taken over an hour to complete what should've been only a twenty-minute walk, I turned down several streets on a switchback path, doing my best to stagger like a homeless bum anytime a car passed by.

Hauling my duffel bag and its bloody contents up the stairs, I went into my apartment and nearly collapsed. But I had work to do still.

I took the first tattoo off the drying rack and set it to the side on the counter. With the new one laid up to dry, I realized I'd begun something big. I'd started a collection to prove the city didn't need to fear the gangs. And with each trophy I added, I'd build a record of my work, something to preserve as a reminder that true justice wasn't lost in this city.

The vest I'd bought had made this possible. Without its protection, I'd have died. I knew I'd need more gear soon, and better gear at that, but the cockroach I killed tonight didn't have any money on him.

Of course he didn't, you numb nuts. He gave it all to the hooker he was with before you squashed him.

Maybe taking out that brothel was the way to go. I'd leave the girls alone, of course, but there had to be a lot of money in there.

And with more money, I could do more to cleanse this city of its rot. Get a new car and rent a place to park it that was close to my apartment but not right out front.

I still had plenty of money left from the first cockroach I'd squashed. More than enough to upgrade my arsenal for an assault on the whorehouse.

With my newest trophy on the drying rack, I grabbed a bag of frozen broccoli and stumbled my way over to the chair in front of my television. I'd left it on but had the volume down low. After I flicked it off, my apartment became a dark cave.

I laid my head back and fell asleep to a dream of gleaming city streets.

16

Emma headed straight to her desk early the next morning, hoping to see a note from Renee Bailey. But her desk was frustratingly bare. With a grunt, she perched on the edge of her desk, bouncing her knee as she read through the unsub's email again.

She glanced back and forth from the email to the stairwell door, waiting for Leo to appear so they could head off to Dalton Renfield's. But when the door swung open, it was Jacinda who marched into the room. "We have another victim."

"Shit." Emma had known another one was coming, but this soon? "Where?"

"Over by the Eighth District. I just messaged the others to head straight to the garage and told Leo you'll meet him there."

Emma logged out of her computer and grabbed her bag. As she went to follow Jacinda, she drew up short, noticing her attire for the first time. The SSA looked more done up than usual and wore her flag lapel pin.

Jacinda caught her staring. "I'm testifying before Congress today, or I'd be right there with you all."

Oh, no. Emma was almost afraid to ask, but she needed to know. "Testifying about Salem?"

The SSA half smiled. "I've been on and off the phone for days, talking to every agency under the sun. Nobody seems to think we're hiding anything. Congress was bound to want a firsthand account. In the meantime, I've appointed Leo to be interim SSA. I trust you'll grant him the respect and allegiance he deserves until I'm back on full duty."

"Of course, and I'm sure the others will too." For a moment, Emma allowed herself to think about the carnage they'd seen in her hometown. The events Jacinda would be testifying about. Before Congress. "You're good with…the Other? I mean, good with me?"

Jacinda took a step closer, almost pinning Emma down with the intensity of her stare. "I am. While I might struggle to understand your experience, I believe in *you*. I won't be throwing you, or anyone, under any bus wheels."

Relief was like a warm blanket on the coldest night. "Thank you, Jacinda. I appreciate your faith in me."

Jacinda winked. "If everything in this world were a certainty, faith wouldn't exist. And we both know there's plenty we can't explain."

Emma considered that. "Like how many people have faith in God, even without proof?"

Jacinda's expression softened. "Exactly. Or faith in love. Or in hope. Or in people. Or in things that don't make sense but still happen. None of us really know what's out there. Doesn't mean we can't one day believe, and it sure as hell doesn't mean we stop caring about the people who do."

Emma was so close to tears that she wasn't sure how she managed to hold them back. "Thank you."

Tears shimmered in Jacinda's eyes too. "No, thank you for reminding me of that lesson. I fear I might have become so jaded by everything humans do to each other that I forgot the human experience is beautifully complex and multilayered. I look at cold facts and hard truths, the certainties, every day. I needed this reminder that not everything that matters can be measured. That sometimes believing is enough."

A single tear broke through, and Emma brushed it away. "Will you adopt me please?"

Jacinda laughed so hard, Emma thought she might fall over. "Haven't I done that already?" She shot her one last wink and turned on her heel. "Go catch our unsub while I deal with this other bullshit."

"Yes, Mom." But the words only met the closing door.

Emma stood there for several seconds before she thought her legs would be steady enough to walk. Grabbing a tissue and her bag, she blew her nose, composing herself as she headed to the garage. No…as she floated to the garage was more accurate. Jacinda's faith in her had released at least a hundred pounds of pressure from her shoulders in an instant.

Leo had a Bureau SUV idling by the stairwell access door. "You got here early." After she joined him in the vehicle, he adjusted the mirror as he drove. "Did I miss something else besides this second body drop?"

Emma checked the mirror to see how red her eyes were. "I wanted to check in case Renee Bailey left us anything last night."

"Did she?"

"Nothing new, so I was rereading the unsub's email before heading out to interview Renfield. Then Jacinda stormed in and told me about the newest victim." She twisted to look at him. "Did you know she's testifying before Congress today?"

"About Salem, yeah. I wouldn't want to be in her shoes."

"She said she won't say anything about the Other, but it sounds like she's gonna be busy on Capitol Hill for a day or two." Emma sailed a light punch into his shoulder. "Speaking of…I'm riding with the interim SSA, aren't I?"

He barked a quick laugh before glancing at her. "No hard feelings, right? I know you have seniority."

She waved him off. He was the best person on the team to occupy the leadership role. Especially with Vance behaving like he was. Having the interim leader so at odds with even a single member of the team could spell disaster for their investigation.

Leo drifted to a stop at a yellow light, and Emma peered out the passenger window. Thoughts of what more she could say to Vance occupied her through the silence, and by the time they pulled up behind the cruisers at the crime scene, Emma welcomed another step in the case.

With police cars stretched along the road on both sides, crime scene tape kept anyone else at bay, though CSI hadn't arrived yet. Agent Wurth waved them past the tape, standing partially up the block.

"Good morning." Emma waved in greeting.

"Not for this guy." He aimed a gloved finger at the victim. "Same as the first one, but worse. Our killer is getting more brutal."

Emma moved up beside him and peered at their victim. She stopped just short of a trail of ants that had already come to consume the victim's corpse. "Forensics won't like these guys interfering. They could affect the evidence, right?"

"Probably not too much, but I don't know what we can do about it without damaging evidence ourselves."

She pulled on gloves and knelt to inspect the man's limbs and neck, checking for signs of blood pooling in the corpse. Remembering what M.E. Miranda Hartford had indicated, she was curious if she could determine if the body had been moved here in the same fashion as the first.

Looking around the area, she saw the only buildings nearby lacked any security cameras.

"If he was moved in a van like the first guy, we'd probably see the same kind of bruising as blood settled while he was being transported." Emma pointed to the victim's face. "I think some of these bruises around his eye and on his jaw might match with that theory."

Wurth shrugged. "Could also mean he got hit a few times, though I didn't spot any defensive wounds on his hands, so maybe you're right."

He'd been killed by two stab wounds to his upper chest, one of which definitely struck his heart. An additional two bullet wounds marred his abdomen.

An incised section of flesh below the man's collar had Emma all but certain they were looking at the same killer's handiwork.

The crime scene was eerily similar to the first one. A body dropped in a public place—this one undeniably close to a police station rather than the Bureau. "I don't see a Skulls tattoo on this guy's arm. Are we looking at a different gang?"

"I'm assuming so. I don't know who he is, but the patch of skin that was removed is an exact match for another outfit in our database." Bending at the waist, Wurth held out his phone to her, the screen showing the collar of a white man with multiple tattoos on his neck and upper chest area. A snake coursed around his collar in the same shape as the cutaway flesh on the victim at Emma's feet.

"This guy was with the D.C. Snakes?"

Wurth dipped his chin. "Close. This is the symbol for the Serpents. If that message your office got is to be believed, our killer is out for any gang in the city, and he's taking trophies."

Leo joined them. "Is there anything going on between the Skulls and Serpents? Just in case."

Shaking his head, Wurth straightened, stretching his back. "Nothing. They're about as distinct as any two gangs can get in this town. Serpents have been around forever, while the Skulls can barely hold down a corner."

Emma raised her eyebrow. "So not exactly blood enemies."

"Not a chance. The Serpents' closest rivals are the Blue Devils. They're literally on opposite sides of the tracks from each other, always trying to push into the other's territory. If you'll excuse me, I need to see what's taking forensics so damn long to get here. They better show up before the ants call in reinforcements."

Emma waved him off and resumed her study of the corpse.

For a moment, she recalled the last gang-related case their team had worked. Denae's brother, Jamaal, had been involved with a major gang, the Drivers, and went by the street name of "Snake."

Leo tapped her on the shoulder. "You in there, Emma?"

"Sorry. The snake…had me thinking about Denae's brother."

"Me, too, but he's out of the Drivers for good and doing okay." Leo smiled. "Denae texted me that he's applying to art school for the fall."

That Denae and Leo were still in touch, even if their relationship had been put on hold, gave Emma a brief, bright touch of joy, which extinguished as Mia and Vance pulled up across the street.

"Anything we can do to help?" Vance seemed his normal self, calm and even-tempered. He met Emma's gaze without a hint of malice or scorn.

He may not believe you, Emma girl, but he's acting normal at least.

"The M.O. is similar but more violent. We have two gunshot wounds in the abdomen, plus two stab wounds over the heart." She indicated each with a gloved finger, then stood up. "I was hoping to interview Renfield this morning. If this is his handiwork, I don't think we should wait a second longer."

A uniformed officer walked over from where he'd been talking with Wurth. "Did you say Renfield? As in Dalton Renfield?"

Emma and the others turned to the cop in unison. "Yes. Was he someone you knew on the force?"

"I worked with him, at the Eighth." He aimed a thumb down the street stretching out behind him.

"Would you say he's capable of doing something like this?"

The cop looked at their corpse. "Murder a gang member?" He scratched his chin. "I mean, that's why he got kicked off the force, for shooting a guy in the back and acting like he was doing the world a favor. The guy was an idiot. Even without that bad shoot on his record, he'd have lost his badge before too long."

"We're more interested in if you think he could do something like this." Vance pointed at the body. "Not just murder a gang member but cut him up this way."

The cop shook his head. "He's been out of work since leaving the force. Maybe he went completely off the rails, I don't know. Last time I saw him, he was at the gym working out. Didn't talk to him."

Emma thanked him, and he wandered back to where Wurth was pacing, still on the phone with forensics, presumably.

Vance pulled on gloves and knelt by the body,

inspecting the symbol carved into his skin. "You think the victims are connected by more than being gang members? They're both white, so maybe the killer is targeting based on ethnicity."

Wurth came up to join their circle. "I doubt we're looking at racially motivated killings. We know gangs tend to group around ethnic similarities, but nothing we've seen matches this kind of…statement killing."

"The mutilation means something to our guy." Vance kept his gaze fixed on the missing patch of skin. "He's taking trophies, or he's removing affiliation."

"I agree. If anything connects the gangs being targeted, that connection only exists in our unsub's head."

Emma shivered in the sudden cold brought on by the Other. The dead man's ghost hovered behind Wurth, muttering in a low, tortured voice. "Need a smoke, man. I'm not a cockroach. Can't even light that one up. Just need a smoke, man, settle my nerves."

The ghost tapped his hands over his pants pockets while trails of crimson poured from his chest, pumping in time with a heartbeat that would never be heard or felt again.

Emma flinched away from the sight, and Leo raised an eyebrow at her.

She'd tell him about the ghost on the drive, but they could look for another calling card now. "Has anyone looked in the victim's pants pockets? Maybe we'll find keys or a wallet or… cigarettes?"

Leo caught the attention of one of the uniforms and asked the same question.

The officer shook her head. "Didn't touch anything yet."

Still kneeling, Vance eyed Emma with a questioning look but patted down the victim's pockets without a word. He fished out a cigarette lighter in one and a smashed packet of unfiltered cigarettes from the other.

He held them up, his gaze still tight on her. "That was oddly specific."

She shrugged. "Lucky me. Any dead cockroaches in there?"

"What?"

She explained about Miranda finding a smashed roach in the first victim's pocket. "If we find one here, we can almost guarantee the same person is responsible for both murders."

Vance popped open the lid on the pack of cigarettes, displaying the smeared remains of a cockroach inside among the crushed smokes. "Bingo. Good memory."

She wasn't about to tell him he should be thanking the man's ghost instead of her.

Handing the evidence to Wurth, who tucked it into a bag, Vance got up. "What's next? You want to interview this Renfield guy, right?"

"Definitely. I'd like to do it right away." Emma drummed her fingers against her thigh, itching to interview a man who checked off so many motive boxes.

"Mia and I can stay here, help process the scene."

"Actually," Leo interjected, "I'd like you both to come along as backup. If Renfield is behind these murders, he's working a vengeance streak that makes him dangerous. We go in with vests on, and I want to bring some uniforms with us."

Emma was glad to hear Leo taking charge and knew Jacinda had made the right choice appointing him to lead in her stead. Vance and Mia seemed to be on board, as well, though neither of them acknowledged Leo's instructions verbally.

The team separated into pairs, with Wurth directing two units of MPD officers to saddle up and follow the agents.

Back in the SUV, Emma pulled up Dalton Renfield's file before starting the engine. "Address confirmed, based on his unemployment records. Hopefully that means we find him at home."

Leo scratched at his elbow, grimacing. "Good catch on the cockroach in our victim's pocket. Guessing you had some help there?"

Emma nodded and put the SUV into drive. "His ghost was talking about needing a smoke and kept tapping at his pocket."

"Vance seems to have relaxed a bit around you, at least."

"What do you mean?"

"I mean you didn't see the look he gave me before he got into the car with Mia. Cold water to the face on a breezy winter day would've felt better. I'm not sure he agrees with Jacinda's decision."

Emma snorted. "News flash for Vance, she doesn't need his agreement to make a decision."

17

Dalton Renfield's apartment complex was a collection of two-story brick buildings taking up one half of a city block. With rigid iron fencing around the lot and cameras hanging from every eave, the complex looked more like a prison than a place to call home. Residents had no green space to enjoy and only a narrow parking lot with too few spaces for the number of units.

Cars on the street filled almost every available spot.

Emma led the way as the team approached building A, where Renfield's unit was located. She went inside and up to the second floor with Leo right behind her. Vance and Mia were next in the stack, and two MPD officers brought up the rear.

The other MPD unit covered the back and side exits.

Cringing at the smell of clove cigarettes hanging everywhere in the hall, Emma wondered if they were about to uncover a den of Goths. "So much for going outside to smoke, huh?"

"Maybe Renfield has his own vampire coven."

Their target's apartment was halfway down the hall.

Emma and Leo moved to the hinged side of the door. Vance and Mia went to the opposite side, and the MPD officers kept watch for anyone approaching from the stairs.

Leo motioned for everyone to keep their hands clear of their weapons before nodding at Emma.

She pounded on the door with three hard strikes. "Dalton Renfield, this is the FBI."

An immediate response, riddled with profanity, erupted from inside.

"Mr. Renfield, this is the FBI! Open your door." Emma listened through another round of cursing. She took a small step back when their guy finally opened the door.

He stood in a ratty bathrobe with a freshly stained t-shirt beneath it. "Show me some ID."

His growl sounded like a cop's, though that was the only thing besides his buzz cut that seemed police-issue. When the agents all held out their identification, he took his time staring before grunting in annoyance. "I hoped they were fake. You want to talk, then talk. I'm gonna finish my coffee."

He turned and moved back into his studio apartment, cradling his left arm across his chest. Emma and Leo followed reluctantly. Vance and Mia stayed at the door.

The place was a pigsty, and Emma would've preferred to wait in the clove-scented hallway. Takeout containers cluttered every surface in view. Renfield's unmade bed sat crammed into one corner, a stack of laundry on top of it. Moving back to the sink in his utility-sized kitchen, the man poured coffee into a mug with his right hand, keeping his left hand held across his stomach.

"What happened to your arm?"

"I banged my funny bone getting up to answer the door. Maybe you aren't aware, but someone pounding on the door yelling 'FBI' can make you jump through your own ass."

Emma stayed in the middle of the room with Leo at her

back. "Mr. Renfield, we're investigating two murders. Can you account for your whereabouts over the last two nights?"

He sipped from his mug and turned around to face them, leaning back against his sink. "Why the hell should I tell you anything? You got a warrant or something? If this is chitchat hour, I have nothing to say without my lawyer present."

Leo stepped up beside Emma, a takeout bag crunching under his boot. "This visit is about taking you off a list. Or leaving you on it. Simple questions, simple answers. Can you account for your whereabouts for the previous two nights?"

The man grunted again, still sipping from his coffee mug, still holding his left arm against his abdomen. Emma glanced around the apartment, searching for any sign of weaponry. And where would a guy like this keep the skin he'd taken off gang members? She certainly didn't see any signs of taxidermy hanging in view.

"I was here. Both nights." He downed his coffee and poured another cup. "I don't go out much anymore. Unemployment covers the basics, not the luxuries, you know?"

"You haven't found anything else since leaving the force?" Leo's question wasn't delicate, but the man didn't bristle.

"Since being *ejected* from the force, you mean. I took my job seriously. Hard to find something like that a second time around." He turned back to them.

The sleeve of his robe fell to his elbow as he held his cup at his mouth, showing that however little attention he paid to his apartment, he kept himself in shape. The muscles of his forearm bulged.

Emma nodded at the exposed arm. "Looks like you still take care of yourself. Maybe you could work at a gym. That might help with the, uh...funny bone hurting you so much."

He sneered at her. "That makes absolutely zero sense." His left arm dropped to his side.

Leo caught her gaze and gave her a short, quick nod. He'd noticed the muscles too. There was little doubt this guy would have the strength to pick up his victims and move them wherever he wanted to.

More importantly, he had the build of the man in the video after the first body drop.

The business with his left arm could be the result of an injury he'd gotten during one of the murders, not from banging it a few minutes ago. But they had no reason or cause to demand he reveal anything. They could ask him if he drove a black van, though.

"What kind of car do you drive, Mr. Renfield?"

"A 1980 Shoe Leather. Like I said, unemployment covers the basics. If you're lucky."

Gesturing around the apartment, Emma tried a different approach. "A guy who takes his job seriously might want to get back into 'our city,' be a member of society again."

"You'd be surprised." He stared at her over the rim of his mug.

She'd hoped using the words from the unsub's email would spark a reaction, but perhaps she'd just chosen the wrong ones.

Beside her, Leo bristled and stepped forward. "Mr. Renfield," he raised his voice, annoyance coming through in each syllable, "do you have any remorse for killing that boy? Or was he just another cockroach ruining our city?"

Seemingly unfazed, Renfield leaned back against the sink again, sneering again. "I did what needed to be done. That scumbag was only going to hurt more people and cause more trouble if he got away. He had priors, which I knew about. That's why I was chasing him down. Not to mention, I thought he was armed and had every reason to believe he was dangerous."

"The investigating committee didn't see it that way."

"No. They didn't."

For a second, Adam Cleaver's desperate face appeared in Emma's mind, and a stab of guilt shot through her. She hadn't even killed him—thanks to Leo—yet she felt guilt for even wanting to, despite the fact that he'd killed Oren.

Meanwhile, this man across from her simply went on with his life after killing an innocent man.

Her throat dried, but she tried to shake away the guilt.

"Mr. Renfield," Emma stepped forward to stand next to Leo, "what were you doing at home both nights? To clarify, last night and the night before."

"Drinking whiskey and watching television. Not that it's any of your business."

Emma pressed further. "And what were you watching last night?"

"*Law and Order* reruns." He took another gulp of his coffee. "Nice to see cops doing their job instead of chasing good cops out of their force. Even if it is all fake."

Leo pointed to a photo hanging on the wall. In the picture, Renfield stood with a teenager. "We read about how your son was killed in an act of gang violence. Did that make you want to do anything violent?"

Renfield slammed his coffee cup down on the counter so hard it shattered, coffee spilling across the counter and splattering his robe and the floor. Emma flinched but stood her ground, though Renfield's gaze remained on Leo. "What the hell's that supposed to mean? You idiots have got no right to talk to me about my son."

"It's a simple question, Mr. Renfield." She hovered her hand near her gun, ready in case the man pulled a weapon.

"If you're not gonna arrest me, then get the fuck out. And you don't got shit to arrest me for." Renfield glared between them as he stalked over to stand in front of the picture and block their view of it. "I'm done talking."

Emma waited for a moment, but Renfield's flat expression made it clear the man had meant what he said. She backed toward the door carefully, and Leo followed her.

Rejoining Vance and Mia in the hall, they all flinched as Renfield slammed the door and turned the dead bolt. Leo approached the MPD officers and asked them if they could maintain a stakeout on the apartment. They agreed and headed down to their cruiser.

The agents lingered in the hall for a bit before following the cops outside. After speaking with the other MPD unit briefly, the officers got into their vehicle.

Watching them drive out of the lot and park on the street, Emma was slightly relieved. "That should at least prevent him from vanishing on us."

"That was my thinking," Leo added, "though I'm not sure he's our guy."

With a shake of her head, Mia disagreed. "You saw how quick he was to get heated and the complete lack of remorse when you mentioned the man he killed. He could absolutely be our guy."

"Maybe." Vance turned to look back at the apartment building. "And maybe he's just a guy who got dealt a shitty hand and doesn't like that he's stuck living in this dump."

"How about you and Mia go back to the crime scene? Catch up with Wurth and see if any other officers there remember Renfield." Leo jutted his chin out. "We might need to talk to the whole precinct, see if anyone recalls him advocating for violence against gang members as a solution, but let's start with whoever's on scene."

Vance stayed quiet for a moment before meeting Leo's gaze. "You like this guy for the killings. I get it. Don't you think we should be looking at the gang angle first, though? What if this is just two gangs taking it out on each other, and one of them gets the bright idea to throw a wrench in the investigation by sending that email?"

Leo leveled a steady gaze at him. "That's a fair point, Vance, and I think Wurth's a great place to start that line of inquiry."

The muscles in Vance's jaw popped for several seconds before he spun on his heel to head back to his vehicle.

Mia hesitated before turning to Emma and Leo. "I'll keep an eye on him. One thing I've learned about Vance is he has a lot of bark, but ultimately, not much bite."

With a little smile of encouragement, she departed and joined Vance in the SUV. They rolled out of the parking lot as Emma and Leo headed to their vehicle.

He must've seen the tension on her face. "What's wrong? Vance isn't still burning your butt, is he?"

She shook her head. "Hardly. He seems more interested in burning yours now."

"So what's up?"

Taking a deep breath, she tried to find the right words, but all that came out was, "Adam Cleaver."

"You're thinking about Cleaver? Why?"

Emma pushed some hair behind her ear as she leaned on the vehicle beside him. "Trying not to. But if you hadn't stepped in, I'd be just like Renfield. Guilty of murder."

"No, you wouldn't." Leo shifted to face her, lowering his voice. "I'm glad you didn't…do what you wanted to in that moment. But even if you had, that wouldn't make you anything like that asshole up there. You'd have ended up feeling regret, and even if you'd been out of the Bureau, you'd have found something fulfilling. You wouldn't be stewing in your own filth and feeling angry at the world, blaming other people for your mistakes like that jerk is."

"If I'd killed Adam Cleaver and ended up like Renfield, I'd have deserved it."

"Well, you didn't, so you don't."

"You're right. Thanks, Leo." She patted his arm and launched away from the vehicle. "How about we solve some murders now? I want to see what all these cameras can tell us about Renfield's comings and goings."

Even as she cracked a smile at him and led the way toward the apartment manager's unit, Emma wasn't sure if the lightness she felt could be trusted. Renfield looked good for the crimes, but she knew better than to trust instinct alone.

And she feared their killer might still be out there, completely unknown to them, plotting his next move.

18

Leo forced away any anxiety that threatened to surface as they made their way around the apartment building. Emma already had so much guilt to shoulder, and the best way to help was to treat her like the trusted colleague she was.

And, as she'd just said, they had some murders to solve.

A sign advertising vacancies hung crookedly on the front door of the apartment manager's office. They entered and were greeted by a woman who looked up from her desk with a less-than-optimistic air about her. Realization seemed to set in as Leo and Emma withdrew their IDs. "How can I help you, Detectives?"

"Agents, actually." He and Emma opened their IDs for the woman to examine. "We'd like to review the footage from cameras around building A."

Twisting her head toward the open doorway behind her, she gave a half-hearted wave. "I'm sure you two know how to work video systems. Go on in. Just let me know if you need copies of anything or if we got some kind of situation I should be worrying about."

Leo was already moving past her. "Thanks, and we'll do our best."

Inside the back room, the security setup wasn't bad, all things considered. He dropped into one of the two threadbare roller chairs in front of a desktop computer. Emma took the other. With some scrolling and mousing, Leo brought up the views outside Renfield's building.

"Let's see if our guy is as good as his word." Leo scrolled the time counter back to four in the afternoon, two days earlier.

Most of the building's tenants carried backpacks and laptop bags. Others wore fast-food uniforms while some wore scrubs.

Leo tapped his foot on the floor. Little activity occurred until after nine o'clock, when a few groups of student types returned, trailed by two women in scrubs. Soon after that, Emma reached out and froze the footage.

Renfield was exiting the building. "He said he was home all night." She restarted the playback. Renfield appeared at 9:20, carrying a bag of fast food.

Grimacing, Leo marked down the time, then paused the playback. "He goes out and comes back between nine and nine thirty, but what's he doing all day?"

"Job hunting online? Sitting in front of his TV with a glass of whiskey, feeling sorry for himself?" She growled a little in the back of her throat.

They restarted the playback and watched the screen, looking for movement. Leo's eyeballs itched with dryness as he stared. Right around eleven at night, Renfield came out again. He had on what looked like jogging pants, black ones. On top, he wore a lightweight jacket over a dark shirt and had a dark watch cap pulled down over his brow.

Leo snapped his fingers, a squiggle of satisfaction in his

gut. "Caught ya. So much for whiskey and television shows. He lied."

Emma leaned toward the screen. Focused as she was, she seemed much less anxious. Scrolling the footage forward until Renfield reappeared on camera, she paused the playback. "Renfield leaves around eleven and comes back close to one in the morning. He's wearing the same clothes, as far as I can tell. But look at his left arm. He's holding it against his stomach. Again."

Leo frowned and made a note of her observation. "You're right. He said he banged his funny bone, but that looks like he might actually be injured."

"Those are really weird hours to be out doing anything legal, and he's not checking his surroundings like he expects to be seen." Emma waved her hand at the monitors. "He has to know he's being recorded right now."

Leo nodded, his gaze fixed on the frozen image of Renfield, as though he could read the man's mind through the footage. "He's not acting like a killer, unless he's the kind who hides in plain sight."

Emma tapped at the desk with a fingertip as she tilted her head side to side. "It's hard to get a good read on his expression, but the way he's just...moseying along. He seems calm."

Leo marked down the times of Renfield's late departure and return the previous night, alongside the times for his earlier burger run. He bounced his knee up and down, running down the list of items that pointed toward Renfield's guilt. "We have him on record lying to us. He wasn't home between nine and nine thirty, or, again, between eleven o'clock and one in the morning."

"We don't have time of death on the latest victim, but this at least shows Renfield had opportunity. And we know he had motive."

"We suspect he had motive." Leo reached for the mouse. This felt too easy, and he knew all too well that cases were rarely this easy. "I agree he looks good for this, but let's see what he was doing two nights ago, when Johnny Duncan was killed."

Rewinding from the point where they'd started, Leo bypassed Renfield coming and going. He played the footage back going forward and marked their guy leaving the building at eleven in the morning and returning shortly after twelve thirty. He was in gym clothes and carrying a duffel bag. "Okay, he has a late-morning workout regimen."

"And a late-evening fast-food regimen to counteract any gains." Emma stabbed her finger at the screen. "Look at his arm, though. No broken wing two days ago."

Leo laughed and kept scrolling backward, stopping at just before one in the morning. Renfield was coming back to his apartment building. Scrolling back farther still, they spotted him leaving the building just after eleven again. Leo straightened, sucking in his breath.

"Two nights in a row, he's out gallivanting between eleven and one, even though he told us otherwise." Emma pushed herself up from the table. "Let's get a copy of this and then ask our boy why he lied. My money's on that injured arm. I bet it has something to do with it."

Leo stood up, tucking away his notebook. "You think he had to work harder to take out the second victim? Johnny Duncan was a quick kill, but the next one fought back and Renfield got hurt?"

She nodded. "That's what I'm seeing, but we need more if we're going to get an arrest warrant. Or we can ask him to come in voluntarily and save us all a lot of time."

When they'd handed over their contact cards and received a copy of the footage for later examination, Leo led the way outside. They followed the same path back to building A and up the clove-scented stairwell to Renfield's hallway. This time, Leo pounded on his door with a bit more force and called his name with a bit more purpose.

There was no answer.

Leo leaned against the door and listened. The television had been turned off, and he didn't hear any indication that someone was behind the door now. He stood back, seething out a breath through his teeth. "Either he isn't home anymore, or he's doing a fine job of ignoring us."

"We'd have seen him leave on the cameras...if we'd been looking at current footage. Dammit. He could've snuck out while we were busy watching him buy burgers and fries."

Leo forcefully shook his head. "He couldn't have known we'd be doing that."

"Renfield used to be a cop. A fallen one, but that doesn't mean he forgot his training. He could've suspected we'd come here and left based on that assumption."

Leo nodded to Emma's point but knew that Renfield could've also gone about his business as if they'd never bothered him. "If he is our guy, it'd make sense that he might try to scoot. But we saw him coming and going around this time yesterday and carrying a gym bag. Let's ask the cops outside if they spotted him leaving."

If the cops hadn't seen Renfield exit, he might still be inside, refusing to answer his door. Leo hated the idea of asking MPD to sit stakeout so he and the team could be free to explore other leads, but they had two murders on their hands. And so far, Renfield was the best lead they had.

Outside, they made a beeline to the MPD cruiser and confirmed the officers hadn't seen Renfield come out. "Coulda used a fire exit on the other side of the building. You want us to sit on him for a while?"

"That'd be great. We'll head around the complex to watch from the other side, in case he did hop out a back door."

Emma leaned down to ask the officer a question too. "Would anyone at the precinct be up for talking about Renfield or his habits?"

"Habits? Other than being a royal pain in the ass, I'm not sure he had any." The officer snorted. "But you can ask the others."

Leo thanked the officers, then followed Emma back to their vehicle, where he called Mia. "I'm hoping she and Vance can get over to the precinct, or maybe they have an update from Wurth about the John Doe."

When Mia picked up, he put the phone on speaker. "Mia, you and Vance still at the scene?"

"Vance is with me now, yes."

"Now? Where was he before?"

She paused, and muffled conversation came across the phone. "He needed to take a quick walk to clear his head. What's up?"

Leo avoided looking at Emma after that bit of information. "I was gonna ask if you could go to the Eighth since you're close by. Renfield told us he was at home the last two nights, but we just caught him in a lie with some security footage. We're wondering if the cops there know of any late-night habits he had."

"What about his apartment? Is MPD sitting on it for you?"

"They are. Emma and I are going to stay here with them." He motioned for the driver's seat, and she climbed in while he went around to the passenger side.

"Okay, gotcha." Mia spoke softly on her end of the call, then came back louder. "We can stop by the Eighth. Wurth has CSI on this scene still, but I think they're almost done."

Leo signed off after asking that she keep them in the loop. He buckled himself into the passenger seat with a sigh. He didn't love that Vance had left the scene without even telling Mia where he was going or informing Leo.

At least he's not here arguing with Emma. I'll take small favors where they come, I guess.

19

Vance did his best to listen patiently as Mia recapped her call with Leo. They'd left Wurth and the forensic techs as the body was being loaded into an ambulance. Mia continued to fill him in as she drove to the Eighth, her voice tight with frustration.

"Leo and Emma are staying there with MPD."

"There? Where's there?"

She glanced at him but didn't reply right away. They'd arrived at the precinct, and she pulled them into an alley alongside the building where cruisers were parked. "At Renfield's place. Emma and Leo are sitting on his apartment with MPD."

She got out without saying another word, and Vance wanted to kick himself.

Try as he might, he couldn't focus on anything except how out of the loop he felt.

First, Emma could see ghosts, and everyone but him was ready to believe her. Even Jacinda, who he thought for sure would be a voice of reason, said she'd "keep an open mind."

Then the SSA got called off to testify before Congress and left Leo in charge.

Not like I've been doing this job longer than him. Oh, no, let's give the interim-SSA slot to the newest guy on the team.

Vance knew Leo and Jacinda were colleagues in Miami, but being passed over, with a double homicide on their hands, did more than rankle him.

You're pissed off, and with good reason. But showing how much won't get you anywhere.

He'd keep his cool and do the job. And maybe he'd consider asking about a transfer to another field office.

Mia held the door open for him but didn't even look his way as he passed. "Thanks." He reached out to hold the next door as she came through and went straight up to the dispatcher's desk.

He pulled out his identification as he joined Mia. The curly-haired Black woman at the desk glanced at their badges. "Special Agent Vance Jessup. This is Special Agent Mia Logan with me. We'd like to speak to anyone who might've worked closely with Dalton Renfield."

The woman's name tag identified her as Sergeant Clark. She typed at her keyboard, and Vance shifted to the side to give Mia more room beside him. Her elbow brushed his, and she flinched in response.

This distance between them wasn't what he wanted. But maybe if this was the path their relationship was going to take, a transfer wouldn't be the worst thing.

"Head up to the fourth floor." Sergeant Clark scribbled something on a sticky note and passed it to Vance. "Ask for Detective Carter. I'll give a call upstairs and see if I can't get him to meet you."

Vance nodded his thanks but had to force the smile that usually came so naturally to him.

Even in the elevator, he couldn't help being distracted by

the swarm of frustrations plaguing him. He shoved himself into the corner, as far from Mia as possible. If the team hadn't been lying, then Emma and her ghosts had helped every one of them, except him and Jacinda.

He still couldn't get his head around the SSA being open to the idea of ghosts in the first place, but Jacinda had made her stance clear. And she'd appointed Leo as her temporary replacement, which put Vance back in the place of feeling passed over.

Dammit, he had a case to work. He didn't have time to be brooding about who said what and when, and why someone else got picked to be team captain.

This isn't high school, dumbass. Pull your shit together.

The elevator door opened, cutting off his next thought. Mia stepped forward, exiting ahead of him.

A muscular Black man who looked to be in his late forties stood across the hall from the elevators. He held out a hand to Mia as she approached. "Detective Rod Carter, at your service. I understand you have some questions about my ex-partner?"

"We do." Mia handed him her card. "Is there somewhere we could speak in private?"

"Not a problem." The detective led them to a bare room with two couches and a square table between them. A coffeepot sat on a laminate counter that ran the length of one wall. When they'd stepped inside, he shut the door behind them. "This space got set up for private, non-interrogation conversations. Mostly gets used for therapy that people don't want to admit is therapy. Grab a seat."

Vance barely succeeded in fighting back a joke about couples counseling. Mia's cold shoulder act dug into him like a knife. He sat at the edge of one couch. Mia left plenty of room between the two of them when she sat at the other end.

Rod Carter took a seat across from them and crossed one

leg over the other, leaning back. "I probably knew Renfield better than anyone here. We were partners for a few years before he was dismissed."

Vance nodded for the man to go on. "What can you tell us about him?"

"This is official, I take it?" Carter glanced from Vance's tablet to Mia's tense expression. "Something to do with the murder down the street?"

"He's a person of interest." Vance waited, and finally the man sighed in defeat.

"I should say I'm surprised, but I'm not. You heard about the incident that led to him losing his job?"

Vance checked his notes. "The eighteen-year-old Renfield shot in the back while the victim was fleeing from him. He claimed the victim was armed, but…"

"Kid had a can of spray paint in his hand. Granted, he was a member of a gang and had priors for vandalism as a juvenile, some of which Renfield had been in on."

Mia sat forward. "Sounds like he had reasonable cause to suspect the victim had a weapon, but that doesn't mean he had to shoot him."

Carter scrunched his brow. "The truth is, Renfield used to say and do a lot of questionable things, and more so after his son got killed."

Vance looked up. "We understand his son was involved in a gang. Was that part of Renfield's…makeup? Did he have it in for gangs everywhere?"

The detective nodded. "He'd say anybody who was associated with gangs was bad news. Capital punishment was 'too uncommon these days,' and cops needed 'more leeway.'"

"*More leeway.*" Mia straightened. "What did he mean by that?"

Carter raised his hands and shrugged. "Coulda meant any number of things."

Mia sat back against the couch again, but she remained silent.

Trying to ignore his growing unease around her, Vance jotted down some of the phrasing Carter had used. "Did any of Renfield's statements get him in trouble, or…?"

"There were moments. A cop would bring in a collar, and the guy would be released on his own recognizance the next day. Renfield always had a fit when a crook got OR. Said he would have made sure the charge stuck and nobody would 'walk out the door' on his watch."

"How did the rest of the precinct feel about that?"

Carter stared at him with a slight smile creeping across his lips. "How do you think?" He waved off any reply. "Everybody hated him. That's no secret, so I don't mind telling you. I told him to calm down at least once a week. I wanted things to work out, ya know? You hate to see a friend let grief and anger tear him apart."

Grief isn't the only thing that tears people apart.

Carter stood and paced the small room. "Renfield was on a downward spiral, and we all knew it. But he didn't do anything actionably wrong until he shot that kid."

"I'm guessing that was the last straw for your captain?"

A sad chuckle came from Carter's mouth. "Mayor, actually. With a lot of the news painting us as the bad guys… don't get me wrong, Renfield had it coming. He made his bed. He just sleeps better thinking he was a political sacrifice."

Vance made notes of everything Carter said and waited for the man to continue. When he just kept pacing, Vance probed as gently as he could. "Anything else you can tell us? Did Renfield have a violent side, or was he prone to excessive force, anything like that?"

"Or anything good you remember?" Mia added.

Carter turned to face them again and leaned on the couch

arm. "The funny thing? I'm probably a lot better at my job because he was such an ass. I had to do both our jobs when it came to interacting with the public, seeing different sides of a situation and de-escalating wherever we could." He folded his arms. "We had a routine after a while. He'd be about to open his mouth, I'd tell him to calm his shit, and he'd back off. I'd take charge of the situation, and we'd be good."

Mia leaned forward. "Sounds like he was more a burden than a partner."

"Sometimes." Carter rubbed a hand down his face. "But to be fair, his collars were solid. I never let him get away with being overly aggressive and arresting people who didn't deserve it."

"Did you have to prevent that from happening often?"

"Rarely. Most of the time, he'd calm his shit like I told him to do. He was a good cop when I met him. Life just threw the man too many curveballs."

Vance wondered if the police captain would be quite so full-throated in his defense. He glanced at Mia, but she'd gone silent again. "Did the captain find a lot of cause to defend your partner? Reason to keep him around, despite headaches?"

Carter fidgeted with the uniform button near his throat. "Renfield never said or did anything out of bounds, far as I know. The captain knew him to be a good cop, like I said."

"Did you see anything suspicious from him other than inappropriate comments and overly aggressive attempts to arrest people?"

Carter shook his head, meeting Vance's gaze to drive his point home. "Far as I'm concerned, he's a garden-variety hothead who became a police officer and did a good job on the force until his son was killed."

Mia stood up and reached out to shake his hand. "If you think of anything else, you'll call?" She passed him a card.

The detective nodded and accepted the card.

Vance stood, extending a hand, and they shook. "We appreciate your time."

Once they were back inside the elevator, Mia shook her head. "I'm glad he's off the force."

"Guy's a gem, but I still don't see him as our killer." Vance wished he was so they could have a quick win, but his gut wouldn't agree. "Anybody can be an asshole and get fired for it."

"I'm gonna call Emma and Leo to share what we've learned. You want to get lunch before we check out the van?"

The words sounded forced. Perfunctory. And she hadn't even looked at him as she asked the question.

Like she was just his partner and nothing more.

Vance turned away from her. "Not really hungry, thanks."

For a half second, he thought she might protest, but instead, she looked back at him, shrugged, and pulled out her phone.

The elevator doors opened, and she was gone. He focused on the staccato beat of her footsteps as she headed for the door. Vance followed for a bit but stopped walking to watch her leave the building. She paced back and forth on the sidewalk, talking into her phone, presumably giving Emma an update.

Letting the tension between them fester wasn't a good thing—Vance knew that—but he needed time to work out his own frustrations.

He couldn't do his job and figure out things with Mia at the same time. One of those problems would have to give.

Taking out his phone, he put in a call to Jacinda and waited while her voicemail picked up.

"Jacinda, it's Vance. I'm wondering if we could sit down for a few minutes as soon as you're back from the Hill." He sucked in a deep breath. "I need to request some emergency leave. Please, call me as soon as you can."

20

Emma and Leo sat in their SUV, monitoring the backside of Dalton Renfield's apartment building. A fire exit let out onto a slim driveway that ran the length of the building. Carports offered covered parking for residents.

They'd been there all afternoon, and now, with early evening well underway, neither of them could do much more than yawn.

She opened her tablet, which she'd been using to review reports of the two gangs they'd come across so far.

Leo noticed and gestured toward the device. "Tell me a story? Something to keep me from falling asleep here, waiting for this guy to show up or come out or whatever he decides to do."

Laughing, Emma obliged. "This one's about snakes. It says the Serpents have a long history of violent crimes. But, except for that homicide Wurth mentioned, they're mostly known for armed robbery, some assaults. And one member was cited for a traffic violation. The responding officer spotted the tattoo."

"Left a note about possible gang affiliation?"

"Yep. The Skulls get similar passing mention, and being a young gang, in terms of activity, they don't have much more than vandalism and some drunk-and-disorderly charges."

"That's going to change if they really are moving into the coke trade." Leo slapped his tablet, which sat darkened on his lap. "I checked vehicles registered to Renfield and even searched for anything that might've been registered under his ex-wife's or mother's name. No vans at all, let alone a black one."

He ran his hand through his hair, closing his eyes for a few seconds.

Emma didn't blame him. "Sitting here watching a building. I keep wanting it to take flight or fall down… stakeouts make me anxious because nothing is happening, except *something* is, and we're not there to deal with it. Whatever *it* is."

They'd been there for hours already, researching, taking breaks to grab tacos from a nearby food truck, and generally getting nowhere in determining if Renfield was their killer.

"Let's go over the basics again. On the gangs, I mean."

Emma groaned. "The basics? Okay, but you owe me for the tacos. Here we go." Scrolling back to the notes she'd taken, she read them aloud. "The Serpents have been in D.C. for about twenty-three years. Membership ballooned in the early millennium but is now considered stagnant, activity minimal. If gangs could fall from grace, they'd be the poster children."

"Meaning?"

"They used to boost cars, knock over liquor stores and other businesses, and rob people on the street. Now the most they get up to is vandalism and some property theft but nothing approaching grand larceny levels or violent crime."

He grunted, and she tabbed over to her notes on Johnny

Duncan's gang. "The Skulls have a three-year history in D.C., with membership barely numbering in the dozens."

"What about interactions between the Skulls and Serpents?"

"As far as I can tell, there are no overlaps in territory, and what toes they've stepped on have been separate, just like Wurth told us."

Leo woke his tablet and made his own notes, nodding. "And the demographics? Anything we might use there?"

"Not really." Emma glanced back to her notes. "Both our victims were white, but neither gang is all-white or known for racism. So, yeah, the crimes could be racially motivated if someone's actively targeting white gang members, but there are three known neo-Nazi gangs in the D.C. area. Any one of them would make more sense as a target. These two have at least a touch of diversity in their ranks, as we saw when we met up with Darius Baker, so I just don't see race being a motive."

"Assuming the gangs were specifically targeted." Leo sighed, drumming his fingers against the dashboard.

Emma glanced at the clock. "I can't believe it's after six. Where did the day go?"

"Down the drain." Leo stuffed his tablet into his bag. "You hear from Mia again? Or Vance?"

"Nothing on my end." Emma couldn't keep the sharp edge off her reply.

Leo cocked his head at her for more.

She only stretched in her seat. "I haven't heard from Mia since she called from the Eighth. She said Vance was going back to the Bureau and that she was getting lunch. She'd have called if she found anything."

Leo pulled his phone out. "I'm texting MPD to let them know we'll swap out with their people in the front. I want to be there if Renfield decides on another late-night walk."

"You still want to wait him out? He's kept us perched on his doorstep all day. What if he decides not to go out tonight?"

Leo frowned before nodding. "Better to wait and see rather than give him the chance to get out without us knowing."

"I kinda think he's going to notice a police cruiser and Bureau vehicle. How about we send MPD home, then move just down the block?" Emma pointed to where a line of businesses stretched into the distance. "We'll leave the car there and walk back to that bus bench across from the apartments."

"Sounds like a plan. I'll pick up coffee at the café down the street." Leo tapped out a text to the MPD officers. After a moment, their vehicle rolled down the block and turned at the next corner.

Emma started the engine and drove in the other direction, parking half a block from Renfield's building, out of sight of his window. They got out, and Leo, true to his word, paid for coffees. They crossed the street and strolled back to the bus bench.

The bench gave them a clear view of Renfield's window and the door to his building. If he were the type to look out his window with binoculars, he'd spot them. But his curtains hadn't so much as twitched all day.

As stakeouts went, at least they had a nice night for it. A crescent moon arched overhead, surrounded by a few stars visible even in the city's light pollution.

By the time ten o'clock came around, Emma was itching to knock on Renfield's door and just ask the man if he planned to go out later. "He didn't even leave to pick up burgers."

"Maybe he ordered in or heated up something from his

freezer. Let's give it more time. Eleven o'clock is his witching hour, remember?"

They continued to wait. Eleven came and went, and she was ready to throw her coffee cup down in disgust when Renfield popped out of his stairwell door and made a beeline for the sidewalk.

He made no move to examine the area and kept walking at a steady pace, heading away from Emma and Leo's position.

She elbowed Leo. "Same black attire. Gloves?"

Leo shook his head. "I couldn't tell." He took out his phone. "Let me text the others."

"I'm going to follow him. Catch up with me."

He waved her off, and she began steadily pacing Renfield, who had his hands in his jacket pockets and was now going at a decent clip. She couldn't tell if he still favored his left arm, as he'd done in the security footage and when they first interviewed him.

By the time he'd turned onto a street that led toward the nearest suburban neighborhood, Leo had caught up to her. "Jacinda and Mia replied and said they're on the way."

"What about Vance?"

"Nothing yet. I miss anything?"

"No. But the night's still young."

21

I crept up the driveway next to the cockroach's whorehouse and crouched behind the neighbor's car. Once I was finished here, I'd have enough money to buy whatever I needed. A new gun, new vest, some new shoes too. Plus, the right materials to make sure my trophies were preserved.

I might even take a few new ones tonight, depending on how many cockroaches I find inside.

Still, coming here on foot was a risk, but I had my escape route mapped and memorized.

The path I'd take to leave the neighborhood would drop me onto the railroad tracks at a place with a lot of overgrown bushes and a few homeless encampments. Once the shooting started, those losers would be bugging out or hunkering down. Either way, the bums would give me plenty of cover to sneak away.

The street was cool and quiet around me, and all I could think about was how poetic my act of justice would be.

My family's home used to be in a neighborhood like this one, with cars in the driveway, just like some of these had. Like the one I was hiding behind. Our neighbor on one side

Last Sign 153

had a basketball hoop, just like the one across the street from where I hid.

And then some dumbass junkie cockroach burned the place to the ground, killing my parents. Sure, I'd eventually bought a place with my ex-wife, but who was living there now? She was, not me.

My victims were gathered right where I'd expected them tonight. A whole swarm in their nest behind that whorehouse. They were still in their pre-party mode, laughing and no doubt drinking or doing drugs.

A neighbor in the house behind me yelled out his window. "Hey, you all need to shut the hell up, or I'm calling the cops!"

The cockroaches, much to my surprise, quieted down. I even heard one of them offer an apology.

Was that a john trying to make sure the neighbor didn't ruin his fun?

I knew the women didn't start taking customers before eleven, and I hadn't seen anyone show up yet. So the only people in the backyard would be cockroaches. But the women were back there too. I heard them laughing.

I needed to be careful not to hit any of them. I'd reloaded my gun and the ones I got from the cockroaches I already squashed, and I carried a spare mag for my M&P 9. I had plenty to get the party started.

Someone else might've wanted to punish the sex workers themselves, but if we got rid of the gangs and corruption in the city, those women could lead regular lives instead of being pulled down with the insects. The women over there had been coerced into associating with the roaches, and I was going to set them free.

Depending upon how much money was in there, I might even share it with them.

That could go a long way to getting them on my side. They

might even conveniently forget what I look like when it comes time to tell the cops what they saw.

I knew there'd be witnesses tonight, and I expected some of them to get caught and interrogated. As much as I hated to do it, I'd worn a ski mask to make sure nobody got a clear picture of my face.

My blood pulsed faster in my veins, and I realized I couldn't even feel the sore spot on my chest anymore. "My mission is healing the city, healing my flesh, and healing my grief. It's good for the body and good for the soul."

I grinned, sliding my suppressed gun from inside my jacket. I stood up halfway, staying behind the car I'd used for cover. "Here we go, you little creeps."

I was ready to move.

But then a guy came down the sidewalk and walked right up to the roach-infested house, pausing at the top of their driveway.

Dammit, I'd waited too long. Now a john was here, which meant I couldn't go in guns blazing.

I dropped back down and watched as he pulled out a pack of smokes and a lighter. If I didn't know better, I'd swear he was a cop. I'd seen him before, back when I was demanding more be done to find my son's killers.

In the glow of the lighter's flame, the guy's face was revealed. Shit, I was right. I'd talked to him at the precinct about finding the roaches that killed Ethan. He blew me off every time.

He'd been so damn useless…I'd wanted to tear the badge off his shirt.

But now there he was. Visiting a whorehouse like a common cockroach.

Or maybe he was on a sting, and I'd had the misfortune of trying to run my mission on the same night. And if he was part of a sting, more cops would be showing up soon.

Last Sign

I stayed crouched behind the car and got ready to leave the way I'd planned. Whatever was happening here, I'd have to wait for another time to take out this cockroach nest.

Once the cop went inside the house, I could bail without him seeing me scoot.

My exit was a utility road between two homes farther down the block. From there, I had a mostly concealed route back to my place, using alleys and lanes between industrial buildings. I knew which ones had cameras and which way they pointed. Avoiding them all was impossible, but I'd mapped out a path that would only put me in view of a few. Plus, I had a mask.

Unable to resist the urge to know what was happening, I peeked to the right to get a look at the driveway next door.

The cop was still there. I could see his feet. A cigarette butt landed on the ground, and he stomped on it. I needed to wait until he was gone.

I bit the inside of my cheek, tasting blood. If he didn't leave soon, I'd have to come back some other night.

Then the extermination could begin.

22

Emma and Leo reached the corner where Renfield had turned.

He stood at the top of an empty driveway, on the next block. He glanced around jerkily before going around the side of the house.

Leo pulled out his phone again. "Giving our location to Jacinda, Mia, and Vance."

"Did he get back to you?"

"Finally, yeah. Says he's coming from the Bureau, so it might take him a bit."

What was Vance doing at the office this late? Whatever his reason, Emma had more immediate concerns. "Tell me you tagged MPD too."

He nodded as Emma unzipped her jacket. Renfield had disappeared into the darkness beside the house.

"Guy's definitely up to something." Emma's whisper barely carried over the night breeze shuffling the branches of the street trees above them.

Leo patted her on the shoulder. "Any sign of a weapon on him?"

Outside the house, a woman appeared beside Renfield. He pushed her up against the house and clutched at her body, groping as they began kissing.

Emma squinted, trying to pick out details in the dark.

Renfield and the woman kept pawing at each other, then he backed up a step and reached into his jacket.

"Freeze, Renfield! FBI!" Emma pulled her gun and ran as Renfield spun around to face them, one hand in his pocket. "Get on the ground!"

The woman shrieked and ran into the backyard. Mouth open in shock, Renfield put his hands up instead of dropping.

From the backyard, a group of people began shouting. Doors slammed, and Emma caught the sounds of feet hitting fence boards. She took in the whole scene, from Renfield's tryst to the sound of women's voices inside the house. Eyes wide, she looked at Leo.

"I think we just unintentionally raided a suburban brothel."

She and Leo reached Renfield, and Leo kept his gun fixed on the man while she approached. Sounds of people making their escape in the backyard continued to erupt into the night.

Shouts from a neighbor in the next house added to the din. "Dammit, I told you all to keep things quiet or I'd call the cops! Now I'm calling!"

"Sir," Emma yelled back, "we are the cops. Please stay inside your home."

Standing before them, Renfield shook his head. "Nice. Couldn't just leave well enough alone, could you?"

"Turn around and face the wall. You know the dance moves, right?"

He complied, leaning his hands against the house and spacing his feet apart.

"I'm going to go through your pockets, Renfield. Make a move, my partner will shoot. You carrying anything that could injure me?"

The ex-cop's face pinched up in a sneer as he looked at her over his shoulder. "I got nothing to hide. You're barkin' up the wrong tree."

Ignoring him, Emma began patting him down. She expected a shoulder harness with a gun, since they hadn't seen one breaking the line of his clothes, but he only wore a t-shirt beneath his jacket. She found his phone in an inside pocket of the windbreaker, along with a packet of condoms. His wallet was tucked into his jeans pocket.

She stepped back, opening up the wallet to glance inside. "He's clean."

Slowly, Renfield lowered his hands. "Can I have my wallet back?"

Emma handed it over but kept her grip on it as he grabbed for it, holding on until he met her eye. "That's a lot of cash for someone who's out of work. A lot of cash for someone who can barely cover the basics with his unemployment. I'm going out on a limb and guessing that cash was meant for the woman we saw you with." She raised her eyebrows. "That about right?"

He scowled, opened up his wallet, and counted the cash. Seemingly satisfied she hadn't taken anything, he stuffed it into his pocket. When he looked up again, his face had grown tired. "I cashed out some of my retirement savings. Been using it for some...comfort." He waved a hand toward the backyard.

"Comfort. Like prostitution." Leo frowned.

Shamefaced, Renfield nodded. "I'm not proud of it, but yeah. This place has been operating for a while now. That's why I lied about where I was on those other nights. I didn't want to get myself in trouble or get the girls in trouble. They should be able to do what they want with their bodies without the law getting involved, far as I can see it."

"Girls?" Leo stepped up close to Renfield.

"Huh?" Renfield jerked back. "Oh, no, I don't mean... they're not underage. I'm not a shithead perv. Some of them are in their forties, and I still call 'em girls."

Tension eased between the men, and Emma relaxed her shoulders. As long as the women were of age, she wasn't concerned about getting them in trouble any more than their ex-cop was. But if he wasn't their murderer, who the hell was?

The air went cold, thickening around her and stealing her breath. Emma flicked a glance at Leo and began searching the street for whatever sign of the Other must have come. Leo grabbed Renfield by the upper arm and led him to the sidewalk.

Emma followed as they marched the ex-cop back around the corner. Whoever had bugged out from the brothel had to be long gone by now, but they'd still put MPD on the place just in case. She wanted to get more info from Renfield, but before she could ask, the ghost of Marty Kaine walked up and stood in front of her, freezing her mid-step.

Both Leo and Renfield noticed, and she quickly mimed a stomach cramp. "Ate something I shouldn't have." Thankfully, Leo caught the look in her eye, and he pulled Renfield aside.

"Give her some space. We still have questions for you."

The ex-cop grunted and followed Leo's pointed finger, aiming him down the sidewalk a few paces.

The ghost stared at Emma as he bled out in death, just like he had in life. Two puncture wounds in his chest leaked rivulets of thick blood, which joined the mass of gore in his abdomen. White-faced, bloody, and with his opaque eyes on her, he whispered into the cold night air. "Bug Man's here. He's gonna stomp."

Emma twisted to look at Leo. As she opened her mouth to call him, gunfire peppered the night air. "It's coming from behind the neighborhood, along the railroad tracks."

Screams and shouting, plus more gunfire, rang out from the same direction. Renfield dropped to the ground with his hands over the back of his head.

"I'll stay here. I promise. Go, go!"

Whatever might be said about the man, he still had a cop's instincts and a sense of duty to the city.

And if he didn't, if he ran during the chaos, they'd find him again.

Running with her gun raised, Emma charged for the edge of the neighborhood. The tracks were just ahead. Leo yanked out his phone and called for backup.

As they rounded the last house, Emma skidded to a halt and took cover beside the neighborhood's boundary wall. Leo huddled behind her, still talking to MPD dispatch and confirming their location.

Lamplight from a nearby industrial building illuminated the tracks, and Emma could see at least two bodies lying prone out there. Farther along, dark figures raced away as more gunfire cracked.

Emma couldn't locate the shooter, but the people running weren't firing back. Another shot rang out, and one fleeing figure fell to the ground. Emma tore from her hiding place, looking around wildly for the shooter.

23

I knew the Feds hadn't come for me once they took the cop. Renfield was the name they'd yelled. I'd known he seemed familiar. Why the hell was that cop acting like a john? Not my problem. As soon as they were around the corner, I'd scooted out from under the car, rolled my ski mask down tight, and raced away on my exit route.

I'd heard the cockroaches scattering and jumping fences. Following them to the railroad tracks was easy, because they'd made so much damn noise.

Once I'd made my exit, using the utility road like I planned, I caught up with them behind the neighborhood. The moment came together like pure poetry.

I used the guns I'd taken off the cockroaches I already squashed, popping off a dozen shots and taking down two more roaches before they could even react. The rest of them, plus the prostitutes, took off like headless chickens running through the light from the industrial buildings across the tracks.

I took aim and dropped a third roach easy, with two shots to his back.

He had no idea where I was hiding, and neither did the Feds.

They were looking for me, though. The woman was shouting for me to drop my gun and come out.

Not a chance, girlie.

I checked my guns for ammo. Four rounds left in the little Ruger I got from the first roach I killed. The Hi-Point I got off the second guy still had three rounds. I could use those to cover myself.

After that, I'd have to switch to my own gun.

The lady Fed yelled again. "Leave your weapon on the ground and come out with your hands up. Do it slow. Now."

A man's voice joined hers, and I started to shake. Dammit, they were both on the hunt for me. Just as the woman finished yelling again, a gunshot rang out from across the tracks. I ducked and heard both the Feds shout. Were they firing or was it one of the cockroaches?

I peeked out to find the Feds hunkering behind a stack of railroad ties. But I couldn't see any of the cockroaches. They'd all run off.

The Feds started yelling again, both of them taking turns to shout their orders.

"Drop the weapon and come out with your hands up!"

"You're not getting out of here. Just put down the gun and come out!"

More gunfire exploded into the night…two rounds fired in their direction. I thought I spotted a muzzle flash from across the tracks, beside a loading dock. Somebody was out there, shooting at the Feds. It had to be cockroaches, but since when did they stick around and shoot at cops? They were too cowardly for that, especially with the FBI. I'd never heard of gangbangers taking risks like that.

Whoever was out there fired off two more shots, and the Feds ducked behind the railroad ties. I saw my chance.

Don't think. Just run!

Keeping tight to the wall around the neighborhood, I sped off toward the homeless camp. I used up the Hi-Point shooting behind me but aiming at the ground.

When the slide locked back, I tossed the gun away and switched to the Ruger, still aiming low. I just needed the Feds to stay put.

I didn't hear them but emptied the second gun as I ran, planning to disappear into the homeless camp and then make my way home. I chucked the Ruger before I reached the cluster of tents and tarps. Once I got there, I snugged myself in behind a bicycle hitched to a small trailer.

Breathing hard, I looked for the Feds. I didn't see them, but police sirens screamed through the night.

"Shit, shit, shit!"

Three cruisers came up the road I'd planned to follow out of the area. A couple of homeless people stuck their heads out of their tents, but they didn't see me. As the sirens grew louder, other people in the camp began stirring. I needed to get gone, fast.

I'd have to chance running through the warehouse district across the tracks. That place was a maze.

But the Feds would see me if I ran into the open.

The mystery shooter fired again, and this time, I spotted the muzzle flash. They were hiding by the loading dock outside the nearest warehouse.

With the Feds still yelling for me and the other shooter to come out and drop our weapons, I took off and hopped over the railroad.

I made it over the first two tracks but tripped over the last rail and face-planted in the gravel, banging up my elbows and both shins in the process.

Scrambling, I got up and ran as the Feds started yelling for me to freeze and put my hands up.

Gunfire kept coming from whoever was shooting at the Feds. I couldn't see the shooter, but the Feds stayed in their hiding place.

The mystery shooter's bullets weren't meant for me.

Do I have a guardian fucking angel? He's covering for me so I can get away.

Saying a prayer of thanks to whoever the heck was helping me out, I kept running. The Feds yelled at me again, even as gunfire continued to split the night. Four shots fired in quick succession gave me all the cover I needed to get clear.

Sprinting toward the maze of warehouses, auto-parts stores, and fabrication shops, I raced away as sirens tore across the night. I had no idea where any security cameras might be, though, since this wasn't part of my planned exit route. Even with the ski mask on, I kept my face down.

Checking every dark shadow and side street, I moved as fast as I could past the darkened storefronts and metal buildings, desperate to get out of the area.

After this shit show, I'd have to lay low for a few months. I might even need to leave the city, and that would eat up every last penny I had.

Dammit, you really screwed the pooch this time.

At the end of a narrow lane, I leaned against a warehouse loading dock to catch my breath. I'd taken a few breaths to calm my pulse when footsteps pounded in my direction.

An FBI agent was practically flying down the street toward me. He saw me and had a gun out.

"FBI! Put your hands up and get on your knees! Get down, now!"

I started backing away, putting my hands up by my shoulders and feeling my M&P 9 hanging in the harness under my jacket.

In the light of the overhead lamp, I could see the guy was

built, blond, with a crew cut. "I said stop moving and get on the ground!"

He had his gun raised, but I was still backing away, not holding my weapon. At the edge of the loading dock, I twisted around and ducked behind the concrete ramp.

A gunshot blasted behind me. A pained grunt was followed by the clatter of a gun hitting the ground. I carefully stood and looked for the Fed. He was down, holding his chest and groaning, rocking side to side. His gun lay a few feet away.

The roar of a big car engine grabbed my attention, and a black SUV squealed out from an alley across the lane. The driver pulled to a stop beside the Fed and got out, leaving the engine running.

I had my gun up and ready, figuring it was another Fed.

When she rounded the back end of the SUV, my hands faltered on my gun.

The woman from the bar—the one who'd talked with me about how bad crime and cockroaches had become—was standing over the Fed with a gun aimed at his face. He started to sit up, and she swung the gun at his jaw, sending his head spinning.

He slumped to the ground, half leaning against the loading dock where I'd stood a few moments before. She held the gun up and studied it like she'd never seen one before, turning it this way and that. "Glad that one hit the mark at least."

Unlike the time we met in the bar, she now had her hair concealed under a black watch cap. She wore a dark denim jacket and jeans over boots. But I'd know her anywhere. She was captivating.

Her dark eyes were just as mysterious and appealing as at the bar. Her round cheeks were flushed, too, with that glow that had made me think she'd been flirting with me.

I took a step forward and froze. "It's you. From the bar."

"Uh-huh. Me."

The Fed started to sit up, and she swung the gun at his jaw again.

Shit. He went down really hard that time.

Before I could react, she had her gun up and aimed at me. "Don't just stand there with your thumb up your ass. Help me get him in the car."

I didn't move. "What the hell?"

"Don't talk. Help. Now."

The command in her voice flicked a switch inside me. I put my gun away, and in three strides, I joined her beside the Fed.

She holstered her gun and pulled out a syringe from her pocket, which she stuck in the Fed's upper arm like a nurse giving someone a shot. "That'll keep him quiet for a bit."

I stared at her. "Look, whatever you think I'm agreeing to, I need to—"

"We can talk later. Right now, we lift together using our legs, not our backs, and we get him in the car."

She capped the syringe and stuck it back in her jacket pocket, then grabbed the Fed's ankles and thrust her chin toward his upper body. "Shoulders. Let's go, friend. Time's wasting."

Sirens continued to echo around us. The cops might turn down this street at any second.

I jumped into action, grabbing the Fed under his arms and heaving him up. Damn, he weighed a ton.

Together, the woman and I muscled our burden into the back of her SUV. We both struggled and made more noise than intended. Her jacket got caught on the bumper and ripped, and she swore like a sailor.

Finally, we had him inside, and she slammed the door shut.

"What're you gonna do with him?"

She looked at me. "Not a damn thing. That's your job, slick. C'mon."

I couldn't help it. I followed her like a puppy being called by its master. She climbed into the driver's seat, and I got in on the other side, rolling my mask up. She was showing me her face, and I knew she'd already seen mine in the bar anyway.

Wheeling us around, she took us back down the alley and deeper into the maze of buildings.

We passed a mechanic's shop, a tire graveyard, and countless unmarked buildings.

Once we'd left the wailing sirens behind, I risked conversation with my rescuer. "What do I call you?"

"Lydia."

I let her answer sit in the air for a bit. Seemed like she wanted to use code names, so I thought I'd play along. "Cool. Nice to meet you, Lydia. You can call me the Bug Man."

She didn't reply, and we drove in silence for a few streets, with her taking turns like a professional driver using the city as her course. After a while, I got tired of hearing my own thoughts, so I tried for conversation again.

"Gonna tell me what this is about? Not that I don't appreciate—"

"What kind of idiot starts gunning down gangbangers with federal agents nearby?"

I didn't have an answer. She was right. I'd gotten greedy, anxious to make a difference, to do something that might change things in this city. "My son was—"

She held up a hand. "I've been watching you work, and I admire the dedication you have for our cause."

"You've been watching me? Were you the one shooting at the Feds?"

She nodded. "Someone had to cover your ass so you

could get clear. I was in the neighborhood anyway and thought I'd lend a hand."

"Bullshit. You followed me here. Admit it."

She flashed a wry grin in my direction. "Guilty as charged."

"And that was you last night, driving past me in this SUV."

The grin widened. "I watched you squash that bug and haul him into your van. He got you good, but the vest saved your ass."

This woman was like a shadow I hadn't known I had.

"What are you, CIA or some shit like that?"

She pulled into a parking lot behind some apartments, and I realized we'd come back to my place. *Just how much does she know about me?*

I stared at her as she turned off the engine. "Who are you really?"

"No one of consequence, but trust me, you do not want to fuck me over. Now open the glove box."

I did and found a thick manila envelope stuffed in there.

"Take it out. Go ahead."

I did. The envelope was heavy, and I could make out the bulky shape of cash bundles. Opening the flap, I whistled low and long. "Hot leaping hell, that's a lot of money."

"It's a hundred thousand dollars, and there's more if you need it. Get a better vest, maybe some better shoes too." She aimed a thumb at my running shoes, which I'd painted black. "If you need ammo or another weapon, I can point you to a seller who won't ask questions and has anything you'll need."

What's the catch?

"A hundred thousand is a lot of ammo, and I'm just one guy."

"Think of it as an exit strategy. When you're done, you'll need to find a way to get gone, and fast. That much money should do the trick. Take the keys too."

I pawed around in the glove box and came out with a set of car keys.

"This car is my new ride?"

The lady shook her head. "This one's mine. Yours is a few blocks over. Standard sedan, registration is up to date. It's nothing fancy, so you'll blend in."

I clutched the keys tight in my hand. "I'm guessing there's a string attached to all this benevolence. Just how big a string are we talking about, and is it around my wrist or neck?"

A smirk curled her lips, and the glint in her eye turned from seductive to evil in a split second. She reached inside her jacket, and I got ready to bring up my gun, but she pulled hers out with two fingers pinching the handle. She passed it to me.

The gun was a .45 with an extended barrel that had been threaded to accept a suppressor. She hadn't given me one of those, and mine was made for the nine-millimeter I carried.

"Any chance you have the suppressor to go with it? I like to work quiet when I can."

She laughed out loud. "Yes, you were so quiet back there I only heard the first dozen shots you fired. After that, my ears were ringing. Sorry, slick, if you want it to be quiet, that's your problem."

"So why give it to me at all? I'm not going to use it this way."

She stiffened in her seat, staring at me with a calm fury behind her eyes. "There's a fresh magazine in there, minus one. It's loaded with special rounds I had custom made."

"What kind of custom?" I jerked my head toward the back of the SUV. "That Fed had a vest on, and your shot didn't break through, so these aren't armor-piercing."

She tutted and shook her head like a teacher about to scold a misbehaving kid. "You have eleven bullets in there.

Every single one of them will hit what you want them to, assuming you can see the target."

I tried not to look at her like she had two heads. "They'll hit whatever I want them to? How—"

"I'll explain more tomorrow night. But I received these from my mother. She worked in law enforcement, and they're her…special invention."

The woman seemed stranger and stranger. "What happens tomorrow night?"

"You and I go hunting together." She narrowed her eyes on me. "You need to learn to trust me and that weapon. And I need to know if you're the right man for the job, because these are the last bullets my mother made."

"And what job's that?"

That devil's smile curled her lips again, replacing the anger that had been seeping out around her words. "I sent the Feds an email yesterday, telling them to stay out of your way."

"You did what? You didn't tell them my name, did you? Dammit, you—"

"Relax. They don't know your name or anything about you except that you intend to keep cleaning up the city, because they're too incompetent to do it themselves."

I stared at her and gripped the gun she'd given me. She didn't flinch as I lifted it. "If you're trying to make me a patsy, this is where we part ways for good."

"Trust me, friend." She flattened her palm on the steering wheel. "The only thing I'm trying to do is help you, and now it's your turn to help me."

My finger hadn't curled around the trigger yet, and I wasn't quite aiming at her. But I kept the gun up, just in case she tried something. "Okay, tell me what you want me to do, and why."

"The why is easy. I feel exactly like you do. I've lost people close to me because the Feds and cops are incompetent morons. We're going to use Sleeping Beauty back there to send them a message."

"And then?"

She reached into her inside jacket pocket and pulled out a new phone and a photo. "I'll call you, and you need to answer when I do." She handed the phone and photo over.

I stared at her. The fire in her eyes and her flushed cheeks told another story. I'd suspected before, but now I knew I was looking into the face of a killer. She tapped the photograph.

The woman in the photo was wearing a dark suit and standing in front of an American flag. It looked like the kind of official police photograph I'd seen in the paper. "Who's this?"

"Your target, slick. Once our message is received, the Fed's friends are gonna go nuts looking for him." She eased back in her seat, those mysterious eyes like two deep pools of darkness. "I want you to use that gun I gave you to kill Special Agent Emma Marie Last."

24

Emma kicked at the ground as she shined her light along yet another stretch of alleyway. There was absolutely no sign of their unsub. The alleys ran between warehouses and small businesses like car repair shops or parts stores. The killer could've disappeared down any of the narrow lanes around her.

And no one had heard from Vance in over an hour. When she and Leo texted the team that they were following Renfield into the neighborhood, Vance had written back that he would join them. So far, he hadn't appeared or picked up when she and Leo called.

Mia and Jacinda had responded immediately too. They were at the crime scene on the railroad tracks now. With a hard sigh, Emma turned around and headed back to join them.

Ambulances bearing EMTs had arrived, but the bodies on the ground were beyond help. And none of the victims had identification on them.

Leo was farther down the tracks, scanning the area.

Emma called to him as she headed his way. "Find anything?"

He nodded and waved an evidence bag at her. "Picked up a knife. The guy you were chasing might have dropped it when he went down. If he's our unsub, we can rule out a psychotic chef using his cutlery."

The knife might be a match for the one used on Johnny Duncan and Marty Kaine, but they'd need to have the blade examined in a lab to be sure. What Emma wanted more than anything was to know she'd been chasing the right person.

Two people were shooting at us tonight, and you only saw one of them running away.

"Any idea who our mystery shooter was or where they went? I only saw the one guy who took off."

Leo shook his head. "I didn't see the second shooter, but techs found a pile of brass near that loading dock." He aimed a finger across the tracks to a warehouse. A concrete slope led from beside the tracks to a roll-up door. "The casings are from a forty-five though. Not a match to Johnny Duncan's scene."

"Dammit." Emma threw her hands up. "Is that all we got? The guy I chased was popping off rounds like crazy."

Nodding, Leo headed back toward the stack of railroad ties they'd used for cover earlier. He waved his hand to indicate the open space between the ties and the tracks. "This whole area is littered with nine-millimeter brass. I also tagged two discarded weapons, a Ruger and a Hi-Point."

"He came loaded for bear."

Emma stared in the direction they'd last seen the man running. He'd skirted around a building near the tracks and disappeared into the maze of warehouses.

As soon as the second shooter had stopped firing, Emma had bolted out of her and Leo's hiding place and gone after the man.

He'd fallen, and she'd have caught up to him if yet another series of gunshots hadn't rung out, the bullets kicking up dirt and chips of rock as they impacted around her. She had to crouch and look for cover.

Emma had no doubt that the second shooter, whoever they were, had been firing the .45 and helped the other guy get away.

She shook her head, frustration burning in her chest. "I feel like we're back to square one here. We have nothing, no sign of either shooter, and no sign of Vance."

Mia and Jacinda stood by a police cruiser, talking with Agent Conrad Wurth. Catching Emma's eye, Mia came over, her face pale. "He's missing. Vance is missing."

"What? I know he didn't report in that he was on scene, but—"

"No, he's missing, Emma. One of the cops told Jacinda they saw 'a tall, built, blond man' in a Bureau windbreaker running into that warehouse maze behind us. They're scouring that whole area, but so far, nobody's seen him, and he isn't answering his phone."

Turning, Emma scanned the industrial streets stretching along and away from the railroad. She kept hoping for any sign of those bright-yellow letters against dark fabric, anything to identify where Vance might be. "We should be out there looking too."

"He was supposed to meet us here. He told me he was on his way, and he was closer than I was."

"Why didn't you come down together?"

Mia pressed her lips into a thin line. "He said he had to follow up on something with Jacinda that he wouldn't tell me about, then he did and we had a fight…don't ask. Please. I was just driving around the city by myself when you texted. I got here right after Jacinda." Mia's gaze went to her phone again. "He won't pick up. It goes straight to voicemail."

Emma drew in a shaky breath. "That man never turns off his phone."

"I know, right?" Mia bit her lip, jiggling her phone in her hand as if to prod it for an answer. "I even tried his desk phone at the Bureau."

Leo put a hand on her shoulder. "Let's check in with Jacinda."

Down the tracks, they joined Jacinda and Wurth, who were talking with two young men in cuffs and three scantily clad women. MPD officers stood nearby. Emma figured the group of civilians had been apprehended attempting to escape.

Jacinda left the group of witnesses with Wurth and moved to meet Emma and the others as they approached. "Wurth has that bunch held for questioning. The men are both members of the Serpents. The women claim to be friends who were on their way home from a club and 'happened to be walking by' when the shooting started."

Leo jerked his chin at the two men in cuffs. "The guys are with our last victim's gang."

The SSA pointed to a police cruiser, where Renfield had been placed in the back seat. "Emma and Leo, wrap things up with our star witness over there, then come back to me. I'm going to check with MPD about their search effort so far. We have an agent missing and need to find him. Mia, with me."

The two women departed, aiming for the makeshift Incident Command post that had just been established by the stack of railroad ties Emma and Leo had used for cover earlier.

Emma touched Leo's arm. "Let's make it quick with Renfield. I want to get out there and start looking for Vance."

"You and me both, and yesterday." Leo walked alongside her as they headed for the cruiser Jacinda had pointed out.

A single MPD officer stood beside the vehicle. "He's been fully compliant, in case that matters."

"Can you open up and let us have a few words with him?"

The officer popped the back door open. Renfield didn't even turn his head. "I'm looking forward to what a solicitation charge does to my prospects. Thanks, guys."

Emma leaned down, resting her arm on the open door. She held up the bagged knife. "Drop something on your way to the brothel?"

No emotion crossed his features as he turned and stared at the knife. "Dust it and let me know when you don't get a match to my prints."

She stood and handed the bag to Leo, who flagged down a passing tech.

While he dealt with getting the blade into the evidence stream, she took another try at Renfield. "I suspect MPD will find physical evidence of prostitution inside that house, but my partner and I didn't see you go inside. All we saw was you and a woman making out against the wall."

Renfield stared at her. "I knew you'd get there eventually." He shifted and turned his back toward her. "Can you take these off now?"

"Almost. Why'd you come here tonight? Why here, instead of some other street corner?"

He hunched his shoulders, as much as the cuffs would allow. "Like I said. The place has been operating awhile. I knew about it when I wore a badge, figured I might as well take advantage of it now that I don't. Not that having a badge ever stopped anybody from buying a little fun."

Emma bit back a burst of laughter. "Only one of us has a badge here, Renfield. Tell me why I shouldn't detain you as an accomplice to what went down here?"

His visible shock turned to anger in a flash. "That wasn't anything I knew about or had any involvement in. You try to pin that shit on me, and I'll make damn sure your badge gets lost too. You have nothing and know nothing." He jerked his arms to the side, rattling the cuffs around his wrists. "So take these fucking things off and let me go."

"I'd love to. I really would. You insist you weren't involved, but it's a real coincidence you happen to show up on the exact night, at the exact time, that everything popped off."

"Shit." Renfield leaned forward, dropping his forehead against the cage dividing the front seats from the back. "I swear I was just here to enjoy a good time with Pamela. That's all."

"Who's Pamela?"

"My usual. She's here every night. And before you ask, no, I have no idea where she lives, what her last name is, or anything else about her."

Emma straightened, searching his face. After a long moment, she asked the officer to release him.

Once Renfield was standing outside the cruiser, rubbing his wrists, she made their position clear. "We have nothing to connect you with the violence here tonight, except your presence on the scene, and your stated reason for being here tracks with what my partner and I witnessed upon our arrival." She handed him her card. "You're free to go."

He pocketed the card with another of his trademark sneers. "You know where to find me. If I'm not at home, I'm at Park Library, applying for jobs, or at the gym on Grant Street."

"Good luck with the job search." She only meant it half sarcastically.

He tossed a sloppy salute her way and headed off on foot. The MPD officer suggested he might get a ride from one of the cops, but he dismissed the idea with a wave. "I'd rather walk. Clear my head a bit."

Emma followed him toward the tracks and informed the remaining officers that he was clear to go. Once he'd wandered off in the direction of his home, she joined the others at Incident Command. Leo was already there.

Jacinda was briefing an assembled group of MPD officers. "We've had no contact with Agent Jessup since shortly after twenty-three hundred hours. His last known location that we can verify was the Bureau offices. MPD have reported seeing someone who matches Agent Jessup's description in this area within the past hour."

She proceeded to divide the assembled search party into pairs of one agent and one officer.

"I don't need to tell any of you how critical it is that we find some sign of where he went." She glanced at Mia. "I do need to stress that at this time, we don't have any reason to believe he has been abducted. That said, we're not making assumptions of any kind. Let's move out."

Turning away, Emma couldn't keep fear from creeping into her face. She caught Leo's eye and could tell he was thinking the exact same thing.

Whatever Vance's absence meant, it couldn't be good.

25

Vance wiggled his hands, fighting against the bonds. He'd been hog-tied, a position that allowed him only the slightest bit of movement at the best of times. But his arm, while out of its cast, was still far from one-hundred-percent. A frightening deep ache had him worried the new bone would snap again. He kept wiggling to a minimum, but he knew he'd try again soon, bad idea or not.

A rope, fitted into his mouth like a horse's bit, prevented him from doing much more than grunting. Another rope around his neck kept his head just off the floor.

Every time he tried to move his head, there was a tug on his ankles. Twisting to the side strained his neck, and he could see the rope extending above his head and looping through a metal shelf bracket a few feet up the wall. The rope ran under the shelf to another bracket, where it descended to his ankles.

Great. Move my feet, choke myself. Move my head, and I can't use my feet to get any support.

He took a deep breath and exhaled slowly. Panicking would not serve him one bit now. He concentrated on flexing his lower legs, attempting to see how far he could move them before constricting the rope around his neck.

Not much. Barely enough to push against the floor or the wall.

The pain in his lower left side reminded him he'd been shot, probably by a large-caliber bullet, given the sharp, stabbing ache that swelled whenever he breathed in. While his vest had saved him, he'd be dealing with a bruise for a long time and might even be bleeding internally.

At least a broken or bruised rib. Fun. When I get out of here, I'm going to write down all the reasons I ever wanted to do this job.

With another long, deep breath, Vance brought to mind his training in survival and escape and took stock of his surroundings.

With his limited vision in the dim light and his contorted position, Vance could only guess at his location. A narrow kitchen extended in front of him, with cabinets on both sides, and the bulky shape of a refrigerator at the far end.

His feet were close to a set of cabinets, with a sink and faucet in the middle. A dishwasher was at the far end beneath a Formica countertop. Vance's head was closer to the stove, which sat between two narrow cabinets.

The refrigerator stood, with its compressor humming, at the end of the farthest cabinet on that side of the kitchen.

Vance looked straight ahead, out of the kitchen and toward a small dining area with a table and two chairs beneath a curtained window.

Weak light from a streetlamp slithered through a crack between the curtains, casting a slender beam on the floor. But outside, the night was still dark as pitch. He could only guess at the time. He'd been shot after midnight, maybe around a quarter past the hour. The rest of his team had been expecting him to join them in converging on Emma and Leo's position by the railroad.

But he'd decided to take a different route, because he'd spotted a man running with a suppressed gun.

Then someone else shot him—someone he hadn't seen.

Of all the days to decide I can do this job alone. Dammit, you know better than this.

He took another deep breath. Beating himself up for past mistakes wouldn't help him in his current predicament.

A heavy snore came from somewhere deeper in the apartment. Vance stilled. He wasn't alone.

He began growling as loud as he could. The snoring continued but cut off as whoever was sleeping either roused or shifted position.

Vance went quiet and listened. A creak got him thinking the sleeper was awake now, and seconds later came the lumbering gait of someone close to his own size and weight.

His captor appeared at the end of the galley kitchen, beside the fridge. The man had dark hair, which he ran one hand through, attempting to smooth down the tufts sticking out in all directions.

A surgical mask concealed most of the man's face, but Vance picked out dark eyes, likely brown, though the dimly lit room made it hard to be sure.

Vance watched the man, waiting for him to act, to say something.

He went to the sink, standing with his hands on the counter's edge.

Great. Hey, Jacinda, I found the killer. He's a psycho with a bondage fetish, and I'm hog-tied in his kitchen. Also, can you approve my leave now?

What he'd give to go back in time and argue harder for his request. When Jacinda had come back from the Hill, she'd been adamant that he stay on the job until the case was closed or for another week, whichever came first.

And now that order might result in him getting killed.

Vance's jaw tightened, as much as it could without twinging the ropes.

The man stood back from the sink and shook his head. He flexed his shoulders and stretched, yawning behind his mask.

Based on the fridge behind him, Vance placed the man's height at around six feet tall. Muscles defined the contours of his shirt, and Vance guessed his captor outweighed him by fifty pounds, even if he might be slightly shorter.

He turned to face Vance. "Doing okay there, buddy? Hope the rope's not cutting off your circulation. I had to work fast when we brought you in."

We? Oh, please keep talking. Tell me everything, you damn moron.

Vance kept his eyes on the man. His face was shadowed, with only the weak light from the window illuminating the kitchen.

"I think she's planning to kill you, and I just need you to know that I'm not going to let that happen."

Okay, so "we" means you and she are working together, but you have different agendas. Now I just need to find out who "she" is.

The man ran a hand over his head again. "Just hang in there. I…I'm gonna go get something for you to eat. It'll have to be through a straw, but it'll be food. Peach-banana smoothie sound good? Just blink once for yes, twice for no."

Survival. Evasion. Resistance. Escape.

Vance blinked once, even though he hated bananas. He was going to get to know this guy up close. Survive him to plot his escape. It was on.

The guy turned around and stumbled through the apartment. A door opened and closed in another room. Sounds of closet doors sliding in their tracks echoed across the space.

Footsteps came back into the room just beyond the

kitchen, followed by an electronic clicking sound, like an older television being turned on.

At his best estimate, Vance figured the apartment had one bedroom with a bathroom and probably a living room with the television in it.

Muffled sounds of a talk show, with lots of audience yelling and booing, began to bleed into the kitchen.

Cool, cool. I'm stuck here, about to lose the use of my hands, and he's out there watching Jerry Springer *reruns.*

His captor had to be standing around the corner by the fridge. Vance heard him grumble about "failed exterminators" before the television sounds stopped with another *click*.

The man appeared at the end of the kitchen again, holding a remote control and wearing a new set of clothes. "I'll be back quick. There's an all-night grocery store a few blocks away. Just sit tight…not that you've got much choice, I guess." He waved and disappeared from the kitchen, leaving Vance alone to contemplate his situation and plan his escape.

26

Emma jittered her knee up and down in the passenger seat of an MPD cruiser while the woman she'd been paired with radioed in their location. The dispatcher directed them to circle up with the others back at Incident Command by the railroad.

"Roger, dispatch. Unit 9524 out."

The teams of agents and MPD officers had worked methodically to cover the industrial zone where Vance was possibly spotted. Leo's and Mia's teams had already returned to IC. Jacinda had stayed behind to coordinate the search effort.

As they drove down a street that bordered the warehouse districts, Emma's phone lit up. "I'm here, Jacinda. Did we find him?"

Jacinda's voice came through the phone with more anger than Emma had ever heard from the woman. "We found his car. I need you back here. Now."

Flooring it, the officer sped back to the railroad, where they jolted to a stop. Even before the engine cut, Emma jumped out and ran to Incident Command, where Leo stood waving for her to hurry. He and Jacinda were under the pop-up canopy by a card table and some chairs.

Floodlights blanketed the area, and teams of technicians were combing the ground for more evidence of the night's violence.

A tow truck carrying Vance's red Chevy Malibu hybrid was parked a few feet away.

Mia was there, standing rigid and staring at the car. She turned as Emma approached.

"We found it. He wasn't inside."

Emma wrapped her friend in a hug, rubbing her back. "We'll find him, Mia. He's alive, and we're going to find him."

The SSA broke in. "I've received another message from our killer. He has Vance."

Emma's gut bottomed out as Mia wilted in her arms. "What does he want? How do we get Vance back?"

Pulling her laptop over, Jacinda tapped at the keyboard. "I'll let you all read it yourselves." She turned the screen so they could see it clearly.

A simple typed message appeared. Like the first email, this one had been sent from an encrypted address and opened with the same salutation.

"'Dear failed exterminators.'" Emma read the text out loud as her friends drew close around her. "'He's alive. If you want him to stay that way, you'll back off and let me work. I'll take care of justice. Try to stop me, and he dies.'"

Jacinda rotated the laptop so she could type again.

"There's a photo attached." She looked up, her brows furrowed. "Mia, brace yourself."

Vance was shown against a wall in a narrow, windowless space that looked like a kitchen. The wood of a cupboard could be seen near his head, but his back was to a blank white wall. He could've been in the kitchen area of an office or an apartment or duplex, maybe a small house.

Bloody wounds and an angry bruise marked his jawline. His hands were tied behind him, and his feet were tied as well.

Ropes around his neck and his ankles led upward along the wall, but the photo didn't reveal what the ropes connected to.

Another rope held his jaw partially open, effectively gagging him. At best, he might be able to groan or growl. His eyes were open, but bleary and unfocused.

Mia sucked in a ragged breath. "I should've been with him." There was an undercurrent of a sob beneath her voice. "I should've been right there with him, wherever he was."

"It's not your fault, Mia." Jacinda spoke gently. "And we're going to get him back."

Emma clenched her fists tight, counting to three before she released them. "We know he made it here tonight. We need to check every business for footage. It's possible his last location is on video somewhere."

Leo frowned. "We should lean on Renfield again too. We know he hates gangs. He could be working with the killer, setting up distractions so the guy can do his work."

Pacing away from the pop-up canopy, Emma tapped her fingers against her thighs. "We saw one man driving the van. One man getting out and dumping the body. Same man both times, from what we saw on the footage. I don't think we're looking at a team effort."

"And he didn't say anything about gang members when I spoke to him." Jacinda nodded at Emma. "He was the first person I saw when I arrived on scene, and he was lying face down next to the sidewalk."

"He waved me and Leo off when the shooting started and promised he'd stay put." Emma thought back to their conversation that night. "I'm prepared to take him off our suspect list, but he might still have information that can help us catch the killer."

"Information such as…?" The SSA's question hung as Leo and Mia looked at Emma.

"He told me he sees a woman named Pamela at that location, and he called her his 'usual.'"

"If he has a 'usual,' he must visit fairly often. He knows more about that place and who runs it." Jacinda pointed at her. "Mia and Emma, you're on Renfield. Get him back here or go to him, just do it fast."

Leo made room for Mia to examine the photograph of Vance on the laptop. "Where am I going, Jacinda?"

"Wurth has those two guys from the Serpents in cruisers. You and I can start with them, and the three women who were 'on their way home from the club' when the shooting started."

Emma and Mia hurried to Mia's car. She unlocked the doors and paused before getting into the driver's seat, her eyes wide. "What if he's already on the run?"

Looking across the top of the car, Emma couldn't ignore the worry on Mia's brow. "I'll ask MPD to send a unit. They can sit on him until we get there."

She flagged down an officer who was helping a tech bag evidence. "Any chance you can ask dispatch to send a unit over to a suspect's address?"

After writing down Renfield's address and description, the officer let out a sharp laugh. "Dalton Renfield? Hell, I'll bring him to you. Wait here."

27

Emma paced in circles beside the IC canopy while Mia stood like a sentinel, staring at the warehouses and repair shops across the tracks. Someone had brought coffee and sandwiches from an all-night grocery store. Emma wolfed down a turkey on rye, but Mia hadn't so much as touched a crumb of food.

An MPD cruiser rolled up, and the driver chirped the siren. Renfield sat in the back.

She went to the vehicle, and the officer opened the back door. Dalton Renfield sat there, his hands free this time, a cup of coffee held in one. He scratched at his unshaven cheek and rubbed his bleary eyes with the other.

"You can't let a guy sleep, can you?" He frowned and scratched a knee through his sweatpants. "Are you that desperate for a man's attention?"

"Don't flatter yourself." Emma resisted the urge to haul him out and fling him to the ground. Instead, she slammed his door and climbed into the passenger seat up front. She left the door open so Mia could lean in and participate. "You're here because you may have information related to an ongoing investigation. Answer our questions honestly, and you'll be home in time for your beauty rest. Keep playing the asshole, and you'll be sleeping in a holding cell for the next forty-eight hours."

He remained smug in his manner but had the decency to refrain from making any more inappropriate comments.

"You can't still think I'm the suspect." He snorted. "I was lying on the ground when the bullets were flying. Or did you forget that part?"

Mia leaned into the car, staring through the cage at Renfield. "We don't think you're the unsub. But we think you might know who is."

"What the hell makes you think I know the guy, guys, or girls who were shooting? I was on the ground. Face down." His sneer went from being focused on Mia to Emma. "I'm over here in the real world, Agent Last. Not the fantasy one you're living in where I have any idea who your killer is."

"You knew that house was run by gangs, right?"

He sat back, sipping his coffee. "To be clear, which 'house' are we talking about?"

Emma wanted to punch him in the nose, but that wouldn't get them anywhere useful.

It would be fun, but not useful. Steady as you go, Emma girl. He's just being a smart-ass.

"The house we detained you at a few yards from this location, where you and a woman you told us was your 'usual' were attempting to rub the paint off the siding using her backside."

Renfield laughed and scratched at his face again. "*That* house is a house the Serpents use for their girls to turn tricks. It's a whorehouse run by a gang, and yes, I knew that. I believe I told you something to that effect maybe one or two hours ago."

"And you knew this how? How did you find out about it?"

"We all knew." He shrugged, taking another sip of coffee.

Mia slammed her hand against the cage. "Who the hell is this 'we' you're talking about?"

He glanced between them. "Everybody at the Eighth knew a gang was running a prostitution ring out of that house. We tried to crack down on it, especially with it being right there in a neighborhood. Not as easy as you think when the girls aren't being coerced and the house is owned outright instead of rented."

Disgust turned Emma's stomach, but she kept her voice even. "We called the owner on record while we were waiting for MPD to bring you in. Turns out he lives down the street and was one among many neighbors awakened by all the noise."

"Allow me to finish for you." Renfield raised his cup to her. "The owner allows a group of young men to live there while they finish school. He's been doing this for 'several years' and 'never had any trouble with the law until now.' Sound about right?"

Emma gritted her teeth. That was exactly the answer they'd gotten. She gave Renfield a short, reluctant nod.

Renfield replied with a smug smile. "That's the exact line of bull he fed us every time we contacted him too. Let me guess, he gave you some phone numbers and said they belong to young men and teenagers. You called, and they all picked up on the first ring, even at this time of night. When you asked, they claimed to live at that address and said they go to school every day and always do their homework."

Emma glanced at the list of numbers she'd collected over the phone from the home's owner. She and Mia hadn't had a chance to call them yet.

Seems like he just saved you a lot of wasted time, Emma girl.

Despite that, she couldn't bring herself to thank him. "Let's try this. Did you see anyone on your walk home?"

He shrugged. "A few cars. One cruiser, going away from the scene, that was probably on the way to a different call. Some drunks huddling under cardboard."

"No one you recognized, no one you knew personally?"

Renfield shook his head.

"What about Pamela? Which way did she go when she left?"

"Nice try." Renfield's lip curled. "I was too busy watching you and your partner aim guns at my face. I suspect she went out the gate in the back fence like everyone else, but I can neither confirm nor deny because I didn't see her or anyone else leave the property."

Emma didn't budge, and neither did Mia.

He looked back and forth between the two of them.

"What's got you so hot about me being there? This isn't just chitchat about some hookers getting away, is it?"

Turning to meet Mia's eyes, Emma prompted her partner. "Do you want to tell him?"

Renfield sat up straighter in the back seat, leaning toward the cage. "Tell him what?"

"Tell him," Mia leaned toward the cage again, "that a federal agent was abducted. If you know anything at all about it, this is your chance to come clean."

Renfield sprang backward and nearly spilled his coffee. Cursing, he slapped his free hand against the cage, a pleading moan escaping his throat. "I swear to you, on my son's grave, I don't know anything about that. You saw me drop so you and your partner could go handle that mess. I stayed right there and let them put the cuffs on me later." He held up his free hand. "Your boss was the first one to show up, and I didn't move until she said I could."

He'd done exactly that, based on Jacinda's report, and his manner had shifted into practically solicitous when they'd told him about Vance.

If he's lying, he should've been an actor instead of a cop.

"You didn't see anyone carrying a pistol on your walk home?"

"Nobody with a weapon of any kind."

Checking with Mia, who gave her a quick nod of agreement, Emma relaxed her posture and waved down the officer who'd brought Renfield to them. "He's free to go. Thanks for bringing him back."

"No problem."

Emma watched Mia head over to the IC table and grab a cup of coffee. She ran her hand over her hair, tugging hard at her ponytail. Whatever forensics could pull from Vance's own car, they had to find something that would tell them where he'd been taken.

Either that, or we start dismantling this city brick by brick, starting with that warehouse district.

28

Leo and Jacinda stood over a pair of white men who had Serpents tattoos above their low shirt collars. They both sat against a railroad tie in the gravel beside the tracks. The taller of the pair called himself Stitchy and had refused, so far, to reveal a legal name. Despite repeated attempts, by both Leo and Jacinda, the man sat mutely on the ground.

The other man, who appeared younger and less convinced that silence was the right move, started to speak. He got an elbow in the ribs from Stitchy. That shut him up fast.

Jacinda offered to get Leo coffee. He nodded. That had been their agreed-upon code for him to adopt a more aggressive approach in his questioning.

The SSA departed, and Leo flicked his tablet closed. He motioned for Stitchy to stand up and waved him away from his partner, who followed Leo with his gaze.

"Can I go?" the unnamed gang member asked.

Leo flashed him a hard look. "Stay here until Stitchy and I get back. We have a few things to discuss."

Two uniformed officers waved to Leo from their cruiser nearby. "We'll watch the other one."

Stitchy's pal slumped back against the railroad tie and muttered something to himself.

Taking the other man a few yards over, Leo indicated Stitchy should stop. "Right here's good. Just wanted to clear the air. I think between you and your partner, you have the brains. Am I right?"

Stitchy sniffed and ran a hand under his nose. "Could be. What'd you want to clear up?"

Leo began reciting a list of possible charges. "Let's start with interfering with a federal officer carrying out his duties."

Stitchy remained unmoved and simply stared back at Leo.

Until Leo added the kicker. "From there, we'd add assault and abduction of a federal officer."

That got the man's attention. Stitchy's eyes nearly popped out of his head, and he started shaking. "Uh-uh. I didn't see no Feds, not until the cops caught up with us and started yelling. We hit the ground, right? We know the game. Comply and do what they say. That's what we did."

"When you saw the Feds, where did you see them? Who took them?"

Leo knew only one agent had been abducted, but he wanted to lean on Stitchy as hard as he could, just as he and Jacinda agreed they would do. Eventually, one of the men might spill a detail that would help them find Vance.

"I only saw you and the lady who just left. Plus them other two women. You all had those jackets on, so it was easy to tell who was who." Stitchy's face had paled, leaving two red splotches on his cheeks.

Leo stood still, gaze locked on Stitchy's as Jacinda returned. She carried two cups of coffee, one for him and one for their witness.

Good cop is back. Let's see if Stitchy notices.

The young man tentatively took the cup she offered and lifted it to his mouth. Jacinda pulled packets of creamer and sugar from her pocket. "Either, both, or neither?"

"Black is fine. Thanks."

Stitchy's genuine gratitude rankled Leo. The man was too at ease and comfortable. If he'd been involved in Vance's abduction, he was doing a masterful job of hiding it.

"Let's revisit that last question, or maybe your friend has the brains after all." Leo aimed a thumb at the shivering man on the ground behind them. "Where did you see the Feds, and who took them?"

Sputtering on the hot coffee, Stitchy repeated his earlier denial. "I didn't see nobody but Cams there and the three girls. We were walking home when you all showed up. A cop car comes screaming up the street, lights going crazy. They hit us with the spotlight and told us to get on the ground. We did, then they called in another car and brought us down to the tracks here."

Jacinda called over to the man still sitting on the ground. "Cams? Is that your name?"

He rolled his eyes. "Yeah. Can I go now?"

"Come join us. Would you like some coffee?"

He nodded, rose on shaky legs, and dusted himself off. The uniformed officers by the cruiser stood ready to chase him down in case he bolted. Leo waved Cams forward as Jacinda stepped away to get another cup of coffee.

The younger man's whining voice was in full swing by the time he joined Leo and Stitchy. "I swear I didn't see nothing. You can just let me go."

Leo laughed. "You 'didn't see nothing.' You, Stitchy, and the three girls were just 'walking home.' Do I have that right?"

Cams nodded, his eyes bugging out just like his friend's. "Swear to God. It was just like Stitchy said."

"Man," Stitchy groaned and ran a hand down his face, "I told you to just shut up. Don't say a damn word."

"What'd I do? I didn't tell the man nothing."

Leo could tell Stitchy wanted to slap his friend in the back of the head. If he was being honest, Leo wouldn't have minded doing the same thing. Jacinda was coming back with coffee for Cams. This was his last chance to let the bad cop routine do its work.

He flung his coffee to the ground where it splashed onto the hem of Cams's jeans. Cams opened his mouth to protest, then closed it quick when Leo stepped up to him, nose to nose.

"A federal agent was abducted. If you are in possession of information that could help us find our man, and you fail to give us that information, you will be prosecuted as an accessory after the fact." He took a small kernel of satisfaction when a drop of spit landed on Cams's chin. "And if that agent ends up dying, you could stand trial as an accomplice to conspiracy to *murder*. Twenty-five to life sound good, Cams?"

Cams held his hands up. Blubbering, he stepped back and nearly stumbled over his own feet. "Me and Stitchy were walking home with some girls we met at a club. That's all. I wish I could help you guys, but I didn't see anything when that guy started shooting."

Stitchy groaned and sank down into a squat, spilling his coffee. "Damn stupid boy. I told you to stay quiet, because you always say shit you shouldn't."

Leo smiled as Jacinda came up with the coffee for Cams. She wore a bright grin as she handed it to him. "Which guy started shooting, Cams? Tell us what you saw."

The young man let out a moan. "He had two guns. Stitchy

and me had the three girls with us and were trying to get away when this guy comes out of the neighborhood, on that little road that goes down to a phone box or—"

"The guy you saw, Cams." Jacinda put her hands on her hips and leaned forward. "Tell us about the guy with the guns."

"He came down that little road and just opened up, like he was in a fuckin' action movie. Took out two of our guys, and we all scattered. I had two girls with me, didn't see where Stitchy or the other girl was. I just ran. Next thing I knew, all five of us are on the same street, next to the concrete plant by the tracks. Somebody's still shooting back there." He looked back and forth between Leo and Jacinda. "I swear, we just ran."

Leo took out his notebook and pen. "What did you do after that?"

"We started jogging, but one of the girls had on these big heels, so we all just walked as fast as we could. The shooting stopped, and we were just trying to get somewhere safe, you know?"

"How much time passed between the first shots you heard and when the shooting stopped?"

He chewed his lip, thinking. "I don't know, maybe a few minutes. It was over quick."

Jacinda motioned for him to continue. "You were walking fast, 'trying to get somewhere safe.' What happened next?"

The young man groaned, and Leo gently toed at his foot. "You're doing great, Cams. What happened next?"

Cams looked at Stitchy, but the older man waved his hands at him. "Go ahead and finish the story, dumbass."

"Okay. Yeah, well…we took a turn down this one street, Packard Lane, I think, or maybe it was, um…I actually don't know what street we were on."

Leo pointed his pen at Cams. "Save us the theatrics,

please. Just tell us what you saw, where you saw it, and when."

"Yeah, well we were walking when a black SUV came around the corner and passed us. When you didn't stop, we thought it was all clear. But the cops rolled up a little bit after that."

Leo traded a look with Jacinda. She looked as frustrated as he felt.

She beckoned for both men to stand. "You're free to go, but give your contact information to the officers." She motioned for the uniformed cops to join them. "Thank you for this information."

The men mumbled a few protests as the cops came over and began collecting their information. Jacinda took Leo by the arm and walked several paces farther down the tracks. "They saw a black SUV shortly after the shooting stopped. You and Emma arrived before the shooting started. Mia and I came in our personal vehicles. Vance's personal vehicle was recovered one block from Packard Lane."

Leo gritted his teeth. "So who the hell was driving a Bureau SUV?"

Jacinda and Leo repeated the interview process with each of the women and verified the story Cams had given them about the SUV. The last woman mentioned seeing two people in the vehicle.

"It was a woman driving. I know that much because I saw her face. She looked like a chipmunk, you know?" The woman cupped her hands in front of her. "Kinda cute-faced, round cheeks."

Leo added the description to his notes. "What about the passenger? You said there were two people in the vehicle."

"Yeah, but I didn't see him clearly. Except I figured it had to be a guy, because his silhouette was kinda big. Bigger than the lady driving anyway. They both had those black hats on, like the kind you can pull down tight."

"Watch caps?"

She shrugged. "I guess? I just call 'em stoner caps because everyone I know who smokes weed is always wearing one."

Jacinda snorted. "Lovely. Don't worry, we're not interested in everyone you know who smokes weed. The officers will take your contact information, and we'll want you to sit down with a sketch artist to provide a description of the woman you saw driving."

"How long's that gonna take? Because I got class in the morning."

"We'll be as quick as we can. Thank you for your assistance."

The woman huffed and pressed her fingers to her temples. "I knew I shoulda stayed home tonight."

While Jacinda conferred with the cops, Leo headed back to Incident Command and made himself a new cup of coffee on autopilot. Remembering the last time he and Denae had shared a cup together, he sagged into one of the folding chairs and rested his head in his hand.

Jacinda surprised him. "Is that second cup for me?"

"Huh? Oh…I thought I was just dreaming about that." He looked at the two cups, one made the way he liked it. He didn't remember pouring the other one. Straight black and no doubt strong enough to peel paint.

Just like she would want it if she were here.

"I was thinking about Denae. It's been a long night." He held out the second cup to her.

"It has." She stirred some sugar into the black brew. "But we have descriptions of two possible perpetrators and a vehicle. We'll find him."

Leo lifted his cup and swirled the contents before putting it down again. "Why was he at the Bureau so late, and alone?"

Jacinda stared down into her coffee, not drinking it. "He left me a voicemail while I was at Capitol Hill, and we spoke briefly when I got back. Vance was in the office with Mia when I left around six. I suspect her departure followed a longer conversation between the two of them."

"About?" The hint of omen in Jacinda's voice hadn't escaped him. "Jacinda? Can you tell me what you and Vance spoke about?"

Jacinda set down her coffee. Running her hand through her hair, she undid and retied her ponytail. Putting her hands on her hips, she stared at the stack of railroad ties that served as a shelf in their command center. "Vance has requested a transfer to another office. This stays between us."

Shocked by the news, Leo could only nod and force himself to his feet, fighting against the fatigue that had suddenly found its way into his bones. Jacinda exited Incident Command to greet Emma and Mia, who were slowly walking up after their interview with Renfield. They moved over to Mia's car after a quick conversation with the SSA. In the empty space between the railroad and where the vehicles had all been parked, Jacinda stood by herself, staring at something Leo couldn't see. Leo left her to her vigil.

He looked at the untouched cups of coffee on the table. In the background, the sound of Mia's car starting caught his ear. He closed his eyes, unable to keep out thoughts of nearly losing Denae. More than anything, he wished she were here.

When he opened his eyes again, Mia's car had vanished into the neighborhood. Leo took a deep breath, trying to keep the anxiety that had crept in at bay.

29

The next morning, Emma and Mia went straight to the Bureau's impound lot to examine Vance's car. They'd clocked a few hours of fitful sleep in Emma's apartment after Jacinda sent them home from the crime scene. The SSA promised to stay with Leo until every piece of evidence had been collected.

Probably worried about losing her career. First me and my ghost shit, and now Vance. Jacinda's going to catch hell from the ADD.

Now, as Mia pulled into the impound lot, Emma hoped for anything that might point them in the direction of the killer and the kitchen where he was holding Vance.

Wurth was waiting for them inside the gate with an odd smile on his face.

"You look too happy." Emma narrowed her eyes at him. "We barely got any sleep last night, so I hope you have good news to share."

"Better than good. An abandoned vehicle came in right after I called you this morning. I got a name and address off the plates and hull number right away. Hank Barnaby, of 118 Shelby Way. Suburb west of the city."

Mia stared at him. "This is important why?"

"The van…it's the killer's van. Has to be, given all the blood inside it."

Emma lit up, but Mia spun around to head back to her car. "Why weren't we told this earlier? Let's go!"

"Agent Logan?" Wurth called to her, the smile dropping from his face. "Wait. I'm sorry. MPD went straight to the house as soon as we got the address. I called SSA Hollingsworth, and she approved the move. The only person there was Barnaby's ex-wife, Heather Alsap."

Mia whirled around. "And? She could be helping him. Covering for him. Tell me they have her in holding right now."

He shook his head. "She was fully cooperative and told the cops she hasn't seen her ex-husband since the divorce was final over three years ago. Even let them search the house for him. She confirmed he drove a black van but has no idea where he's living now."

Emma blew out a hard breath. "Did we get any trace evidence from the van itself?"

Rallying a bit, Wurth scrolled on his tablet and showed her the screen. "Evidence teams are all over it. So far, we've collected multiple prints, all partials. Looks like someone wiped the inside down pretty good, using an ammonia-based material. Probably a glass cleaner."

Mia planted her hands on her hips. "Any matches to Barnaby?"

"Not enough to get us anywhere for certain, but we do have his prints in the system. Seems he applied to the academy two years ago. Didn't get past the psych eval and has no record of employment, or even filing for unemployment, for the past year."

Mia gave an exasperated grunt. "Awesome. He tried to be a cop and failed. That doesn't help us find him or find Vance. This stupid van is useless."

"Hardly." Wurth rotated his tablet. His screen showed four photographs of shoe marks in spilled or smeared blood. "Lots of red on the van floor, and our guy walked all through it. One guy, same set of shoe marks each time. Size eleven, running shoes based on the tread. No match on the brand yet."

"How does that explain two shooters last night?" Emma tried, and failed, to keep the edge from her voice.

Wurth's shoulders slumped. "Well, it doesn't. Hair fibers recovered from the driver's seat are all the same color. DNA tests aren't back yet, but I put a rush on them. We'll need samples from Barnaby to run a comparison and analysis. We already have an APB out for him."

Mia turned away, pacing up and down parking lot aisle.

Emma could practically see steam pouring from her ears. She fought the urge to comfort her, because the techs had dropped everything to start working the van—she wasn't about to waste their efforts.

Turning back to Wurth's tablet, Emma swiped to the photographs of shoe marks. "Do we know if the blood was from multiple victims or just one?"

"Condition of the blood pools suggests over twenty-four hours had passed before we found the van. Additional trace evidence could be from our first victim. There's dried blood in the nooks and crannies, and in places where the surrounding area had been wiped clean."

"So he cleaned up after the first kill, but the second was messier, and he decides to dump the van rather than clean up."

"Or he knew we'd be onto him and decided not to maintain possession of the vehicle." Wurth nodded at the tablet. "Either way, he dropped it and gave us a lot to work with."

Emma stared through the open doors into the body of the van, imagining the horrific events that must've unfolded within. "You said at least twenty-four hours passed, which narrows down our last victim's time of death to around midnight on Thursday."

He nodded and folded his tablet case closed. "Good news on victim number two, or as close to good as you can get, considering. Tattoos and dental records gave us Martin Kaine, also goes by Marty and Murda."

"Has anyone spoken to his family yet?"

"No known associates or family, beyond other members of the Serpents. Body's being kept at the morgue for now."

Emma's phone buzzed. She fumbled for it in her pocket before she read Jacinda's name on the screen.

"Hi, Jacinda. I'm here with Mia and Wurth. He's catching us up on Barnaby's van." She put the call on speaker and headed over to where Mia was still pacing.

"We saw the APB for Barnaby. That's great news, despite the address not panning out. Leo and I also have a lead. The men and women interviewed last night reported seeing a black SUV driving in the area where Vance's car was found. We also have a description of a woman at the wheel. A sketch has been produced and is being circulated."

Emma furrowed her brow. "I don't think the person I chased was a woman."

"She wasn't alone in the vehicle. Our witness says a large man was in the passenger seat."

Mia pulled Emma's phone toward her. "A large man who looked like Vance? Jacinda, why didn't you tell us this last night?"

"I didn't say he looked like Vance, and I kept this information quiet because we all needed to rest." The SSA's voice had a bite to it. "Leo and I just got to the offices five minutes ago. I did give MPD the descriptions, and they put out a BOLO for the vehicle and passengers. So far, no joy."

Gently tugging her phone from Mia's grip, Emma tried to get the conversation back on track. "Was 'large' the only description of the man? Did we get hair color, anything else?"

"Nothing, but the eyewitness claimed both passengers wore dark watch caps. MPD has already collected footage from last night from any businesses that had cameras. We got a brief image of the SUV on one, heading north from the area."

"Are we sure it was the same SUV and not one of ours?"

Jacinda sighed and said the vehicle had been driving in dimly lit areas, which made it impossible to confirm who was inside. "Whoever was behind the wheel either knew the area or had taken pains to plan an exit route."

"Okay." Mia jumped into the conversation. "So we canvass every building from the scene up to the Capitol Mall. We have to find out where they took him."

"That effort is underway, I assure you. I'm collecting phone numbers for every business in a one-mile radius from where Vance's car was found. Leo and I will let you know the instant we get anything. If you and Emma want to go down there in person, I'd suggest starting on Packard Lane."

Emma told her they'd get on the road immediately, then ended the call. She stared down at the phone for a moment. Who was this woman who'd been spotted driving the vehicle? Her mind started to spiral out into possibilities, but when she looked up into Mia's worried face, she reined it in.

"We're close, Mia. I know we are." She reached out, holding the other woman's shoulder. Mia managed a quick, watery smile in return.

We may not know where he is right now, but there's a trail that will lead us to his location.

30

Pins and needles prickled Vance's hands, and he shifted onto his opposite hip. The guy holding him prisoner had loosened the rope around Vance's neck, just enough to let him roll side to side and keep his head flat on the floor.

The water and smoothie bottles, with straws sticking out of them, had toppled over at some point when Vance was asleep. He must've bumped them. At least he'd finished the water first.

A small, sticky pool of pale liquid coming from the smoothie bottle covered the floor in front of his face. From the faint morning light that sneaked in between the curtains, Vance saw cockroaches scurrying around the edge of the puddle, enjoying the remains of his smoothie.

So much for breakfast. His stomach churned.

His captor had replaced his gag anyway. Even if Vance had been hungry or thirsty, he wouldn't have had an easy time getting anything through the straws.

His throat had been so raw and sore from dehydration that when the gag came out, the most he could manage was a pained cough and to jut his chin toward the water bottle.

The guy had helped him drink at first, then gave him a flexible straw that allowed him to drink while lying with his head on the floor.

He'd been stuck there for hours now, maybe ten or twelve. Keeping track of time wasn't easy when all he could see was one thin strip of sky through the curtains more than twenty feet away.

Most of his muscles had cramped up, but he'd been flexing them as often and as much as he could. Every little bit helped, despite most of one side of his body aching from where he'd been shot. And it kept his mind busy and focused.

His best hope for escape would be to convince his captor to change his ways, turn himself in, and let Vance go free. Doing so would at least get him a hint of leniency from the judge.

A killer's capacity to feel remorse could make all the difference between a life sentence and death sentence, and the man had already confirmed his intentions to turn on the mystery woman he was working with.

Or working for. The way he talked about her made it sound like she was his boss or someone he owes some kind of allegiance to.

Vance stretched his hands, flexing his fingers and wrists, but the knots wouldn't give. This guy knew how to tie someone up.

He yanked at his hands again.

His bonds were too tight, made of material he couldn't break or sever without a tool of some kind, and he was held with his neck tied to a metal bracket supporting a wall shelf a few feet above his head. His feet were tied to the bracket at the opposite end, so he could neither stand nor kneel to relieve pressure around his neck.

And pulling with his neck to try and yank the bracket out of the wall risked tightening the rope, which would cut off his airway. Dying of slow self-strangulation wasn't on Vance's bucket list.

Sagging against the wall behind him, Vance kicked a heel at the kitchen cupboards.

The force of his bound feet barely made a sound, but he kicked again, just to do something. His feet impacted the wood with a loud *thunk*. He kept doing it, as much to keep his blood circulating as to hopefully alert someone in a neighboring apartment.

All he got for his trouble was a *thump* from the other side of the wall and a muffled demand to *"knock it off!"*

His shoulders slumped, as much as they could within the confines of the binds.

Mia. Think of Mia for a little while. Something good.

But all he could hear in his mind was her frustration as they'd fought the evening before in the Bureau offices. The pain in her voice as she told him how *he* had to understand Emma's situation. How her face, in his memory, drooped with pity when he told her he was planning to transfer to another field office.

Even she saw what he'd been slow to see. That the biggest reason for his anger was that he felt deceived by his friends, left in the dark when it came to what was really pushing Emma to close cases. They'd hid it from him, even after she'd told Mia and Leo.

And it didn't matter that Jacinda didn't know either. Jacinda hadn't almost died on a case.

But Vance pushed his anger aside, even if Spooky Last deserved every ounce of his rage. He needed to conserve his energy for his survival.

Blocking out thoughts of Emma or Mia or anyone else, he concentrated on what he knew of his predicament. He closed his eyes, trying to recall the sounds he'd heard when his captor had moved around the apartment. His footsteps had grown louder, and harsher, as he came around the corner at the edge of the kitchen.

This place has carpeting out there, but it might be an area rug. Flooring is vinyl or linoleum in the kitchen.

One of the roaches drinking up his smoothie skittered right at him, and Vance snapped his head up off the ground quickly.

He turned to the side, looking for the insect. The roach was out of sight, and he hadn't felt it crawl on him.

Not yet anyway. As soon as that jackass wakes up, I'm getting him to put me somewhere else.

Vance ground his teeth against the gag, the only movement he could safely make without choking himself. Hell, even a bathtub would be better, unless the damn things were crawling out of his drains too.

31

Emma and Mia headed out in a Bureau SUV, leaving Jacinda and Leo behind to call businesses in the neighborhood where Vance's vehicle had been found. Lacking a warrant, Jacinda would ask the businesses to review their footage.

If any cameras had picked up the perpetrators last night, Emma and Mia would be alerted. Until then, they'd canvass the area on foot and talk to as many people as they could.

Emma gave herself no choice but to believe they would find Vance. He was counting on them and deserved nothing less, as their friend and colleague.

He was only released from the hospital a few weeks ago, Emma girl. The man can't catch a break.

The thought sparked a question she'd been meaning to ask ever since Vance had pulled her aside and challenged her.

"I need the truth."

"Do you think his behavior lately is because of the bomb?"

"What behavior?" Mia turned to her, coming into Emma's peripheral vision.

Vance's sneering aggression echoed in her thoughts, and

she let everything out. "He doesn't believe me. He thinks I'm making everything up for attention, like I have some kind of grudge against him."

"No, he doesn't, Emma. You can't really think that about him."

"Then explain him pulling me aside and demanding I tell him the truth. Explain him blowing me off every time I try to clarify what I *know* is true but can't prove because I've yet to encounter a ghost who knows him. I mean, yeah, I'm asking him to adjust his entire worldview, but you're making the same request, and so are Leo and Denae. And he still won't accept what we're telling him."

Mia sat quietly for a moment as Emma drove them deeper into the industrial zone adjacent to last night's crime scene. "You think because the bomb caused a brain injury… that it's affecting his judgment."

Emma swallowed hard before answering. "I think it's possible."

"The doctors cleared him to return to duty." Mia's voice held a defensive edge that almost made Emma drop it. But she couldn't.

"I know, but how else do you explain the man going off on his own last night?" Emma shot Mia a sidelong glance. "He didn't even check in when he arrived. That's not like him."

It's more like you, Emma girl. And even you've learned not to fly solo anymore.

They reached Packard Lane, and she parked beside a food truck serving coffee and breakfast burritos to a crew from a nearby car wash.

"We'll start on Packard and spiral outward one block. If we don't run into anyone or find anything, we'll widen the search. Jacinda and Leo will call if they get any hits."

Mia nodded and got out. Emma turned off the engine and joined her on the sidewalk.

They entered each business they passed and spoke with someone inside. Most of the businesses were happy to share their security footage, none of which captured enough of a street view to be useful.

A few of the business owners balked at the lack of a warrant. Emma sent their names and numbers to Jacinda.

After close to two hours of canvassing, Emma and Mia grabbed something to eat at the food truck. They'd just taken their first bites when Jacinda called with an update.

"We got a batch of footage from a delivery operation down there. They wanted a warrant, so I got one. We spotted Vance." She described the location and gave them the business address. "See if you can find anything to confirm that was Vance's destination. We only have a brief image of him running in that direction."

"Got it. We'll let you know ASAP."

Wrapping their burritos for later, Emma and Mia raced down the street to the address Jacinda had provided. They arrived at a long building with a concrete platform running the length of the block. Ramps led up from the street, and workers carried boxes or operated forklifts, filling delivery vans and flatbed trailers.

Emma flashed her badge at the first person they met, a middle-aged white man wearing a hard hat and carrying a toolbox as he came down the ramp.

"Manager's inside, first door on the left."

Through a window beside the entrance, Emma spotted a figure hunched over a desk.

Mia stepped onto the ramp, but Emma put a hand on her arm. She'd spotted a glint of blue in the crack between the pavement and concrete platform. "What's that?"

Pulling on gloves first, Emma crouched and used a ballpoint pen to fish a capped syringe out of the crack. Holding it between her gloved fingers, she placed the item in an evidence bag.

The worker who'd spoken to them was watching and let out a laugh. "Probably just another junkie leaving his trash for us to find. I saw that this morning and kicked it out of the street. Didn't need anybody catching hepatitis, you know?"

"Where was it when you first saw it?"

He pointed to a spot on the street, about four feet from the platform.

Mia got the worker's information, just in case, and said she'd stay outside to keep looking for additional physical evidence. Emma went inside to speak to the manager, a Black man named James Hutch. He extended a hand and welcomed her into his small office.

Emma held up the evidence bag. "We just collected this outside. One of your employees suggested a junkie dropped it. Have you had trouble with intravenous drug users before?"

James sighed. "We have. I've found maybe a dozen of those things out there over the last year. Even set up an extra camera pointed out the window." He indicated a device aimed out his window. "I was thinking y'all might want it to go along with what our outside cameras picked up."

Coming around the desk, Emma watched over his shoulder as he played back footage from the previous night. "Can you speed it up to midnight?"

He did, and they watched the empty street for a few minutes. James sped the playback to double speed. After another minute, Emma's breath caught in her throat. "Got him!"

On the screen, a man dressed in dark clothing and a ski mask moved backward through the camera view with his hands raised. Seconds later, Vance appeared with his weapon aimed at the other man, who had now stepped out of view.

Vance suddenly staggered as if struck by a heavy blow and fell back against the concrete platform. Emma watched, dumbstruck, as a dark SUV sped into view.

Another person dressed in dark clothing exited the SUV. A woman. A shiver ran down Emma's spine as she fixed her gaze on her. She wore a dark watch cap that concealed most of her hair. Some strands stuck out on one side above the collar of her lightweight jacket.

The woman held a gun trained on Vance, who was mostly obscured from view by the platform. Her arm came up as she pistol-whipped him across the jaw.

Vance tried sitting up, and the woman struck him with her gun again. He went down hard. Then she knelt by his side for a moment before pocketing something.

Emma continued watching as the woman motioned the other guy over. He came back on-screen, and the two dark-clad figures gathered around Vance.

As the pair struggled to get him into the back of the SUV, the woman's jacket caught on the bumper. Emma paused the footage.

She tore the jacket when they were loading Vance into the SUV, and I'd bet that's where this syringe came from.

Her chest burned with worry for Vance, but this brought them a step closer to finding him.

"Please send the full file to the Bureau right now and give me a copy of what we just watched." She pulled a thumb drive from her pocket and had him upload the relevant section of the footage.

After they finished up, Emma thanked him and left her card. As she headed outside to join Mia, she couldn't get the image of the black-clad woman out of her head. A suspicion was starting to form, but it wasn't one she wanted to put voice to just yet.

Mia met her at the bottom of the ramp, and Emma led the way to their vehicle. Shoving aside thoughts of the mystery woman, she faced her friend. "We have him, and we know the exact time when Vance was attacked. Did you find anything out here?"

"I collected some flakes of metal that might be bullet fragments. Vance had his vest on, so if he was shot—"

"He was."

What color was left in Mia's face drained away. "You saw what happened?"

Emma held up the thumb drive. "I'll explain on the way back to the Bureau." She reached out and squeezed Mia's shoulder. "We're going to find him, Mia, and get the assholes who took him."

32

Inside the conference room at the Bureau offices, Emma and her team sat around the table while Jacinda projected her laptop screen to the whiteboard at the end of the room.

"We received footage from multiple cameras, but none give us a better view of our perpetrators than the one Emma obtained." Jacinda tapped at her keyboard, and the image zoomed in on the two figures standing over Vance as he lay against the concrete loading platform. The side of an SUV was just visible behind them.

"We can't confirm who's who, but I believe the individual on the right, the man, is our primary suspect in the killings so far."

"He looks like the man Vance and I saw in the footage from Darius Baker's body dump." Mia leaned forward, squinting at the screen as if she could pull identities straight from the recording with her will alone.

Jacinda nodded. "The woman on the left is possibly an accomplice or might be directing his actions. She's the one who shot Vance, which has me leaning on the latter." She clicked her mouse button, and a new image appeared, showing a dark SUV from the rear but without a clear view of the license plate.

Emma gnawed on her lip. The most important thing at the moment was getting Vance back safely. Now was not the right time to bring up her inklings about who this woman might be.

Leo aimed his pen at the screen. "Is that the same vehicle from the previous image? Can we be sure?"

"It is, based on additional footage that shows a dark-colored SUV driving through the area at approximately the same time." The SSA clicked her mouse, and another image of the vehicle appeared—this time from the side with two figures visible in the front seats. The woman was driving. "They departed the area where Vance was abducted, aiming north. We lose them after two blocks, though." Another click, and another image showed the vehicle again, but from the opposite side.

Emma slapped a hand on the table. "We have a trajectory. It's not an arrow to Vance's location, but we know their starting point."

With a sigh, Jacinda sat down. "The syringe you found may prove to be more helpful. Toxicology confirmed trace amounts of a veterinary tranquilizer called xylazine. Given the bruise we saw on Vance's jaw, and what we saw in the video, I believe his captors struck him to stun him and then injected him with a powerful sedative, so he wouldn't rouse before they got him to a secure location."

"Vance has been in the hands of that maniac for over twenty-four hours." Mia's knuckles were white as she clasped her coffee cup. "We know how they got him and which direction they started moving in, but…how will this help us find him?"

Emma reached across the table, gripping Mia's elbow. "We'll figure this out."

Mia looked down into her cup. Emma spotted tears gathering on her eyelashes. Jacinda tapped at her keyboard again, and the screen went blank.

For a second, Emma pictured Vance's ghost showing up beside her, railing at her for not saving him.

The darkness of the thought made her throat close up. No matter what memories she had of nearly losing her colleagues before, she couldn't afford to dwell in hopelessness. "Jacinda, you said the syringe contained a veterinary tranquilizer. Would that be used for horses?"

"Yes. I looked it up the minute toxicology sent the results." Jacinda tilted her head. "Why do you ask?"

"Agent Holland, with Richmond's BAU, recently worked a case involving horse racing. He might have information we could use to trace the source."

"Call him but do it while Leo's driving. Wurth has three MPD units on stakeout around the area where Vance was taken." The SSA jerked her thumb toward the door. "Liaise with him and add your eyes to the coverage."

Mia angrily pushed up from her chair, almost spilling her coffee. "We need to be out there looking for him, not sitting in our cars watching buildings."

"Agent Logan." Jacinda's sharp tone was like steel in Emma's ears.

Mia froze halfway to the door. She turned around, squaring her shoulders before meeting Jacinda's gaze.

The SSA kept her voice level. "You and I will be out there looking for him. We'll each do a ride-along with MPD on their patrols through Skulls and Serpents territory, in case our killer targets those gangs again."

Dropping her chin, Mia let out a breath. "Thank you, Jacinda. I'm sorry."

"Don't mention it." Jacinda got up and joined Mia at the

door. "We're all tense. Save it for the perpetrators when we catch them."

"Jacinda?" Emma hoped her question would be received as the honest inquiry she intended. "How long is the stakeout planned for?"

"As long as necessary. Mia and I will take over in six hours, so the two of you can get some time on the streets." She glanced around at everyone in the room. "Nobody's off duty until Vance is located."

With that, Jacinda and Mia left.

Emma grabbed her phone. As she and Leo followed them out and headed for the garage, she was already tapping out Keaton's name.

33

Danny "Stax" Stoko flicked the butt of his cigarette to the ground and demolished it with his boot. The nearby buzzing of a drugstore sign reminded him he was almost out of cigarettes, but that'd have to wait until tomorrow.

Maybe his girlfriend, Mixxie, would stop talking by then.

"Baby, you just need a good night's sleep in my bed to get you right." She had her arm around his waist and hugged him tight to her side. Stax did like the way she felt, snug up against him, her hip rubbing his, and the way she smelled.

He could almost see himself doing what he always did. Following her home and climbing into her bed.

But tonight was different. He'd been running with a no-name crew, knocking over liquor stores and doing smash-and-grabs out of cars. All he had to show for it was a scar down one arm from breaking a window with his elbow and a whole lot of nothing else.

"I don't know about tonight." He shrugged. "I'm thinking I need to tell the guys I'm gonna quit."

"Quit? Baby, what are you gonna do if you quit? You

didn't even finish school or work a real job except for that one time you drove for Uber."

"I know, but that doesn't mean I can't find a job." He snugged her in a bit closer.

Mixxie turned up her face to his. "Who's gonna hire you at twenty-three years old when you can't show them where you've worked since high school?"

He'd already run into that problem, trying to get work doing deliveries for a paper-supply company. The manager took one look at all the blank lines on Stax's application and just shook his head.

"Try again after you've got some experience you can tell me about. Sorry, I can't help you."

Staying with the crew wasn't going to get him any experience like that.

Mixxie shook her head and pulled her arm from around his waist. She took his hand in hers, though, and kept walking with him. "What's got you wanting to quit now? Really? Tell me the truth."

Stax wished he could just fly away into the night. He took a deep breath. "Being in a gang isn't how I want to go out. One day, you might feel on top of the world. Next day, you're getting shot at or arrested, or both."

"You think being out there alone is easier? At least with the gang, you got people you can ask for help when you need it."

Trying to ignore the empty ache in his stomach, Stax focused on the lines in the sidewalk. "We're ripping off liquor-store owners who live in the same buildings we do. Some dudes I know harass every woman they see. Smacking a server on the ass, then stealing her tips? I don't wanna be part of that."

They'd reached Mixxie's place, and she put her hands on his shoulders, leaning in for a quick kiss. "Why don't you come up and let me help you forget all that shit?"

He wanted to, so badly, because she was right. When they were together, Stax always felt better.

But tonight just felt so damn different, like he had to make a change or he'd be stuck walking down this same sidewalk forever. "I need to take a walk. It's not you, I swear. I just gotta get my head clear."

She stared into his eyes and stepped back, her hands falling to her sides. "Take your walk, I guess. But don't think I don't know you got someone else's bed waiting for you somewhere in this city." She waggled her finger at him. "And don't try getting back in mine after this. We're over."

Before he could say anything, she spun around and marched into her building.

Stax threw a frustrated curse into the air and headed out. He'd get things right with Mixxie later. Right now, he needed to get things right with himself.

He headed home, planning to do his thinking while he walked.

Around him, the apartments and businesses faded into row houses and abandoned lots. Sirens echoed far away, and someone shouted in a building down the street behind him.

A woman's voice got his attention, and he stopped to see where she was. A lady dressed all in black was coming his way. Stax looked around, in case she had a partner who was going to jump him.

He only saw her, though. She was still walking his way but looked pretty harmless. "What do you want?"

"Nothing at all, my sweet boy. Nothing at all." She stopped and put her hands on her hips. A streetlight cast just enough glow that he could see she was white.

What the fuck is she doing walking in this neighborhood at this time of night?

"Lady, you're on the wrong street. You need to get gone.

Two blocks back the way you came, then take a left and don't stop until you see the freeway overhead."

She stepped closer, coming fully into the streetlight's halo. "I'm right where I need to be."

Her hair was tucked up under a watch cap, but wisps of dark brown showed here and there above her cheeks.

He took a step back, holding his hands out. "Girl, you're crazy. I'm gonna get home like I was planning. If you know what's good for you, you'll get out of here and fast."

"Like you want to get out of the gang?"

Stax's eyes popped wide open, his body on full alert now. She'd been following him and overheard him talking to Mixxie. "Who the hell are you?"

"Call me an exterminator. I'm here to deal with the city's cockroach problem."

He jerked his chin up. "You want to make jokes, bitch? I don't need that shit tonight. Get lost."

She stepped closer. "Do you want to run? Make it interesting?"

Whatever this lady was tripping on, Stax'd had enough. He flipped her the finger and spun on his heel.

A man's voice joined the woman's, and for a moment, Stax thought he should turn around and see how tough they were once he started swinging. He wasn't the best fighter in the crew, but he could hold his own.

The woman laughed out loud, and Stax twisted to look over his shoulder. A guy was standing with her now and had something in his hands.

Shit, dude's strapped.

Stax started running as the woman laughed again.

The clap of a gunshot reached him an instant after something slammed into his back, sending him sprawling forward. He threw his hands out, but his head smacked on a concrete step in front of an abandoned row house. Stars exploded through his vision to join the blazing agony pouring from his chest.

Stax tried to roll over, get onto his back. His arms wouldn't work. One hand flopped against the step he'd bashed his head on.

The concrete felt cold, so cold, like everything around him was made of ice. A shiver raced through him, and Stax coughed, tasting blood on his tongue.

The man's voice called out above him, something about cockroaches. Stax pushed with both hands, using all his strength to move his body off the ground, to stand up so he could fight back. No matter how hard he pushed, the concrete stayed cold and pressed tight against his body.

Warmth spread beneath him, cutting out the cold. It took Stax a moment to realize that it was his own blood, pooling beneath him, and his last thought was how he wished he'd stayed with Mixxie after all.

34

This cockroach was more awkward than heavy, tall and skinny in a way that should've made him a pro basketball player instead of a gang member.

"Crushed you like a baby bug, didn't I?" I grunted with the effort of moving him. As one of his hands fell from my grip, I recentered myself. Lydia was sitting in the driver's seat, waiting for me. I wasn't going to ask for her help. That would show weakness, something I didn't want her to see.

I struggled with the dead body some more, hoisting him into the back seat, onto the tarp we'd laid down. She just sat in the driver's seat and watched me, tapping her fingers on the steering wheel.

"Hurry up, slick. Someone's going to see you."

She knew my name, too, since that night at the bar, but hadn't once spoken it.

I looked around. The street we were on only had empty buildings near us. A few apartments farther away had lights on, but most had dark windows.

She wasn't wrong, though.

The longer this took, the greater the chance somebody might stick their head out and see what was happening.

You could get off your ass and help, lady. That would make things go faster.

I didn't know what kept my tongue tied, but I couldn't bring myself to challenge her. She'd given me all that money, and she hadn't lied about the bullets in my new gun being special.

When I shot this guy, I just looked at the middle of his back, but I pointed the gun at the ground and fired.

And down he went, face-first onto the sidewalk, like I'd been aiming dead center mass.

The puddle of blood on the sidewalk would be noticed, but I wasn't worried about anybody having camera footage of me. None of the buildings on this street had doorbell cameras, and most weren't even occupied.

I hopped into the passenger seat, and she took off. As the vehicle rattled through the street, I couldn't stop thinking about my son. Ethan wouldn't have liked what I'd become. I knew that now. But I couldn't just give up. For his memory, and for my parents, I had to keep going.

So other innocent people could be saved from the pain I've been forced to endure.

Was Agent Emma Marie Last innocent, or was Lydia telling me the truth? Had the Feds and cops failed her the same way they'd failed me?

"Penny for your thoughts." She slapped me on the thigh with the back of her hand.

"Eh? I was just thinking about the guy we kidnapped. The Fed."

"He's still alive, right?"

I nodded. "I left him with some water and a smoothie. He's probably pissed himself by now, but at least he won't die of dehydration."

"Thoughtful of you, given how useless he and his colleagues have been."

I didn't know what to say to that, so I went for a more familiar topic.

"Lydia." I narrowed my gaze at her. "This gun you gave me...I gotta say, I'm impressed. Where'd you get the custom loads anyway?"

"My mom. Someone who'd been doing her job when Emma Last killed her in cold blood. Now shut up and let me drive."

I didn't like the tone she used or the way she'd been treating me in general. When she called me, all she'd said was to meet her at an intersection three blocks from my apartment.

"And don't be late. If you're not there when I arrive, the deal is off."

She kept treating me like I was hired help, and I didn't like it one bit.

Hired help is exactly what you are, ole buddy. Hired to do a helluva job for a helluva lot of cash.

I gave up trying to be her friend, for now, and let the city roll by as we drove through the night.

We ended up in some warehouse district. Could have been the one I'd run through the other night when we met, but I wasn't sure. They all looked the same. She stopped at a metal garage door and took out her phone.

Lydia tapped in a code, and the door opened. We drove inside, and the door rolled down behind us. She got out, but I sat in the SUV for a moment, wondering what the hell was going on.

Lights glowed in a small office at the back of the space and at workstations around the large room. I could make out metalworking tools, what looked like CNC machines, and plenty of crates and boxes.

Some of those looked like they might be military surplus. I got out and went to inspect the boxes nearest to me. But she was at my side and pulled me away. "You have work to do."

She pointed to the back seat.

I faced her, planting my hands on my hips. "Look, you haven't told me why we're here, what 'work' you want me to do, or why you're being such a stone-cold bitch all of a sudden."

If I didn't know better, I'd have guessed she knew one of the martial arts. She stood like a fighter, hands loose at her sides, as she looked me up and down. I braced myself, ready to catch her foot if she threw a kick at me.

But she started laughing again, like she had back on the sidewalk after I'd shot the cockroach.

"Oh, slick, you just don't get it." Her laughter kept going, getting under my skin, and I whipped out the gun she'd given me.

From the shadows around us, behind the boxes and crates, six guys appeared like they'd just popped out of thin air. They all wore hockey masks and were pointing guns at me.

Lydia walked up and pushed my gun to the side. "Why don't you put that away?" She nodded at my weapon. "Trust me. Even if you did get off a shot, that would be your last one. And after these men are done killing you, they'll kill your ex-wife. Slowly."

Shit, how the hell does she know about Heather?

My hands suddenly trembling, I tucked the gun into my pants at the small of my back.

She smiled and handed me a slip of paper.

"What the hell's this?" The paper had a drawing of a cloud with a lightning bolt coming down.

"The mark you're going to leave on him. Take whatever tattoo you want, but make sure that's clearly cut into his chest. Work slowly, so you don't screw it up. And since you lost your knife, here." She reached into her coat and brought out a knife in a sheath.

"How'd you know I lost mine?"

"I watched you fall on your face at the railroad and saw it drop when you stood up."

My hand instinctively went toward my hip.

One of her guys was in my face with his gun, growling at me. "Try it, and you'll get dead."

I backed off and held my hands up. Looking at her, I shook my head. "This isn't going the way I like. Who are these guys, and why are you acting like I shit on your shoe when I'm the guy you hired to do a job?"

With that smug smile still in place, she stepped up beside the guy who'd come forward. She put a hand on his wrist, and he brought the barrel down. "I need to send another message, to flush Emma out." She pointed at the cockroach we'd brought with us. "This is how we're going to do it. Once you get started, I'll fill you in."

The guy next to her muttered something, and she smacked him in the back of the head. "You can help him get the body out of the car. The rest of you, back to work."

Like they were all trained dogs, the other five guys lowered their guns and melted into the shadows like ninjas or something. I could see them now, all sitting at little card tables, hiding behind the stacked boxes and crates.

Some of them opened laptops, others tapped at phones. Little glows emerged from the devices, lighting up the hockey masks they wore.

This is some freak show I've landed in.

The guy who stayed behind helped me muscle the cockroach from the back seat and lay him on the floor. I pulled back the tarp and lifted his shirt, looking for a gang tattoo. I didn't see any and had to cut the whole shirt off him. Seeing his bare brown skin sent a tremor of fear through me.

I killed an innocent man. He wasn't a cockroach, after all. She told me he was, and I believed her. I was so ready to believe anything she said and now...

Her helper punched my shoulder. "She said get to work. We don't have all night."

I looked up at him, the hot sting of anger welling in my eyes. Whoever Lydia was, and whatever her plans might be, tonight was the last time I'd be hanging around with her crew of psychos.

My goal had only ever been to clean the streets of criminals, not to become one myself.

I carefully made the storm cloud image she wanted, cutting it into his chest on the right side, away from the exit wound the bullet made when I shot him.

Making the cloud wasn't easy, and the guy's body was starting to stink. He must've had something in his guts when he died. I didn't look forward to hauling him anywhere after this, but at least I had the tarp to wrap him in.

Once I was done, she gave me another magazine and another slip of paper, this time with an address written down.

"That's twelve more loads. The address is to Emma Last's apartment building. Drop him there and make sure the body's visible to anyone leaving by the front door. When Emma shows up, you know what to do." Her lips curved up. "Make it messy. For me."

She blew me a kiss and walked away without another word.

35

Sometime in the middle of the night, Vance swallowed, the taste of blood still tainting his saliva, thanks to the split in his bottom lip.

His arms were both numb. Part of him wondered if that was a blessing in disguise. His old injuries were starting to blend with his new injuries until his whole body thrummed with pain.

He tried to picture the woman who'd shot him and gave him a crack on the jaw with her gun. Try as he might, he couldn't remember any details. He'd only seen her briefly, distracted as he was by the sledgehammer blow he'd taken from her bullet. He knew she was a woman because he'd seen her silhouette right before she hit him.

Vance went out like a light after the butt of her gun connected with his jaw for the second time.

She knew where to strike and how hard. Someone trained her.

The front door opened and closed in the other room, and one set of footsteps approached. Vance had just enough time to imagine Mia's face before the killer appeared at the end of the kitchen.

He still wore a medical mask and had a watch cap snugged down over his hair. His manner remained…friendly, though. Vance could imagine the guy charming someone in a different situation. "You awake over there?"

Vance grunted and kicked the cabinet again, as hard as he could, but his bound feet didn't make more than a dull *thud*.

"Shit, man. I'm sorry about this. Honest to God, I am." The man came into the kitchen and turned on the light, sending the roaches scurrying away. He stomped on several of them, angrily cursing and muttering to himself. When he noticed the spilled smoothie, he grabbed a roll of paper towels from the countertop.

"I'll…I'll get something better set up for you. Smells like maybe you pissed yourself." He recoiled a bit and sat back on his heels. "I gotta get you out of here. Gotta do that really quick."

Vance hadn't been able to hold his bladder earlier and was just happy he hadn't eaten much of anything the day before. Surviving on a liquid diet wouldn't keep him going for long, though.

His captor wiped up the spilled smoothie, using almost the entire roll of paper towels to do so. Vance tracked his every movement carefully.

"No hard feelings, I hope. Just…until I can get things sorted out for you, try to keep things neat if you can. The damn cockroaches are all over the place."

He stood and threw the wad of paper towels into a trash can at the end of the counter. With that done, he went to the sink and opened the cupboard beneath. He pulled out a plastic dish tub, set it on the floor near Vance's abdomen, then reached over and undid his fly.

"I'll, uh…you should be able to figure it out, right? You can use that tub as a bedpan."

Yeah, because my dick has an opposable thumb. I'll be fine.

His captor stood, and Vance glared at him, observing the man and committing his face to memory. Even with the mask on, his captor's round cheeks and dark eyes were unmistakable, and his unruly dark hair stuck out around his watch cap.

Vance cataloged every detail, making a mental portrait he could recite to a sketch artist once he escaped. Assuming his captor wasn't already in custody at that point.

"Guess you should know, this wasn't my idea." He pointed at the ropes and makeshift bedpan. "None of this was part of my plan. She's got something going on with a woman named Emma, though. Wanted me to drop a body outside her apartment."

At the sound of his colleague's name, Vance stiffened. He hadn't wanted to reveal anything to his captor but couldn't stop himself from reacting.

Jacinda told us other people might be trying to hurt Emma after what happened in Salem. You were so ready to blow her off.

Vance schooled his face to appear mildly interested.

The man crouched in front of him and stretched his neck side to side, making several pops and cracks. "So you know Emma. Figured, since she's a Fed too. I did leave the body on her doorstep with a little love note. Gotta go back and make sure she finds it. I just wanted to make sure you were okay first."

Rage flooded through Vance at his captor's easy manner when talking about leaving a body anywhere. He fought off the urge to show any objection to the man's words and actions, making his body go slack and moving his gaze from his captor's face to the floor.

Let him talk all he wants.

His captor stood up again. "Hey, don't go anywhere while I'm gone, okay?" He laughed, left the kitchen, and shut off the light, dropping Vance into darkness again, with nothing but the scurrying of insects nearby to keep him company.

That's not true. You have your SERE training, and you know it.

Survival. Evasion. Resistance. Escape.

You are surviving. And he's not completely on board with the woman who shot you. You have a way out of here, if you can convince him that cooperating will be better for him in the long run.

The woman had a reason to want Emma dead, or at least to hurt her. And she seemed to be using Vance's captor as a tool, perhaps as a weapon.

Either way, their alliance was shaky at best, and that weakness would provide Vance with his means of escape.

36

After a night of staking out warehouses and riding along with MPD, Emma and the team returned to the Bureau for a brief reprieve. They'd been running on minimal sleep and suffering for it.

Jacinda had nearly bitten Leo's head off when he suggested they take a break, but she'd reined in her frustration in the end.

"You're right. We all need some downtime, but it's going to be brief."

Now, with four hours of sleep behind her, Emma stirred her coffee across the conference table from where the SSA slept, her head resting on her crossed arms.

Jacinda's phone chimed with a series of alerts. She snapped awake and snatched it off the table, wiping at her eyes. "Shit, another body drop."

"Where is it this time?" Emma was already heading out to the bullpen, where Leo and Mia had both fallen asleep across their desks. Jacinda's voice pulled her back into the conference room.

"Emma, tell me this address isn't where I think it is." Jacinda turned the phone for her to see.

Her stomach plummeted as she stared at the screen. *That's my apartment building.* "Do we know who the victim is?" Everything clenched inside her.

Checking her phone again, Jacinda touched her arm. "It isn't Vance. The victim is a Black male. Wurth is on scene. Body was reported by a passerby."

Shoulders slumping in relief—relief she felt bad about, because this was another person dead, even if it wasn't Vance—Emma went to the break room to make coffees for Leo and Mia while Jacinda woke them up. Groggy, yawning, and bleeding stress, the team assembled in the garage, with Jacinda directing them into two vehicles.

Fortunately, given the early hour, the streets weren't too congested. Emma and Leo pulled in behind Mia and Jacinda. Three police cruisers with lights flashing filled the parking area immediately outside Emma's building.

They got out and headed toward Wurth, who was talking with the officers. A small crowd of onlookers had formed at the building entrance. Joggers and dog walkers stopped or changed course on the pathways ringing the parking lot.

From where she stood, Emma couldn't identify anyone who looked like Hank Barnaby, but that didn't mean he wasn't present.

Keep your eyes open. He could be dressed like a jogger, for all you know.

Wurth and the police officers stood around a body that had been covered by a sheet. He separated himself and met them in the middle of the parking lot, out of earshot of the small group of Emma's neighbors who remained gawking at the scene.

"You'll want to see this." Wurth held an evidence bag up,

containing what looked like a sheet of paper torn from a notebook. "Another message, written by hand this time."

When they'd circled around him, he read the note out loud but kept his voice low.

"'Dear failed exterminators, it seems we still have a lot to talk about. But you're not listening, so I'm leaving this here for you. Somebody's trying to make me look like a bad guy.'" Wurth snorted but quickly rearranged his face to match the gravity of the situation. "'And I'm telling you, we're on the same side. We both want the streets to be clean of cockroaches, and that's all I care about. I mean it. Just let me do my work and you can have him back. Sincerely, the Bug Man.'"

"Is the victim in the same condition as the first two?"

"Surprisingly, no, and that's worrying me. Our guy might just be targeting people he *thinks* are in gangs."

Jacinda held out a hand for the evidence bag, which he passed to her. "What makes you think this victim isn't gang-related?"

"No tattoos, for one thing." He led them to the body and lifted the sheet, revealing a tall, wiry Black man.

He lay on his right side, with his arms extended in front of him. A gory exit hole above his heart showed the fatal injury had been a gunshot wound to his back.

Emma knelt and pulled on gloves, examining the wound site. "This isn't consistent with the previous two victims. They were gut shot, then stabbed. Can we even assume it's the same killer? What if this is a copycat? A sloppy one?"

"We haven't released any details about the first two murders. That doesn't mean the information isn't in the wild. The bodies were left in public places. But I think our guy is either escalating or working under duress."

Leo scoffed. "Duress? He killed a man. He's killed multiple men."

Jacinda tapped her fingers against her lips thoughtfully. "I think Wurth is saying the killer might not have chosen *this* victim himself. This victim is different. Not a gang member. It's possible his accomplice is more of a puppet master, is that right?" She turned to Wurth, who stood and stared down at the victim.

He nodded. "We're looking at a choice that was made for him. The drop location, specifically outside your team member's residence, coming on the heels of two other drops near LEO offices, starting with the one across from your front door."

Jacinda stiffened and flashed Emma a stricken look. "You think Emma is the target in all this? That he's been aiming at her the whole time?"

"I hate to say it, but that's where my thinking goes. Except I'm not sure I'd put the killer in the driver's seat. Like you said, he's working for a puppet master, not with an accomplice."

Emma balled her hands into fists. Wurth's suggestion ran right alongside her growing suspicions, that the woman working with Barnaby was the mysterious sister who Celeste had warned her about. But she couldn't say that to Jacinda, not with Wurth standing right there.

Instead, she looked down at the victim. Peering between the victim's outstretched arms, she spotted what looked like scratch marks on his chest, to the right of the exit wound. "Did he add a calling card like with the first two?" She turned to Wurth. "Like the cockroaches. There's something on his chest. Can you help me roll him over?"

Leo stepped up beside Emma and came down in a squat, tugging on gloves. Together, they rolled the corpse onto his back and set his arms at his sides. "What is it this time?"

A series of cuts over the victim's right pectoral were undeniably purposeful.

Only very faint traces of blood marked the edges, and no blood from the exit wound had leaked out to conceal them. Emma squinted at it. "He was dead when this was made. Looks like a head of broccoli, though."

"A what?" Leo leaned in for a closer look and pointed to the bottom edge of the markings. "That looks like a lightning bolt at the bottom. I'd say it's a storm cloud."

Jacinda and Wurth stepped away for a moment, then the SSA returned. "We're going back to the Bureau to review public CCTV footage for this area. If the SUV is spotted, we'll let you know. For now, stay here and assist with the scene, starting with camera footage from the apartment security." Jacinda put her hand on Emma's shoulder. "Emma, I wouldn't blame you if you wanted to go upstairs and catch some more sleep. Feel free to take breaks in shifts, but get that footage first."

"Thanks, Jacinda. We're on it." She nodded at the SSA, but her mind churned, spiraling between images of the mysterious woman and Celeste's dying warning.

"When your sister learns of what you've done to me, she will find you, and she will end you."

37

I sat at a bus stop across from Emma Last's apartment, unable to believe my luck. Lydia had been right to send me here to drop the dead guy. Even if I'd killed an innocent man instead of a cockroach, we'd lured Emma into the open, and I was looking right at her while she and the others circled up to read the note I'd left.

Even without her FBI jacket, that sandy-brown hair was unmistakable. Plus, the way she stood, like she was always ready to take off running. That was definitely her over there, surrounded by other Feds.

As soon as Emma was standing on her own, I'd take my shot and get gone, just like Lydia and I had discussed.

Lydia might be ten different kinds of psycho, but she knows how to plan.

She'd promised to double my money if I killed Emma by tonight. I was wearing a money belt with half of what she'd given me. The other half was under the front seat of the car, parked down the block.

I just needed a safe moment, when I could be sure the cops wouldn't look in my direction. Then I'd finish the job.

Emma would die, the crowd of lookie-loos, joggers, and dog walkers would go apeshit, and the cops wouldn't know where to look for the shooter.

Not like the gun would ever leave my jacket anyway.

Its weight hung under my left arm, heavy and solid, like an anchor. I resisted the urge to reach in and grip it.

Don't get scared now. You're in control here. The cops are dancing to your tune.

The redhead I'd seen talking with Emma moved off with one of the detectives who'd shown up earlier. I still had six cops to worry about, but as I waited, a pair of them got in a cruiser and drove away.

The other four remained, handling crowd control as people started coming out of the apartment building in larger numbers. The workday was getting started.

On my side of the street, a few people wandered up to wait for a bus that was arriving. Not wanting to be conspicuous, I pulled out the phone Lydia had given me and dialed her number, the only one in the contact list.

The bus picked up its passengers and pulled away as the phone rang in my ear.

Lydia answered after nine rings. Nine. "All done?"

"Not yet. Got too much blue in my eyes."

"Why the fuck are you calling me, then? Get it done, then call. In fact, just come to me. Same place as last night. You'll get the rest of your paycheck on arrival."

She disconnected the call, and I pulled the phone away from my ear to stare at it. "You can be such a bitch sometimes."

I put the phone away, remembering how she'd threatened me last night. When I was doing the work and her hired goon squad had their guns in my face.

"They'll kill your ex-wife. Slowly."

Heather. I couldn't pretend my love for her died with our

divorce. I knew she had her faults, and I certainly had mine, but she didn't deserve to be murdered just because she had the bad luck of being my ex.

Taking out the phone again, I called her number, hoping she hadn't changed it since the divorce. The phone rang and rang, and Heather's name was finally spoken by one of those robots with an option to leave a message.

"Hey. It's me, and I know you're thinking you should delete this message before listening to all of it, but, please… let me say I'm sorry. I am. And you should know…shit, I'm sorry for this too."

I imagined her beautiful face crinkling in worry and confusion. She'd place the palm of her hand on my cheek, begging me to explain.

No…that was Heather in the beginning. The current Heather probably wouldn't give a damn. But I had to try.

I took a deep breath. "I got mixed up with some people who might try to hurt you. I'm doing some work for them right now. It's not good work, not clean. Just know I'm doing it for Ethan's memory, and I'm going to keep doing it so no other family ever suffers like we did. You should go to the police and ask for protection, though."

I apologized again and told her I was sure the cops already knew who I was. At the end, I kept saying I was sorry more times than I could count and finally hung up.

Across the street, the crowd outside Emma's apartment had gotten bigger. An ambulance had arrived, and I could see Emma talking with the curly-haired guy she'd pulled up with. He stepped aside to help deal with the gawkers.

Can't blame them, really. It's not every day you see a dead body on your doorstep.

I had to laugh at that but covered up the outburst with a fake coughing fit. Two women in scrubs got into a rideshare near me, and one looked my way, shaking her head.

She probably thought I was some drunk or crackhead. Well, that was fine. I knew what I was.

I'm the Bug Man.

As I looked across the street, I knew my time had arrived.

Emma was standing by herself near a lamppost in the parking lot.

I reached into my jacket and put my hand around the butt of the gun. The roughness of the grip against my palm brought a faint smile to my face.

38

Emma leaned a hand on a lamppost as she pulled her phone out to answer.

"Hey, Jacinda. My apartment manager showed up five minutes ago. Leo and Mia are with him, getting the footage."

"Get them, now. We have Barnaby's home address and a new vehicle to track. A blue Toyota Camry was spotted driving in your area around midnight last night on a trajectory to your building. The same vehicle was seen on the same road but departing approximately fifteen minutes later."

"How do we know it wasn't late-night pizza delivery?"

"The driver matches the description Barnaby's ex-wife gave us. CCTV coverage isn't thorough across the city, so we don't have his full path of travel. But the vehicle was spotted parked outside an all-night grocery store at close to one in the morning. MPD have contacted the business owner, who confirmed Hank Barnaby as a regular customer. They live in the same apartment building."

Emma clenched her fist. Finally, they had him. "I'm going

inside to get Leo and Mia now. We'll have my manager send you the camera footage."

But as she stepped away from the lamppost, four gunshots crashed through the morning. Bullets impacted on parked cars, setting off alarms.

Emma ducked as four blasts of Other chill rippled across her skin, pulling at her and dragging her to the ground. She fought against the oppressive cold, her whole body shuddering.

Nearby civilians panicked. They ran in all directions, ducking for cover. Traffic pulsed by on the street. Some farther-away pedestrians stood frozen in fear, while others crouched, lay down flat, or took shelter inside doorways.

Police officers shepherded some people inside and into sheltered spaces around the parking lot. Dogs barked, pulling at the leads their walkers held. Emma continued her fight against the cold that struck her just like it had outside of Salem, when she and Leo had driven through last month on their way to Boston.

Letting out a scream of frustrated rage, she forced herself into a crouch beside the lamppost. A cop had taken shelter beside a car a few feet in front of Emma's position. She yelled for his attention. "Where is he? Where's the shooter?"

"No idea. I don't see a weapon anywhere."

Emma huddled behind the lamppost and scanned her surroundings but couldn't see any weapons either.

Jacinda's voice screamed at her through her phone, which she'd dropped by her foot. "Emma! Emma, tell me you're all right!"

"I'm here, Jacinda." She snatched up her phone. "Still here, unharmed. There's a shooter, but I can't see him."

Leo and Mia appeared at the door to her building, waving her toward them. She shook her head. Whoever had been shooting, they were aiming at her. Where she went, danger would follow.

Four shots fired, and four waves of the Other pulled you into the ground. That's not a coincidence, Emma girl.

She'd experienced this same sensation not long ago, in the forest outside of Salem, when Celeste had shot at her.

"Jacinda, I'm going—"

"Go straight to the address I'm texting you. Now." The SSA's voice bit into her ear. "Barnaby's blue Camry has been spotted again, five blocks from your location. He's out of camera range now, but we're going to assume he's heading home, probably to use Vance as a hostage." Jacinda was almost growling. "Get there first."

❄

Emma, Mia, and Leo pulled up outside a grimy two-story apartment building. Barnaby's car hadn't been seen yet, but their trip from Emma's apartment had taken longer than expected. Even with sirens and lights running, their vehicle was slowed by morning traffic still clogging the roads.

The agents got out and took position at the rear of their SUV. Emma gave the narrow parking area in front of the building a quick scan.

No blue Camry yet. But that doesn't mean he isn't home.

"He could've parked anywhere nearby and walked in. Jacinda wants us to go in with MPD. An ambulance is on standby."

The cops had beaten them there by a few minutes and were collecting gear from their vehicles. Two officers would handle breaching. The other two would stack on the hinge side of the door, ready to flood into the apartment. Emma and her team would be on the handle side, ready to do the same.

Emma double-checked her vest and weapon, making sure a round was chambered. Leo and Mia followed suit, and they were soon moving up the nearest staircase to the second-floor walkway. At the opposite end, the four cops climbed another set of stairs.

The walkway had a rusty railing that stood between empty planters. Cigarette butts and bits of trash filled the planters. Barnaby's apartment was in the middle, with one unit to either side.

Emma rapped hard on the door. "FBI! Open up now!"

A thud sounded somewhere on the other side, followed by a deep, pained groan.

That was the only response, so she motioned for the breaching team to do their part. Raising the ram, the officers slammed Barnaby's door open.

The agents flooded in with Emma going left, into a living room. Leo and two cops came in behind her.

Mia went right with the other officers. A moment later, her cry echoed through the apartment. "Vance!"

Heart in her throat, Emma quickly cleared the bedroom and bathroom opening onto the living space, Leo at her side.

Mia's voice came across the room, a steady stream of comfort and encouragement. "We found you. You're gonna be okay, Vance. You're gonna be okay."

While the cops radioed their precinct with an update, Leo did the same for Jacinda. Emma rushed to join Mia in the kitchen, which stank of urine and the foul smell of old garbage. A trash can sat overflowing next to the kitchen counter.

At the end of the dim room, Vance was lying, limp and exhausted, against the wall. Ropes hung from metal shelf brackets above him. A cop was helping Mia carefully unwind the rope that had been wrapped around Vance's throat and used to gag him.

Keeping her focus on Vance, Emma knelt beside Mia, putting her arm around her friend. "We found him, and he's okay."

Vance rocked slowly on his back, holding his hands together in front of his chest. "Wrists…can barely feel my fingers." He tried to flex his hands and cried out. Mia shrugged off Emma's arm and reached out for him.

Leo appeared in the doorway to the kitchen. "EMTs are inbound."

Vance continued to groan and wince as Mia gently massaged his wrists.

"Can you move? Is anything broken?"

"Maybe a rib from when that woman shot me."

"Did you see her, get a description or anything?"

Slowly shaking his head, Vance groaned as he worked his ankles in small circles. "No, not that lucky." His voice was weak and crackly. "Just get me out of here."

Emma went to his side, clutching his elbow. "As long as you think you can move."

"Watch me, ghost talker." He flashed her a grin, which she returned. At least he hadn't lost his sense of humor.

Mia crouched by his other side, bracing herself to help. "Do you want to stand up?"

Gripping Vance's other arm, Emma tried not to flinch at the groan that left their teammate as she and Mia lifted him. He whimpered and swore under his breath as they moved toward the door, slow step by slow step.

Leo was there, ready to catch him if he pitched forward. "Looking good, Jessup."

"Don't bullshit me, Ambrose. I look like hell."

"Fair enough. Let's get you out of here." Leo went out the door and kicked away splintered bits of frame.

Vance coughed a few times and paused. "Before we get outside, can somebody zip up my damn pants?"

A little huff of amusement broke from Mia's set lips as she casually reached down and did up Vance's fly. The three of them gingerly moved out the door to join Leo on the balcony.

"Hold on." Vance swallowed, and his gaze focused more loosely on Emma. "I get it, and...I believe what you said, about someone wanting you dead. The guy who had me in here said all of this was some woman's idea. He kept insisting he was just acting on her orders."

Emma peered into his face. "Did he give you a name? Description?"

With a shake of his head, Vance dashed her hopes. "Sorry. He just told me she called the shots and that he wasn't into her game. I don't know what else to tell you."

"I suppose I should thank him if it means you're willing to believe me now."

"Let's not jump to conclusions." The lines of pain on his face softened into a weary smile. "That second body drop, the guy with the smokes in his pocket and the roach in his smokes...how'd you know to ask about them? Really, tell me the truth on that. Please."

Taking a breath, Emma told him how Marty Kaine's ghost appeared, patting his pockets. "He kept mumbling about wanting a smoke to calm his nerves and how he wasn't a cockroach."

"You couldn't have just said that, though, not with Wurth standing there." Vance took a slow breath, in and out. "Consider me tentatively on board the ghost bus, I guess. I reserve the right to ask questions, but we're cool. I mean, I am...with you." He tilted his head. "Forgive me for being a dick about it?"

She clucked her tongue. "Mia, have the EMTs check this man for shock."

That got her a genuine laugh from Vance, who weakly

lifted his hand to her. "Just close this case for me. I'll be with you in spirit. No pun intended. I mean that."

Mia waved her and Leo off just as his phone chimed.

Leo pulled the device out, putting the call on speaker as two EMTs climbed the stairs, carrying a stretcher. "Jacinda, I'm here with Emma, Mia, and Vance. Ambulance just arrived."

"Glad to hear it, and welcome back, Vance."

Vance groaned in reply. "Glad to be here."

The pleasantries ended there, and Jacinda was back to business. "Barnaby's blue Camry was spotted again, near Packard Lane this time. Get down there and link up with Detective Carter from the Eighth. His people were first on scene and have set up a cordon. If Vance tries to tag along, he's suspended, effective immediately."

With a pained laugh, Vance confirmed he wasn't going anywhere except to the hospital.

Leo and Emma raced down to the parking lot. "We're on our way now. Mia's staying with Vance until he's loaded up, then she'll join us."

"Be careful, all of you." The line went dead.

At the SUV, Emma dropped into the driver's seat and started the engine, barely waiting for Leo to get in.

Leo buckled his seat belt and raised an eyebrow. "I'd normally tell you to drive safely. Right now, I'm just telling you to drive."

Emma grinned and floored it. "That I can do."

39

Emma pulled to a halt behind a line of MPD vehicles on Packard Lane. Before she and Leo made it out of their SUV, another Bureau vehicle pulled up behind them. Mia swung out the door as Emma and Leo grabbed radios and took in the scene.

Agent Wurth and Detective Carter stood nearby, leaning against a cruiser. "Welcome to the party."

"Why aren't we moving in?"

"We spotted your guy's car but lost him in that maze of alleys and loading docks." Detective Carter jerked his chin at one of the offending lanes. "Two units are patrolling the streets in there, and another four are setting up barricades between this zone and the neighborhood on the other side. We're holding the cordon on this side."

"Are any civilians inside the perimeter?"

"Shouldn't be. We closed off everything connecting to Packard Lane for two blocks."

A rattle of automatic-weapon fire from within the warehouse district sent them all crouching behind the cruiser.

Carter had his radio in hand. "Where's the shooter? Any units with a visual, report your location."

Reports crackled over the speaker. "Unit 9524 to base, gunfire is coming from a warehouse near us. Dropping a pin."

Carter lifted his phone and confirmed the unit's location. "They're two blocks north. Let's close the net." He ordered the mobile units to tighten their roving patrols, even as the gunfire continued and more weapons were added to the din.

Carter cursed and called for SWAT support. "Active shooter, multiple automatic weapons."

Dispatch confirmed SWAT was inbound.

Frustration boiled through Emma. She couldn't wait for SWAT to arrive. Their killer was in the maze of industrial buildings and actively shooting at people.

Including someone who might be your sister. Even if she is the woman who shot and helped kidnap Vance, she can't be gunned down by a maniac. Not before you get some answers.

She tapped Leo and Mia on the shoulders and motioned for them to step aside with her. Waiting until they were out of earshot of any cops, she suggested they split up and search for Barnaby. "That's our best chance of finding him. We need to get this guy before he hurts anyone else."

Leo held his hands out, pushing back on the idea. "Jacinda made me Incident Commander for a reason. With SWAT on the way—"

"He might kill her before they get here."

Both Leo and Mia stared at her. He put a hand on Emma's shoulder. "Kill who? Who's out here that we should be looking for?"

Fearing she'd lose their support so soon after finally earning Vance's, Emma braced herself to share the burning terror that had been building ever since she'd heard about a mysterious woman being involved in Vance's kidnapping.

"I think my sister might be here. With what Vance told us, I think she's the one who was helping and even directing Barnaby. But Vance mentioned the two weren't seeing eye to eye. I'm worried Barnaby might be turning on her and planning to kill her, so she can't set him up to take the fall for everything."

Leo looked up, as though he were asking Heaven for guidance. With a sigh, he double-checked that nobody was near enough to overhear their conversation. "From the look on your face, you're hoping some *friends* might be around here to help us find your sister."

She smiled tightly. "They might, yeah. I haven't seen any yet, but…if she's alive, she's the only family I have left. Maybe she's a psychopath who's out for revenge, but I don't know that for sure. I couldn't live with myself if I didn't try to get answers from her, so I have to save her from Barnaby, and I can't wait for SWAT to get here."

Searching Leo's face for agreement, or at least acceptance, all Emma saw was concern. The same brotherly worry he'd always expressed for her, for everyone on their team.

"Leo, please. She's my sister. She might want me dead, but I can't know that until I've at least had a chance to talk to her." She reached out and touched his arm. "I can't get the answers I need if she's dead."

He cleared his throat and looked up and down the street, but not at her. "I need to confirm change of command with Detective Carter. I'll ask him to advise his people to be on the lookout for friendlies. You should be easy to spot since you're wearing your jacket."

She exhaled a tiny bit of the tension building in her lungs. "Okay."

He slapped her on the shoulder and spun on his heel. "Mia, let's make sure Carter has told us everything we need to know."

The briefest touch of panic flooded Emma's chest as Mia met her gaze, then wrapped her in a hug. "You have a radio and your vest, and you're not stupid." Mia released her and stepped back. "The instant you spot him, let us know. Drop a pin, and don't get yourself killed."

40

I ducked behind a stack of boxes as one of Lydia's goons stalked by my hiding place in her warehouse. I'd shown up, like she told me to, and I'd been ready to give her an earful and then some. But the only thing waiting for me was a welcoming committee. Three of her goon-squad guys.

Good thing my father didn't raise an idiot, or I'd have walked right into that ambush.

Only a dumbass would blindly go into a warehouse where someone had pointed a gun in his face the night before.

I'd taken the car to the door Lydia had used, and I texted her that I arrived. Before the door started rolling up, I was out of the car and hiding beside the entrance. As soon as the door cleared the car's front bumper, the goon squad started shooting, sending lead flying through the windshield.

When they stopped, I flicked a glance around the edge of the garage door and spotted a goon. A quick squeeze of my trigger had him on the ground. The bullets still worked on them, at least, even if every shot I'd fired at Emma Last had gone wide for some reason.

One of Lydia's minions fired off a burst in my direction, so they must've heard me, but I kept moving deeper into their hideout, ducking behind crates and boxes, staying low and in the shadows.

Now I was as safe as I could get and just had to hope I spotted those guys before either of them spotted me.

I should've known better than to trust someone who called herself Lydia. After the bullets she gave me failed to kill Emma, I knew all bets were off between us.

All I'd wanted was to do right by my son's memory, to make sure his death wasn't tarnished by my inaction. The police had done that already, and Ethan needed someone to stand up for him. Even in death, he was still my boy and deserved the best I could give him.

Lydia's money had been seductive. With half of it in my money belt now, the other half was still stuffed under the front seat of my bullet-riddled car. I'd take care of Lydia's goons and go back for it.

A hundred thousand was a nice chunk of change. I thought of all the things I could do with it, all the gear I could buy, the weapons and ammunition. I'd be able to set myself up with anything I needed to squash cockroaches left and right.

I could've cleaned the streets in double time with Lydia's help.

But she hadn't really wanted to help me. She'd wanted to use me and never planned to let me live after I'd done her dirty work.

I'm one step ahead of you, you cloudy bitch.

She promised me the bullets would hit home if I was merely looking at my target.

I'd been staring right at Emma's head when I pulled the trigger. I even fired four times to make sure, to make it messy, like Lydia wanted.

And not a single bullet hit her. The cars next to her and behind her got hit instead. I knew, because the alarms started wailing like mad.

That helped me escape while the cops handled all the chaos I'd created. But now I was stuck hiding from Lydia's goons while those same cops waited outside.

Their sirens kept whistling in through the open garage door.

Footsteps clicked on the concrete floor, coming my way from both directions. Either they'd found me or they were coming together to make plans. Carefully easing my way around the crate I was using for cover, I peeked into the dark space of the warehouse.

More boxes and shadows filled my vision, but I managed to spot a figure stepping into the aisle between my hiding place and the next stack of crates. He was partially outlined by light from the open garage door. I stayed hidden and curled a finger around my trigger.

Now was my chance. I fired, and the goon dropped.

His partner must've seen me, because a spray of bullets punched into the crate above my head. I spun around, running down the line of crates and boxes I'd followed on my way in here. Gunfire followed me, and bullets whistled past my head.

I flicked a glance over my shoulder, looking for any sign of him. He fired again, and his muzzle flash gave him away in the darkness.

I fired two times, and was relieved when he screamed.

Rushing back the way I'd come, I found him. I'd hit him in the hand and stomach, just like the first cockroach I squashed. "Sorry, pal. Your boss probably thought she hired an idiot. Turns out she did, except it wasn't me."

I shot him in the chest and between the eyes, emptying

my magazine. I quickly swapped it with the spare and grabbed the little machine gun he'd been using.

More sirens and amplified voices echoed from the streets outside. They were closing in on me.

I dug into the dead guy's pockets and pulled out a set of keys. With those in hand, I ran back to my car and grabbed the second belt with the rest of my money, then hightailed it through the long building to the other end. Sure enough, I found my way out. The goons had come in a car just like the one Lydia had given me—another blue Toyota Camry, this one a little darker—only they'd entered from the opposite end of the warehouse.

The car had a garage door opener clipped to the driver's visor.

Now, for a distraction.

When Lydia had brought me here last night, I'd seen warning labels on some of the crates, but she'd pulled me away before I could examine them. Sirens kept wailing outside, and I heard the cops driving around out there.

They'd noticed the gunfire and were pinning me down.

I went to the stack of crates I'd been curious about last night…and found my answer.

"TNT, huh? Well, Lydia, I guess I owe you one after all."

41

Emma hadn't wasted any time when Mia turned her back and jogged to catch up with Leo. Heading down the street in the other direction, Emma turned on the next block.

Weapon drawn, she chanced running across the street to the warehouse on the opposite side.

The Other clawed its way toward her as she reached the building. The victim left outside her apartment stood in the middle of the street. His eyes were ghostly white, and he extended his arm, pointing toward a neighborhood street where MPD had set up barricades.

A single cruiser sat angled across the street.

Icy rage poured from the ghost, radiating toward Emma like a wave of sleet she feared would cut her skin. She backed away, and the ghost followed her, still pointing down the street. "Bug Man's gonna blow. Better duck and hide." He vanished, winking out of sight.

Emma didn't move, scanning the area.

A shock wave erupted from a warehouse across the street, flinging her to the ground. Flames shot out in every direction, sending a plume of smoke into the sky, the acrid smell sharp in her nose.

Automatic gunfire rattled from somewhere. Emma's mind spun from the disorienting blast. Sitting up, she checked herself for injuries and tried to steady her vision.

Sirens screamed from every direction. A police cruiser had been flipped over by the explosion and teetered on its side in the street. Emma spotted another cruiser racing up as the officers in the flipped vehicle kicked out the cracked windshield and crawled free.

Her radio crackled with Leo's voice, and she pulled it from her belt. "I'm here, outside the building. Not hurt, but there's a pair of cops whose car was tossed by the blast. They're mobile, and another unit is helping them, but they need medical assistance."

"The second unit already called. Looks like we found Barnaby's location. Stay there. Mia and I are coming down with Carter."

"Okay." Emma continued to scan the area, looking for any movement in the nearby buildings. With the police cordon going up earlier, no civilians had come in to work for the day.

So anybody moving out there is likely a suspect.

Smoke billowed out from the building, and smaller secondary explosions began to fill the air. In her periphery, Emma spotted a dark sedan racing from an alleyway. The vehicle sped past the overturned police cruiser, and the officers there ducked as another burst of automatic gunfire riddled the cruiser's underbelly.

The sedan swerved in Emma's direction, but the driver wasn't looking at her. He had his eyes on the rearview mirror.

She darted aside and brought her weapon up. The driver returned his attention to the road and swerved toward her.

That's Hank Barnaby. Shit!

She fired twice at the windshield, then spun aside as the car continued racing her way. He jumped the sidewalk and flew around the police barricade.

Emma was on her radio as she ran after the car. "Suspect is fleeing in a dark-blue Toyota Camry. He broke the cordon at Grable Avenue, heading toward Shade Street."

The officers at the barricade were in their vehicle and moving in pursuit of the speeding Camry, but it whipped around a corner and vanished from Emma's view.

A crash, followed by screaming, echoed back to her. The police cruiser rounded the corner and came to a stop as she followed. Both officers exited the vehicle, drew their weapons, and began shouting commands.

Emma joined them, taking shelter beside a parked vehicle on the curb. Down the street, the Camry had smashed into a car backing out of a driveway.

Barnaby raced away from the scene on foot as the cops called in for backup. "Suspect fleeing north on Shade Street. Possible civilian injuries. Ambulance required."

Emma took off, keeping her eye on the man in black, who was ducking and weaving around parked cars. The cops were behind her and approached the crashed vehicles. She spared a moment of her attention to confirm the Camry was empty.

A submachine gun lay on the ground beside the driver's door.

She radioed Mia. "Barnaby fled on foot. I'm pursuing down Shade Street."

"Is your…is she with him?"

"No sign of her. MPD have his vehicle. It's empty, and he dropped a weapon. He might still be armed. Can we get a drone over here?" Emma spied Barnaby racing through a yard and turning a corner. She chased after him.

Mia's reply came after a short pause. "Drone operators are converging on your location."

"Okay. I'm with one unit from MPD and will stay on Barnaby. We need support to pen him in, at least two more units."

"I'll tell Carter. Be careful, Emma."

"I will." Emma raced forward to the corner. Barnaby was running down the street, past homes and small businesses.

A gun was clearly visible in his hand.

She cued her mic again. "Barnaby spotted and still armed."

Leo's voice crackled in her ear. "Mia and I are coming with one unit from MPD. We'll alert Jacinda."

Emma kept pace after Barnaby, who'd made it to the next block. She reached the car he'd previously been using for cover and took position, lifting her weapon. "FBI! Drop the gun, Barnaby! Get on the ground!"

He kept his gun by his side and continued running but glanced over his shoulder at her. He fired, and sparks flew from the car as a bullet struck the metal beside her.

Emma spun away as a wave of Other cold tore against her skin. She put a hand to her face, expecting the sharp burn of a grazing shot, but it came away clean.

No blood, no injury at all.

Just like in Salem, when Celeste was shooting at me.

Scanning the street from her hiding place, she took off on Barnaby's trail, weapon at the ready. Her breath came fast as she ran, her gaze darting from side to side as she watched for any ghosts.

As she entered the neighborhood, the amplified voice of an MPD officer came across the air. "Attention, residents, this is the police. Please remain inside your homes. This is an active shooter situation. Stay away from all windows."

Another bullet whistled through the air beside her head,

bringing with it a violent gust of Other cold that raked across Emma's face.

She couldn't see Barnaby, but clearly, he could see her.

The house to her right had a porch that would provide her with cover, and she ran for it, crouching and cueing her mic. "Leo, I'm down Wharton Avenue from the intersection with Shade Street. Barnaby is within a block of my current location."

She dropped another pin while Leo replied that he and Mia were minutes away. "Just one more street, and we'll be coming into the neighborhood from the opposite side. We'll get him surrounded."

She risked poking her head out to scan the street. Barnaby was on his heels, in a crouch behind a truck, two houses down.

"Barnaby, you're not getting out of here unless you cooperate. Put the gun down, and let's talk. All right?"

"No deal! This isn't over until every cockroach in this city is smashed under my boot." He sprang from his hiding place and raced away from her.

Emma stood, taking aim, but he glanced over his shoulder and fired at her over and over.

Three waves of Other cold washed over her, forcing her backward and down.

The bullets struck a car parked along the sidewalk, setting off the alarm.

But she realized that every time Barnaby had fired at her this morning, progressively stronger blasts of cold covered her skin.

You need to concentrate, Emma girl. This man has no qualms about killing people, and you have to stop him before he kills again.

Another gunshot rang out up ahead, and a bullet whistled past Emma's ear. A fiercer and more threatening pressure from the Other tugged at her. She stumbled against a car parked on the street, feeling a heavy pull to just stay there, to sit down and go still.

Her breath heaved in and out as she stayed put. *But how can a maniac like Barnaby reach into the world of ghosts? And why would he want to?*

Unless this had something to do with Celeste, through her sister.

She bent and glanced around the corner. Barnaby was on foot again, running.

"Freeze, Barnaby! Drop the gun!"

She hauled after him and took position beside the car he'd been using for cover. She kept her aim on him. Pedestrians stayed hidden and crouched along the street, behind cars and out of her line of fire.

Flicking a glance over his shoulder, Barnaby fired behind him, and the bullet impacted on the wheel beside Emma, letting loose a whoosh of air as a blast of Other cold pushed her back a step.

Emma steadied herself against the car's fender again and lifted her weapon. The incessant chirping and wailing of all the triggered car alarms assailed her ears, but she aimed center mass and fired five times, knowing that stopping him was essential.

Pitching forward, Barnaby went down in the middle of the street. He lay still but kept ahold of his gun.

Emma remained partially behind the car. "Stay on the ground and take your hand off the weapon! Do it now!"

Leo and Mia were running in her direction from down the street.

The air went cold with the Other again, thickening the atmosphere. Mia skidded to a halt beside Barnaby, kicking the gun away from his hand. She holstered her weapon and lifted her radio. Her words crackled through Emma's radio. "He's dead."

Disappointment shuddered through Emma. She turned as Leo ran up beside her and asked if she was okay. The chill came with him, but she relaxed.

Barnaby was surrounded by his victims, standing in a cluster. Their white eyes were all turned toward their murderer's corpse.

She took them in, making herself appreciate their sad expressions, milky gazes, and bloodied bodies.

"Yeah. I'm good. Thank you."

The street went colder around her, icier than she'd felt even in Salem. Emma fell back on her heels, reaching for Leo's hand as a ghost appeared directly in front of her.

Hank Barnaby stared down at her, white-eyed and with half of his head translucent, leaking brain matter. A stray headshot must've been what killed him in the end.

He grinned and let out a haunting bark of a laugh. "A storm sent me for you, Special Agent Emma Marie Last. And it's still coming. This is your last sign, pun intended."

Leo's hand gripped hers tightly. "What is it, Emma? What's happening?"

She shook her head, unable to answer. *How does he know my name? How the fuck does he know my full name?*

42

After a week of administrative leave to investigate discharging her weapon, Emma was grateful to settle into her regular seat at the conference table. Across from her, Vance shifted his bruised and battered frame in his seat. The bandages on his face and peeking out from beneath his collar testified to his ordeal, but his eyes drew Emma's focus.

He no longer appeared angry or confused or resentful. If she had to pin a word to his expression, it would be *sad*. But a slight smile tugged at his lips, and he nodded at her, his eyes brightening just a touch before some ache or injury inside seemed to remind him not to move more than was necessary.

"I'm glad we got you back, Vance. The team wasn't the same without you."

Mia sat beside him and gently rested a hand over his. "You're going to heal up fine. If a bomb couldn't kill you, I doubt you'll suffer long from a few kicks and a bullet."

A raspy chuckle left his throat. "It was a couple of pistol-whips and a bullet, for the record. I'm just glad I missed the exploding warehouse party this time."

Leo came in with Jacinda. They sat, and Jacinda focused

on Vance first. "You should be in bed. As long as you'll take the day off after this, we can continue."

He gave the slightest of nods. "You have my word."

The SSA leaned forward. "I'll make this as brief as I can." She tapped at her keyboard and scrolled for a moment.

Emma sat still, content to remain silent. After the chaos of last weekend, she and Leo and Mia had remained on-scene into Saturday night. Sunday had been consumed by a debrief with Jacinda, Wurth, and the MPD.

Looking up from her computer, Jacinda began. "The warehouse 'party,' as Vance so eloquently put it, was finally brought under control without much damage to neighboring buildings. The existence of explosive ordnance complicated matters."

Vance coughed. "Can't imagine they found much. The fire could have cooked things off, destroying any evidence."

"True. We may never know who was responsible for the explosion or what the building was used for. Property records may tell us more. For now, I want to share some news about our primary suspect, Hank Barnaby."

Jacinda glanced down at her tablet, and Emma braced before learning more about the man she'd killed.

"Four years ago, his son, Ethan, was killed by gang members conducting a drug deal on a neighborhood street corner. The killers were identified but never caught. To clarify, the Barnabys lived in a suburban neighborhood not typically affected by gang activity. Regardless, you should all know that Heather Alsap, formerly Heather Barnaby, has requested police protection based on a voicemail she says her ex-husband left her that Saturday morning."

Emma clasped her hands on the table. "What did he say?"

Jacinda looked up. "Only that he'd warned her some 'bad people' might try to hurt her." She paused and scrolled on her tablet. Emma looked over at Vance as he shifted in his seat, wincing. He turned his head, stretching his neck, and flinched against some unseen source of pain.

The SSA cleared her throat. "Eight years prior to Ethan Barnaby's murder, Hank Barnaby suffered the loss of his parents and family home. The official cause was listed as arson, but Barnaby insisted, and I quote from his statement, 'The junkies next door started the fire by cooking heroin in the driveway.'"

"He had plenty of reasons to hate gangs in D.C." Leo sat up straighter in his chair, his eyebrows knitting together. "But what triggered him to start slicing off their tattoos and dumping their bodies like calling cards?"

"When his son was killed, Barnaby devolved." Jacinda pointed to her tablet. "He lost his job due to what his employer referenced as 'psychological disturbances and antisocial behavior.'"

Mia shook her head, frowning. "And he was an accountant? Do we know how he went from crunching numbers to crushing gangsters?"

"Journals and other items recovered from his apartment paint an ugly picture of a man losing his mind day by day. At some point, he became fascinated with vigilantes and read every account he could find, from true crime to wild fiction. Stacks of paperback novels were collected from his apartment, along with newspaper articles going back decades. He'd done his research and printed off scores of them, which he kept in three-ring binders, organized by date."

When Jacinda sighed, shaking her head, Emma couldn't help but mirror the gesture. "He got drunk on the fantasy of being a hero who uses violence to solve problems."

"Exactly."

Lifting a hand slowly and revealing the bruises around his wrist as he did so, Vance added to their summation. "He was off his rocker, no question about it. But he wasn't working alone. I think the man we saw at the end wasn't the guy who dropped that body across the street last week. Something happened when he and this mystery woman connected."

"Thank you, Vance. That was my next point." Jacinda rotated and checked the screen behind her. She slid her chair to the side and tapped at her laptop.

The screen lit up with images of email messages, side by side.

"These are the messages we received from our anonymous sender, using an encrypted address. Cyber is still working on tracing the source, and probably will be for some time."

"What should we be looking for?" Leo stood and walked up to the screen, standing to the side, opposite Jacinda.

"Our resident linguist, Renee Bailey, agrees these emails were written by the same person. Now look at this." She tapped at her keyboard, and the screen flicked to a slide, showing a page of handwriting. "That was taken from Hank Barnaby's journal. The writing is clear and legible and is an exact match to the handwritten note found with the victim left outside Emma's apartment. Also, notice how the email writer used the exact phrasing that Barnaby did when he described law enforcement as 'failed exterminators' and gang members as 'cockroaches.'"

Vance flicked a look at Emma. "I heard him use that phrasing about us at least once. He had a lot to say about roaches too. Based on how many I shared that kitchen with, I'm not sure if he was talking about gangs or bugs, to be honest."

Everyone, even Vance, managed a laugh, and for the first time in a long time, Emma remembered how good it felt to be a part of her team. To have these people around her, with her in the trenches, at her back when she needed them, and filling her sails with their presence.

She smiled at him across the table. "Thanks for that, Vance. I think we all needed it."

He blinked too fast a few times as he nodded at her, before Jacinda called everyone's attention to the screen again.

"Renee wanted us to notice the differences too. The emails contain phrases like 'tide of vermin' and 'useless leeches,' neither of which appear in any of Barnaby's journals she's examined so far. That's not to say she won't find them, but she would've spotted them immediately."

Emma got up and joined Leo by the screen. "She thinks these were written by different people. Our mystery woman, the one who helped kidnap Vance, wrote the emails."

The SSA nodded. "That's her suggestion, and I'm inclined to agree. Barnaby was wearing a pair of money belts, each containing close to fifty thousand dollars."

Leo turned to her. "She was paying him."

"And very well."

Stepping back to lean on the table, Emma stared at the images on the screen. "Why would she do this? Why pay Barnaby that much money and put words in his mouth like that?"

With a quiet cough, Jacinda clicked her mouse, and the screen went dark. "I received another image from the technicians working over Barnaby's apartment. Emma, you might want to be seated."

"I'll stand. Whatever it is, I've probably seen as bad or worse."

With a quick, silent nod, Jacinda clicked her mouse again.

The screen showed an evidence bag containing a photograph of Emma taken after her graduation from Quantico. She stood in her best suit with the flag behind her and a smile on her face. Jacinda clicked again, and the bagged photograph was shown flipped over, revealing Emma's full name written on the back in Hank Barnaby's precise lettering.

Emma swallowed down the fear rising in her throat. "Why did he have this?"

The SSA stood and faced Emma, putting a hand on her shoulder. "Whoever Barnaby's mystery woman is, she has access to a significant amount of money and, I hate to say it…you're a target."

The End
To be continued...

Thank you for reading.
All of Emma Last series books can be found on Amazon.

ACKNOWLEDGMENTS

The past few years have been a whirlwind of change, both personally and professionally, and I find myself at a loss for the right words to express my profound gratitude to those who have supported me on this remarkable journey. Yet, I am compelled to try.

To my sons, whose unwavering support has been my bedrock, granting me the time and energy to transform my darkest thoughts into words on paper. Your steadfast belief in me has never faltered, and watching each of you grow, welcoming the wonderful daughters you've brought into our family, has been a source of immense pride and joy.

Embarking on the dual role of both author and publisher has been an exhilarating, albeit challenging, adventure. Transitioning from the solitude of writing to the dynamic world of publishing has opened new horizons for me, and I'm deeply grateful for the opportunity to share my work directly with you, the readers.

I extend my heartfelt thanks to the entire team at Mary Stone Publishing, the same dedicated group who first recognized my potential as an indie author years ago. Your collective efforts, from the editors whose skillful hands have polished my words to the designers, marketers, and support staff who breathe life into these books, have been instrumental in resonating deeply with our readers. Each of you plays a crucial role in this journey, not only nurturing my growth but also ensuring that every story reaches its full potential. Your dedication, creativity, and finesse have been nothing short of invaluable.

However, my deepest gratitude is reserved for you, my beloved readers. You ventured off the beaten path of traditional publishing to embrace my work, investing your most precious asset—your time. It is my sincerest hope that this book has enriched that time, leaving you with memories that linger long after the last page is turned.

With all my love and heartfelt appreciation,
Mary

ABOUT THE AUTHOR

Nestled in the serene Blue Ridge Mountains of East Tennessee, Mary Stone crafts her stories surrounded by the natural beauty that inspires her. What was once a home filled with the lively energy of her sons has now become a peaceful writer's retreat, shared with cherished pets and the vivid characters of her imagination.

As her sons grew and welcomed wonderful daughters-in-law into the family, Mary's life entered a quieter phase, rich with opportunities for deep creative focus. In this tranquil environment, she weaves tales of courage, resilience, and intrigue, each story a testament to her evolving journey as a writer.

From childhood fears of shadowy figures under the bed to a profound understanding of humanity's real-life villains, Mary's style has been shaped by the realization that the most complex antagonists often hide in plain sight. Her writing is characterized by strong, multifaceted heroines who defy traditional roles, standing as equals among their peers in a world of suspense and danger.

Mary's career has blossomed from being a solitary author to establishing her own publishing house—a significant milestone that marks her growth in the literary world. This expansion is not just a personal achievement but a reflection of her commitment to bring thrilling and thought-provoking stories to a wider audience. As an author and publisher, Mary continues to challenge the conventions of the thriller genre, inviting readers into gripping tales filled with serial killers, astute FBI agents, and intrepid heroines who confront peril with unflinching bravery.

Each new story from Mary's pen—or her publishing house—is a pledge to captivate, thrill, and inspire, continuing the legacy of the imaginative little girl who once found wonder and mystery in the shadows.

Discover more about Mary Stone on her website.
www.authormarystone.com

Printed in Great Britain
by Amazon